The storm appeared to have died down briefly, and a hush fell over everything. Christy shivered and held out her hands before the fire which flickered brightly and then died for no apparent reason.

Then, as if an invisible hand were at work in the room, the candles in the pewter candelabra went out. The room was plunged into total darkness.

Gripping the arms of her chair, she rose, peering into the inky blackness. She took a tentative step forward before stopping and holding her breath in ghastly anticipation.

There was someone in the room with her....

FALCON'S ISLAND
is an original POCKET BOOK edition.

FALCON'S ISLAND

by

Antonia Scott

PUBLISHED BY POCKET BOOKS NEW YORK

FALCON'S ISLAND

POCKET BOOK edition published May, 1973

This original POCKET BOOK edition is printed from
brand-new plates made from newly set, clear, easy-to-read type.
POCKET BOOK editions are published by POCKET BOOKS, a division of
Simon & Schuster, Inc., 630 Fifth Avenue, New York, N.Y. 10020.
Trademarks registered in the United States and other countries.

Printed in the U.S.A.   Cover art by Vic Prezzio.

Prologue

Pre-Colonial Settlements in America

Published 1924

Falcon's Island (Previously known as *Awwanee Island*)
Original inhabitants: Blue Heron Indians (Currently extinct)

AWWANEE Island was discovered by one Rufus Falcon and bestowed upon the Falcon family in perpetuity by King Charles I of England in the year of our Lord 1624. It was the first such manorial grant in the New World and exists entirely intact unto the present day.

The island is 28 miles in length and 7 in width at its widest point. There is but one major peak, with an altitude of 2,628 feet. The terrain is generally rocky with little arable land suitable for cultivation. The settlement of Pirate's Cove is the sole township and has a population of between 100 and 135 souls.

Awwanee Island was officially proclaimed Falcon's Island in 1683 by a sovereign act of the Colonial Legislature. It is historically notable in that it was used as headquarters for the British fleet during the American Revolution. It once again came to public prominence during the infamous Salem witchcraft trials, when the trial judge referred to the island as "a boiling cauldron of Satanism."

The island is blessed with a wide variety of flora and fauna. Great herds of deer still abound and the rare and beautiful hooded falcon is known to have once flourished, although the bird is now believed to be entirely extinct. The present inhabitants are engaged solely in the pursuits of farming and fishing. The only exports are carded wool, piñon nuts, and salted codfish.

NOTE: *Under the original land grant, the Falcon family retained the feudal right to judge, punish, and, if they deemed necessary, put to death any who might be found guilty of crimes.*

This right has never been abrogated by United States law, allowing the surviving Falcon heirs the same prerogative as their ancestors.

FALCON'S
ISLAND

One

MILE after mile Christy kept her eyes set dead ahead and tried not to allow her growing sense of apprehension to get the better of her.

Thoughts could only bring about doubt and confusion, something she could ill afford at this point. No. She had made her decision and it was by now far too late to do anything but continue on to Falcon's Island.

She had hired a car and driver after getting off the bus in SeaPort, Maine. Since she had left the outskirts of town the road had grown steadily more winding and treacherous, the storm increasingly violent, buffeting the car with high winds and driving rain.

Fortunately, due to the lateness of the hour, the narrow road had proven free of traffic, a blessing in view of the almost total lack of visibility through the streaming windows.

The storm that had been predicted on the radio early that same morning had overtaken her while still aboard the bus bound for Bangor. From there she had been instructed in the letter to change and take another to Sea-Port.

The trip north had been long and tiring. Christy had started out from Boston before dawn, and now with a weary sigh she pondered the fact that the worst was still ahead of her.

She dreaded the thought of setting out to sea in such a

tempest, but there seemed to be no other alternative, unless, of course, Mrs. Falcon had made other arrangements
at the last minute, which didn't seem very likely. Surely
she would have left a message for her at the bus station if
that were the case.

Mr. Findley, her elderly driver, had proven some conso-
lation. He handled the car with skill and prudence, his
hands clinging tenaciously to the wheel as he squinted out
into the stormy night.

For over an hour they had driven in silence as the windshield wipers slapped monotonously back and forth, barely clearing the rain-splattered windows.

Finally he glanced up to see her pale, tense face reflected in the rear-view mirror of the car. "It won't be long
now," he said, his voice nasal and monotone, tinged with a
New England twang. "Just about another twenty minutes."

Christy appreciated his obvious concern and rewarded
him with a wan smile. He reminded her of the grandfather
everyone wished they had, and she was glad of his company for at least part of her journey.

Mr. Findley was a kindly, bespectacled man, whose
beaked nose and craggy face conveyed a fierce sense of
rocky Northeastern independence. He had been obviously
taken aback when she announced her intention of traveling to Land's End that night. After some discussion he finally agreed to drive her there but only after she had produced her letter of instruction from Iris Falcon.

What she could expect to find upon her arrival she
wasn't quite sure. Mrs. Falcon had said only that she
would be met.

At twenty-one Christina Randolph appeared to be several years older. She was an attractive girl of better than
medium height, whose youthful prettiness and finely chiseled features were verging on the ripening bloom of
young womanhood.

A perfect peach-pale complexion set off light brown eyes flecked with amber gold and spaced wide beneath heavy, arched brows. Her nose was classic if slightly commanding, the long chiseled effect softened by a full mouth, high cheekbones, and delicate chin punctuated by a soft indentation.

Although her hair appeared to be almost black indoors, it was actually of the deepest reddish brown, and she wore it softly waved about her shoulders.

On that particular morning she had dressed carefully in a beige linen traveling suit, frilly lace blouse, and voluminous leather bag strung over her shoulder. Now after an exhausting day she felt rumpled and disheveled. The outfit —her best—had not been at all practical for the journey.

Although it was too late for regrets, Christy realized that she would have been far smarter to have worn slacks, sweater, and a warm coat. Still there was nothing to do now but make the best of it and hope she would have a chance to freshen up before meeting the Falcon family once she arrived on the island.

Jason, her Welsh terrier, slept beside her on the back seat, his muzzle resting lightly on her knee. Occasionally his back paws twitched expectantly, as if he were anxious to be off in pursuit of some stray cat he had conjured up in his dream.

Glancing down at the sleeping dog with a look of fond caring in her lovely eyes, Christy was glad of his company on this, the first real adventure of her young life. Until that day she had never been further than fifty miles outside of Boston.

With a slim, tapered hand—the fingers tipped by clear-lacquered nails—she patted the well-shaped head and stroked the wiry silver coat. She and Jason had been inseparable for the past four years. He had been a present from her Aunt Ellen upon her graduation from high school, possibly the only gesture of genuine kindness the

woman had ever expressed toward her. It had gone far to
smother Christy's grudging dislike and resentment.

"It's a difficult time of year you've picked to go out to
the island," Findley called from the front seat. "The
winter will soon be upon us from the looks of this storm."

"I don't suppose many people travel out there during
the winter months," Christy suggested, intent on learning
all she could. Thus far Falcon's Island remained only a
small dot on the map, barely visible off the coast of Maine.

In addition she had located an obscure reference book
entitled *Pre-Colonial Settlements in America,* but it had
given little information other than that of historical signifi-
cance.

Mr. Findley's laugh was a skeptical cackle. "No, miss.
Don't get many visitors out there in winter or any other
time for that matter. Fact is I only remember a score or so
being permitted on Falcon's Island for as long as I can remember, and that's goin' on seventy-five years now.

"Lived all my life in these parts and to my knowledge
the only people the Falcon family ever allowed on the island were those that work at the mansion and the local
people themselves."

Finley's craggy face grew thoughtful, his bright, highly
magnified eyes reflective behind wire frame spectacles.
"Of course there was Miss Iris. She married Abigale's son,
Willard, 'bout seventeen years ago. Fact is everyone considered her an outsider even though she was born and
raised in SeaPort. Mighty particular those folks. They
don't take kindly to foreigners."

"Well, as you saw by the letter," Christy announced a
bit defensively, "I am going to the island on the express
invitation of Iris Falcon, the Mistress of Falcon's Eyrie."

Findley laughed once again, this time emitting a delight-
ed chuckle followed immediately by a rheumatic wheeze.
"Old Abigale would turn over in her grave if she heard her
daughter-in-law called that. Those two never did get

along. Always acted like two hens sittin' on the same nest." He shrugged his narrow, suspendered shoulders. "But I suppose someone had to take charge after the old lady's death."

With a shake of his head he nipped off a plug of Bull Durham chewing tobacco. "Her son, Willard, ain't much to speak of . . . but then none of the Falcon men has been for some time. My guess is the male blood line's all worn out. Has been for a couple of hundred years now."

Findley chewed contentedly for a few moments before adding, "Only the Falcon women are worth their salt. Strong they are . . . like those Amazons you hear tell about."

Clenching the wad of tobacco fiercely between his teeth, Findley gripped the wheel and swerved adroitly to avoid a fallen branch that partially obstructed the road. Then with the danger past he breathed a deep sigh and said, "Too bad about old lady Falcon up and dyin' of a heart attack. Abigale was the last of a breed."

As Findley lapsed once again into silence, Christy thought back to the unusual exchange of letters that had ultimately resulted in her trip to Falcon's Island.

She had first seen the ad in the *Boston Globe* some three months previously and had been immediately intrigued. It had read in large bold type:

GOVERNESS WANTED

Twenty-one to 28 years of age. Must be of at least medium height with fair coloring and dark hair. Prefer someone well versed in music, letters, painting, and subjects suitable for tutoring a 7-year-old girl. Send particulars and recent photographs in order to receive full consideration.

The advertisement went on to request that anyone interested should contact Mrs. Iris Falcon of Falcon's Island, Maine.

Iris Falcon's return letter in answer to Christy's application expressed interest in her qualifications and requested that she send additional photographs, both profile and full face.

She mentioned in addition that if Christy should be selected, she would be given a house of her own as well as a salary almost double that which she could hope to receive as a primary school teacher in Boston.

It had seemed a golden opportunity and after their second exchange of letters Christy had waited eagerly for a favorable reply.

It came within two weeks. She had been offered the position of governess to Mrs. Falcon's niece, Amanda. No other details had been given.

Somehow to Christy this strange and fortuitous turn of events appeared to have been fated.

In a word, Falcon's Island was freedom. Freedom from her Aunt Ellen and the unreasonable demands that her guardians, the Lacy family, continually made upon her even though she had by now reached her majority.

Christy had decided after her graduation from teachers' college that if she were ever to mature as an individual, she would have to escape from the shadow of her domineering aunt.

It was inevitable that if she remained to teach in Boston as Ellen Lacy wished, she would eventually be forced into an unsuitable marriage with someone of her aunt's choosing. Most likely, a cast-off suitor of her cousin, Marylou.

Christy expected far more than this from life. She not only wanted to discover her own potential as a woman but to find her own place in the world. That special place where she could feel genuinely needed, a place where she belonged. Eventually there would be a man she loved, a home and children, but all that would come later.

This desire for independence and the million small humiliations inflicted over the years had played a large role in Christy's decision to accept the position of governess on Falcon's Island in spite of her aunt's open opposition.

She had become so involved in her thoughts that she failed to notice the fork in the road or the weathered sign pointing to the right and reading, "Land's End. Five Miles. Proceed With Caution."

The road quickly dwindled to little more than a country track, overhanging trees forming a ghostly arch mushrooming overhead. Spectral branches flailed at the car with leafy arms as they sped past, hurtling on into the rain-wet darkness.

Christy was growing extremely weary. So much had happened that day and her eyelids were leaden with fatigue. Still, sleep was an enemy she was determined to resist.

The steady hum of the tires and the slap-slapping of the windshield wipers had an almost hypnotic effect and in spite of her determination to remain alert, she began to doze off.

Up ahead the headlights barely penetrated the wash of rain and pockets of fog swirled up like ghostly manifestations to engulf the car. Feeling dazed and groggy, Christy cranked open the window a crack and took several deep breaths. The air was chill and icy pellets of rain splashed in against her cheek.

After a few minutes the fresh air began to revive her and almost immediately she felt refreshed.

"We'll soon be there," Mr. Findley called from the front seat. "Land's End is about a mile on down the road."

To her surprise his words struck a fearful chord somewhere deep within. Suddenly Christy dreaded the moment when Mr. Findley would switch off the key and the engine would fall silent.

Even the name, "Land's End," conjured up visions of the furthest reaches of the known world. In many ways their arrival there would signal the beginning of an entirely new life, one that was fraught with the strangeness of the unknown.

"That'll be Matthew Parrish up ahead," Mr. Findley informed her, guiding the car in the direction of the beckoning beam of a powerful torch. "He'll be waiting for you at the dock."

"Who is Matthew Parrish?" Christy asked, an uneven quaver betraying her apprehension.

"Matt's got the only power boat on the island. He brings in all the supplies and makes the mail run every two weeks."

As the car slowed to a bumping, jolting halt, Christy glanced down at the phosphorescent dial of her watch and saw that it was almost four in the morning.

For a brief instant all was silent. Then, to the accompaniment of thunderous cannonades on the horizon, the storm gathered in intensity and driving force. As Mr. Findley helped Christy from the car, the rain swept across the muddy road with sheets of water and a driving wind that almost whipped her coat from her shoulders.

"Better bundle up," Findley called as she turned to lift the reluctant Jason into her arms, sheltering him as best she could beneath her coat.

At that moment a figure materialized out of the rain and mist, a glistening black slicker flapping wildly about his tall body like the wings of a great bat.

Mr. Findley's mumbled introduction was lost on the wind. The man drew close and looked down into her face. Christy stood transfixed by the magnetic eyes that seemed to peer into her very soul.

For what seemed an eternity Matthew stood staring at her, his tall powerful body hunched against the wind. What was it she saw flash in his eyes? Surprise? Dislike?

The look came and went so swiftly that before she could read his reaction, the man's features were once again granitelike and closed.

Then with an unintelligible grunt he turned abruptly to help Mr. Findley unload her luggage from where it was strapped to the roof of the car.

"You'd better get on board," Matthew called out, in a gruff commanding voice as Christy stood watching helplessly. "No sense just standing around in the rain."

Feeling useless and painfully puzzled by his hostile attitude, Christy hurried toward the dock where the waiting boat was moored. Each step accompanied by sucking sounds, she sank deeper into the wet, oozing mud.

Land's End would have been a bleak and lonely spot in any weather: a desolate place of broken rocks and treeless dun-colored terrain used primarily as a staging point for Falcon's Island some thirty-five miles out at sea. It was surrounded by dunes, low lying cliffs, and a weedy ooze of swamp.

Rimming the squat cliffs Christy could just make out a shadowy grouping of clapboard houses surrounded by stunted pitch pines, warped and tortured by the wind. The glimmer of lantern light showing in several of the windows barely pierced the night. Other than that, there was little sign of habitation other than a few dilapidated storage shacks fronting the pier.

Stumbling on board Matthew's pitching, bobbing launch, Christy huddled into the comparative shelter of the open cabin as the fog closed in around her like a soft, gray winding sheet.

Jason whined and burrowed his head beneath her arm as if seeking the warmth and assurance of her body.

After helping Matthew transport her trunk and bags to the launch, Mr. Findley came aboard to bid her "Godspeed" and accept the ten-dollar bill she thrust gratefully into his hand. It was far more than he had asked for bringing her to Land's End, but she wanted somehow to thank him for his concern.

As he climbed stiffly back to the dock and turned to wave, Christy's heart caught in her throat. Now she was alone with the storm, the sea, and the strange and silent man standing at the wheel.

At that moment the powerful engines roared to life, churning the black water to a white froth. Without a glance or a word Matthew spun the wheel and the launch shot off amid towering plumes of salt spray and the deafening roar of twin Diesel engines.

"Best put this on," he shouted, tossing her a rubber rain slicker identical to his own. "It's going to get pretty rough once we hit the open sea."

Christy did as he suggested, settling the trembling Jason beside her on the cushioned bench.

Even though her teeth were chattering with the cold, she drank in the pure salt air and experienced a surge of excitement. She was on her way.

As they skimmed across the small harbor, Christy took the opportunity to examine more closely the man standing with his legs spread wide apart as if rooted to the swaying deck. His face was illuminated by the faint orange light emanating from the instrument panel.

It was an arresting face. Unusual and, in that subtle light, positively medieval. Unbidden, visions of her favorite El Greco painting came to mind. That was it exactly. Matthew's was the classical El Greco face—long, lean, and slightly disdainful, yet with a certain rugged attractiveness.

His body was perfectly attuned to his features. Tall, broad shouldered, with a mass of unruly black hair graying slightly at the temples. Although he couldn't have been more than thirty-six or thirty-seven, his skin was creased and weathered as if he had spent long years exposed to the sun, the wind, and the sea.

As he stood there straining to see out into the night, there was no smile on his lips and his eyes were icy blue and distant. It was as if his thoughts were far from that place, that particular moment in time. Christy wondered where they might be. About whom they might be.

The hands that gripped the spoked wheel were strong, the fingers blunt yet playing over the wheel with a sensitive master's touch. There was something strong and sure in the way he handled himself. A sense of command that caused her to feel secure and protected in spite of his gruff manner.

As they reached the open sea, the launch began to pitch and roll through the heavy swells, plunging down into the deep troughs like an onrushing train.

Thirty-foot showers of spray shot up on either side as waves thundered against the breakwater. The blinking buoy marking the harbor entrance with its flashing red light was gradually lost to view, although the tolling bell continued to ring out in the pitch-black night.

The launch began to pick up speed even as towering waves broke over the bow. They were quickly drenched in spite of being inside the open cabin.

On and on they went, foaming and hissing through the heaving black sea. Below the flimsy wooden planking the sea was a place of hollow boomings, great watery tumblings, and long hissing seethings. Again and again they plunged down into the deep watery troughs only to rise again to be soothed by splashes, whispers, and the comforting throb of the engines carrying them on into the night.

In spite of her discomfort Christy took some strange assurance from the presence of Matthew Parrish at the wheel. Within minutes after they had left the harbor she tucked a kapok life jacket beneath her head and, with Jason clasped in her arms, drifted off into a fitful slumber. Even then Matthew remained a presence—her troubled sleep shot through by his booming voice heaping imprecations on the wind.

As it worked its way into her dreams, the sea was constantly changing in tempo, accent, and rhythm. Now loud and thundering, then again growing placid, solemn, and slow. A pause in time before the monstrous rhythms began to swell once again, rising in concert with the elemental howling of the wind.

Christy awoke at dawn, drawn from sleep by a calloused hand proffering a bottle of whisky. "Better have a drink of this," Matthew instructed. "It'll take the chill out of your bones."

As the smell of the liquor reached her nostrils, a sick nausea welled up within her and Christy turned her face away with a bleak shake of her head.

"Suit yourself," he retorted shortly, tilting the bottle into his mouth and turning his attention to the wheel once again.

Christy closed her eyes, trying to wish away the queasy sensation in the pit of her stomach. She was chilled and sore from her cramped hours on the narrow bench.

"There it is," Matthew called after what seemed an eternity but was in reality a short ten minutes. "Falcon's Island, dead ahead."

Getting unsteadily to her feet, Christy clung to the railing and peered out into the pewter-gray dawn. The storm had slackened and the sea was by now a mass of heaving oily swells.

In the far distance the island swam up out of the sea, green and beckoning in the faint light. It formed a star shape, looming above the glowering horizon still misty with the dawn.

As they drew closer Christy could see the mountains enveloped in banks of mist and cloud while sea spume sprung high against the rocky limestone cliffs.

There was an austere beauty to the place. Craggy peaks

surfaced through green forests of ash, pine, and cypress, while on the lower slopes, orchards, and farmland stretched away as far as the eye could see.

"We'll be landing at Pirate's Cove," Matthew informed her, taking another long pull on the bottle and drawing his sleeve across his mouth. "It's the only town on the island."

"Is that where the Falcon family live?" she asked, placing the unsteady Jason on the deck. With great pleading eyes he remained pressed close against her legs, dejected, his tail drooping, and his tongue lolling forlornly from his mouth. He looked just as ill as she herself felt.

Without answering her question, Matthew raised his arm and pointed along the shore beyond the town, where the cliffs rose high and sheer above the turbulent sea.

"That's Falcon's Eyrie," he said, a note of bitterness creeping into his voice. "Up there—where they can keep an eye on everything that goes on down below."

Christy allowed her eyes to follow his pointing finger and sucked in her breath sharply.

Falcon's Eyrie was perched high on the towering cliffs, a commanding view of both the sea and the town of Pirate's Cove.

The mansion itself was an ancient Victorian structure of time-mellowed brick. Crowned by turrets and towers, its myriad banks of windows reflected the first pallid rays of the rising sun. They stared out like vacant eyes and Christy couldn't help but wonder what might lie behind them.

The house was surrounded by wide, sloping lawns and ornamental gardens, while beyond, Christy was greeted by a sweep of verdant mountains enforested with pine.

"Why, it's beautiful," Christy breathed after she managed to regain herself.

Matthew's laugh was harsh and toneless. "Yes, isn't it? A beautiful hell."

The depth of resentment honing his voice caused her

skin to crawl. "Exactly what do you mean by that?" she challenged.

For the first time Matthew smiled. A narrow, twisted smile that faded as quickly as it had appeared. "I'm going to let you discover that for yourself, my dear Miss Randolph. And so you shall. Whether you know it or not, you are about to step back into the past."

Matthew paused to give emphasis to his next statement. "To be exact, four hundred years in the past."

Christy remained transfixed, staring at his face in profile, his strong, masculine features clearly etched by the dawn.

"On that island out there you are going to encounter people whose ancestors worshiped the Devil," he went on to relate. "People who may appear to be perfectly good Christians on the surface but whose lives are governed by the superstitions and myths of the Middle Ages."

"It's not entirely their fault if they're backward," Christy offered defensively. "After all they are almost totally isolated."

"More than you might imagine," he replied. "There are no newspapers, radios, or telephones on the island and the only electricity to be found is up at Falcon's Eyrie."

At the look of surprise that blanked her features, Matthew added, "You might as well prepare for the worst, Miss Randolph. Your arrival here will not be welcomed by the islanders. I suspect they will look upon you as an emissary from the arch fiend himself."

He turned to regard her critically, his eyes a bright hard blue. "And the only thing the Falconers fear more than God is the Devil."

Christy was growing panicky. "I'm afraid I don't understand," she pleaded. "Why should they be afraid of me?"

"Because you're an outsider," he stated flatly. "Outsiders have always been considered to be the bearers of misfortune."

Christy opened her mouth to speak, to defend herself, but the words were stillborn on her lips.

"Let me give you an example," Matthew continued. "Several years ago a boat full of picnickers from the mainland were discovered in a secluded cove on the north shore." He turned from the wheel and once again that strange bitter smile flashed across his face and was gone. "When the islanders heard about it, they went there en masse."

"Oh, what they found was innocent enough. Men and women enjoying a summer afternoon on the beach. Eating, drinking, swimming, and generally behaving themselves."

Matthew paused to make an adjustment in course and then continued with his story. "The men were tarred and feathered on the spot. While the women, who were considered to be dressed immodestly, were stoned and driven through the streets of Pirate's Cove in a manure cart."

"They had no possible means of escape because the Falconers had burned their boat." Christy saw his teeth clench and grind together with ill-concealed indignation. "They might have been killed if I hadn't heard about it and taken them to safety in my boat."

"But what about Mrs. Falcon?" Christy demanded, by now thoroughly frightened by the picture he painted. "Surely she must have tried to put a stop to it."

Matthew uttered a low derisive snarl from deep in his throat. "There are two worlds here on the island, Miss Randolph. The world of Falcon's Eyrie and that of the village. They have existed in a state of uneasy truce for over four hundred years.

"Each knows enough not to interfere with the other's prerogatives. Both have tried in the past . . . and both have paid the price for meddling in blood."

"And what about yourself?" Christy challenged. "Just whose side are you on?"

It was a long moment before Matthew answered.

"The most important thing you can learn if you are to remain on this island, Miss Randolph . . . is not to ask questions."

He turned and fixed her with a steely gaze. "Have I made myself quite clear?"

Two

SHORTLY before nine they entered the small harbor of Pirate's Cove. The air was filled with the smell of pine and woodsmoke. The small town sprawled over the surrounding hills in a haphazard patchwork of cottages, barns, and garden plots.

The buildings of the town itself were uniformly old and weathered, the walls vine-covered, with trailing wisps of smoke rising from stone chimneys.

The sun had by now burnt off the morning mist. Above, a salmon-colored sky was rippled with feathery clouds, the sea beyond a crumpled parchment map inked a teary blue.

As they drew up to the small pier, the engines throttled down to a steady muffled throbbing. There was a jarring bump and after shutting down the engines, Matthew leaped ashore to secure the launch to the pier with thick hawsers.

"I'll be back shortly," he said, helping Christy ashore. "My wagon's up at the blacksmith's." Then without further explanation he was gone, moving away with his rolling seaman's stride. Christy watched him go, his powerful masculinity worn with an easy grace she found very appealing in spite of herself.

Then, feeling suddenly abandoned and terribly disappointed that Iris Falcon had sent no one to meet her, she turned her eyes toward the town.

At the end of the pier a cluster of fishermen were gathered together. They appeared entirely occupied with boiling lobster vats, baskets of shell fish, and freshly caught herring glinting silvery in the bright autumn sunlight.

Immediately she took notice of the fact that the islanders were given to similar physical characteristics. They appeared uniformly short in stature, spare of frame, with eyes that were widely spaced and deeply set beneath hooded brows.

One by one they began to take note of her presence on the dock, their narrow faces remaining dour and unsmiling.

When her wave and friendly smile brought no visible response, Christy began to feel uneasy and turned her attention to the town itself climbing the hills beyond the wharf.

Bathed in early morning light, it appeared to be quiet and peaceful. From where Christy stood she had a clear view of the grassy commons surrounded by mellow old stone cottages with steeply pitched slate roofs. The single cobbled street was intersected by a rushing stream neatly spanned by a sturdy wooden bridge.

The stream tumbled down from a millrace above the town, where a venerable water wheel turned in slow creaking cadence at the top of a mossy waterfall. At the foot of the falls was a still and silent millpond, its surface a glassy shimmer swept by the branches of trailing willows.

Christy couldn't help but think that Matthew had been partially right at least. The town of Pirate's Cove was something out of a bygone century. But surely, she reassured herself, people living in such a lovely, idyllic spot—

a veritable Eden—couldn't be as backward and narrow minded as he had suggested.

Most likely he was nursing some personal grudge that had colored his attitude toward the local inhabitants.

At that moment she saw him emerge from a low wooden building leading a horse and wagon. What could possibly have taken place in his past to have embittered him to such a degree, she wondered?

As he passed along the wharf, Christy realized with a sense of shock that it was now completely empty. Where only moments before the fishermen were busily mending nets and arranging tackle, there was now no one to be seen. For his part Matthew appeared to take no notice of their disappearance, glancing neither to the right nor to the left as he came toward her.

After transferring her trunk and bags to the back of the wagon, Matthew helped Christy up onto the buckboard seat and then swung up beside her. As she cast a curious glance at the wooden crates packed full of groceries and household goods stashed in the back of the wagon, he spoke as if in answer to an unasked question.

"You'll be needing supplies out at the pond," he offered by way of explanation. "This ought to last you for at least two weeks. When you run short, just make a list of what you need. I'll be dropping by every so often to make sure you don't run out of anything."

It was the first time that he had spoken agreeably to her, and Christy was completely taken aback.

"That won't be necessary, Mr. Parrish. I'm perfectly capable of doing my own shopping."

Matthew's voice dropped into an apologetic key. "I'm afraid the truth of the matter is, the townspeople won't sell to you, Miss Randolph."

She stared at him in disbelief, her mouth falling open in surprise.

"Like I said. Falcon's Island consists of two different

worlds. Not only are you a stranger, but you're part of the great house. It's best that you don't try and trespass where you're not wanted."

Making a sharp clucking noise, Matthew grasped the reins firmly in both hands and they started off across the quay at a brisk trot, the horse's hooves making hollow clopping sounds on the cobbles. "You'll see what I mean soon enough," he added with a grim smile.

As they passed along the single main street of Pirate's Cove, the women of the town scurried indoors at their approach. Jason raced from one side of the wagon to the other barking and wagging his tail frantically, but all to no avail. They received not a glance as doors slammed behind the retreating women and shutters banged closed.

From what little she saw of them, the women of Falcon's Island, like the men, were dressed alike. They wore black multilayered skirts that swept the ground as they walked, with shawls of a somber blue draped about their shoulders. Uniformly their heads were covered by cowl-like bonnets that gave their sharp, angular faces a spectral mourning look.

Were it not for the difference in costume, it would have been impossible to tell the men and the women apart.

"How strange they are," Christy said in a voice that was full of wonder and disappointment.

"You'll get used to them in time," Matthew offered. "It's fear that makes them act the way they do. Fear and ignorance."

"But why do they treat you like this?" Christy demanded. "Surely they don't consider you an outsider."

Matthew's jaw muscles knotted together and his features hardened. Then the look drained away, leaving his face totally empty of expression.

"As I said earlier, Miss Randolph. You'd be wise not to ask too many questions here. There are things better left unsaid."

For an instant his eyes sought hers, ice blue and piercing. "I'm sorry to have to be so rude. But for your own good, you'd be better off if you listen to what I say."

Turning his attention to the road, he flicked the whip gently along the horse's flanks, sending the wagon jolting along at a brisker pace.

The two of them sat perched on the wooden seat in silence, lurching slightly with the swaying movement of the wagon. The road had begun to grow steeper and more winding as they left the town, the old mare laboring and the cart creaking and groaning as they climbed the hill.

Turning to look back, Christy marveled at the magnificence of the view—the sea gleaming like a silver platter in the distance.

After cresting the hill, they began to descend into the open countryside that stretched away as far as the eye could see. The road meandered on ahead of them, rutted and muddy from the previous night's storm.

An uneasy silence had settled over the wagon since leaving the village. It was counterpointed, however, by the creaking of the wheels, the clopping hooves of the mare, and occasional bursts of birdsong from the thick foliage bordering the road.

Off in the west, thunderheads were once again glowering on the horizon, the promise of rain implicit in the moist, heavy air. A marbleized sky stretched above, with fleecy clouds scurrying in formation, line upon line, to join the steadily darkening mass.

Staring out at the lovely rural scenery vanishing on either side of the wagon, Christy felt rumpled and exhausted. The linen suit was a mass of wrinkles; her shoes and silk stockings were splattered with dried mud. She was growing anxious to reach their destination and wondered only at its distance from town.

They crossed a second wooden bridge, this one covered and spanning a smooth flowing river, with bulrushes standing tall in the placid green water. According to Matthew the river commenced at a spectacular falls high in the mountain.

Coming out into the fast waning sunlight on the other side, Christy saw two figures approaching along the road. As they drew closer, she noticed that the first was a boy with a shriveled arm and great painful eyes. His manner of dress was identical to that of the adults she had seen in town, if slightly more threadbare.

He shuffled past with head bowed, the narrowness of the road forcing him to draw close to the wagon. When Jason began yapping excitedly and tried to lick his face, the boy broke into a grudging grin and reached out to stroke the dog's head.

Following directly behind, the figure of a man—tall and spare with the trailing beard of a Biblical patriarch— lifted a gnarled walking stick and brought it down hard on the boy's back, sending him sprawling in the muddy track.

Looking back, Christy was horrified. "Stop the wagon," she cried, her voice quavering with outrage.

Behind them the man was standing over the boy, bringing the stick down on his back and shoulders again and again.

Unable to watch further, Christy turned her face away and once again ordered Matthew to stop the wagon. When he showed no inclination of doing so, she attempted to wrest the reins from his hands only to be rudely shoved to the far side of the seat.

"But you saw what he did," she shrilled. "The boy only wanted to pet Jason. There was no harm in it."

Matthew glanced over at her and suddenly she saw the pain and helplessness flash in his eyes. "There's nothing you can do," he offered in a toneless voice. "I know you mean well, but it's just no good interfering. If you do, you'll only make it harder on the boy."

She sat there staring at him in stunned silence, a slow

realization coming over her. The man with the stick, who bore a striking resemblance to the boy, was as well afflicted with a withered arm.

Steeling herself, she turned to look back at the two figures now proceeding down the road once again. "How strange," she said in an empty voice. "I just realized that——"

"I know," Matthew cut in. "They both have a deformed right arm. It's a freak genetic inheritance afflicting the men of that family. They've all had it. Every last one of them for over two hundred years."

"Why I've never heard of anything like that."

"Here abouts they call it the hanging curse," Matthew informed her. "At the time of the Salem witchcraft trials the local preacher talked the people here into hanging the island witch. It was that boy's ancestor who pulled the rope, and ever since that time the local people believe the family to be cursed because of their part in the deed. They're outcasts, barely surviving on food that's left outside of town for them."

Christy listened intently as Matthew went on, telling her of the boy, whose mother had died at his birth. He spoke as well of the half-mad sister and the father, who was known to hitch the children up to a wooden plow each spring in order to scratch a meager living from his fields.

Although shocked to the point of tears, Christy realized for the first time that Matthew spoke well and with a high degree of intelligence, scarcely what she would have expected from a common fisherman. She found that in spite of his initial ill humor she was impressed with the man.

"But that's barbaric," she commented when he had finished his story. "Positively medieval."

"It's ridiculous of course," he went on, "but the old legends die hard out here. You must bear in mind that this island is a backwater of civilization still closely bound to the past, its primitive legends and superstitions, its myths."

"But aren't the children taught differently in school?" she demanded. "Surely the minister of the church knows better."

Matthew shook his head sadly. "There are no schools and the church has been closed for years. No preacher has been willing to visit the island since they tarred and feathered the last one."

"But then . . . what do they believe in?" Christy demanded, almost dreading his answer.

"If I told you," he responded, choosing his words carefully, "you wouldn't believe me. Nor would you remain on this island one day longer than necessary."

They drove on through the rolling farmland paralleling the eastern coast of the island. Off to the left the mountains rose majestically, craggy peaks surfacing through forests of pine, beach, and ash. On either side of the road orchards were clothed in the gold and russet colors of late autumn, interrupted occasionally by somber clusters of ancient white oak.

As they rode along, it was plain to see that Falcon's Island was a virtual paradise primeval. Herds of deer scattered at their approach while flocks of wild turkey took ponderous flight from roadside thickets at the sound of the wagon's wheels.

Strung along the island's twenty-eight-mile length were moss-grown stone fences, built, according to Matthew, centuries before by the first settlers to the island. All about them the air was filled with the song of birds. Many of them exhibited rare and beautiful plumage as they darted swiftly through leafy glades like brilliantly hued butterflies.

As they emerged from the cool, resin-scented shade of a pine grove into the sunlight, Christy looked up to see a windmill cresting a hill in the distance. It appeared to be beckoning them onward, its ghostly arms revolving slowly in the faint breeze. The sails caught the light of the dying sun, casting revolving shadows on the fields of waving barley grass.

"What a lovely old mill," Christy commented. "Can we stop for a few minutes?"

"I'm afraid there isn't time," Matthew responded, glancing apprehensively at the darkening sky. "It's too far off the main road and the storm will soon be upon us."

Christy masked her disappointment with a lighter tone of voice. "Is the mill still in use?"

"Not any longer," he answered slowly, his eyes darkening and distant. "It belongs to Falcon's Eyrie."

Raising his hand, he pointed to where the chimney and cupolas of the mansion were etched against the sky, only barely visible above the treetops.

"In the old days they used it to signal pirates when it was safe for them to land," he went on to say. "Although, now . . . no one goes near it. The islanders are convinced that it's haunted."

"Pirates?" Christy repeated with some surprise.

He nodded. "Falcon's Island was used by Captain Kidd to bury the treasure stolen from Spanish galleons. There are those that say that the Falcon family themselves were in on it, but that's never been proven."

The clouds overhead were moving together now with dark certainty. There was a brief flash of lightning, announcing the quick anger of an autumn storm, while off on the horizon thunder boomed an elemental cannonade.

With a great flapping of wings a flock of Canadian geese lifted gracefully from a roadside marsh and swiftly climbed the sky in a westerly direction.

About a mile further on, Christy noticed a stone cairn beside the road, marking a turn-off. Flicking the reins, Matthew guided the wagon into a tree-shaded lane that wound its rutted way over the low-lying hills. Beyond, the sea glimmered like a tarnished mirror in the distance.

The road eventually dwindled to a sandy track winding

through meadowland and marsh before ending altogether beneath a stand of ancient oak festooned with Spanish moss.

"There it is," Matthew exclaimed as a house appeared among the trees. "Witch's Pond. Your new home."

To Christy the sight was anything but reassuring. The cottage itself was enclosed by a wall of mossy stone and sheltered by venerable white oak. It was of two stories and crouched on the shore of a tidal pool. Swamp grass stood waist high in the yard and there was a general air of disuse about the place.

The pond itself was a flat swamp choked with weed and backing on the dunes that faced the ocean beach, an inlet spaced with gloomy islands, dark with spiny pitch pines and traced by meandering creeks.

From beyond the ghostly mushrooming dunes Christy could hear the somber thunder of surf breaking on the outer beach.

She shuddered at the desolation of the place. Even as they drew up in front of the house, the fog began to billow up from the beach and waft slowly through the hanging Spanish moss. It came in wave after vaporous wave, rolling inland to envelope the house and its surrounding trees, carrying along with it the smell of brine and seaweed.

Matthew's voice jolted Christy from her gloomy appraisal. "The place belonged to old Mistress Cory," he informed her. "She's dead now. Died about six months ago."

He pointed to a low shed barely visible through the rising mist and very nearly enshrined by a thicket of sea grape. "You'll find an old mule back there who answers to the name of Robin. I've been keeping him out at my place but I brought him back when I heard you were coming.

"There's a buckboard in back of the shed that you can hitch him up to. It's not exactly the last word in modern conveyance, but it should get you around well enough."

The sky was by now completely overcast, so changed

from the earlier sunlit morning. As the wagon jolted to a halt, the rain, which had let up before dawn, returned with a few warning drops accompanied by a splintered flash of lightning.

With a sinking heart Christy climbed down from the wagon and moved toward the cottage as if in a trance. Jason trailed reluctantly at her heels, sniffing along the path and making short forays into the high grass as unseen creatures scurried off at his approach.

The door swung open on creaking hinges and Christy found herself standing in a darkened room, the furniture shrouded with yellowed sheets. The air was damp and close, smelling of mildew, and a fine coating of gritty sand covered everything.

Biting her lip with disappointment, she fought back the stinging tears that threatened to engulf her. For a moment she simply stood there listening to the past whisper in the dimness. Then drained and entirely exhausted, she crossed the room and sank down on the window seat.

As the choking sensation rose in her throat, she brushed a shaking hand across her eyes. She was determined not to break down completely. Perhaps later, but not now. Not in front of Matthew Parrish.

Hurriedly she located a handkerchief in her bag and dabbed at her eyes. Then hearing Matthew's approaching steps on the gravel path, she rose quickly to her feet and set about pulling dust covers off the furniture.

After carrying her luggage inside, Matthew moved about the cottage with an easy familiarity. He threw several logs into the large stone fireplace, touched a match to some kindling, and stood watching as the firelight crept up the walls to extinguish the shadows.

Then turning from the fire, he found Christy staring in mute fascination at an old barrel she had discovered in the corner. It was constructed of oaken staves with a seat built inside. Overall it was covered with a voluminous canvas, while at the top there was a narrow opening just large enough to enable a person to enter and sit down.

"What on earth is that?" Christy asked.

Matthew laughed. A deep hearty boom of pure masculine amusement. "That, my dear Miss Randolph, is your bathtub."

"But why is it . . . ?" She gestured toward the canvas cover that would surely obscure the bather from anyone who happened to be inside the room.

"It's called the Devil's shroud," he responded with a wry smile. "The Falconers believe it is the greatest of sins to view the human body. They traditionally undress in the dark, and as you can see. . . ." At this point his smile grew broader, displaying strong white teeth. "Even when bathing they take no chances of being seen. Either by themselves or by anyone else."

Christy shook her head in perplexity and returned his smile. "I can see I still have a lot to learn."

"Don't worry about it. You'll get used to our primitive ways in time."

With a friendly salute Matthew turned and started for the door.

"Oh, Mr. Parrish," she called out a bit anxiously, dreading the moment when she would be alone in the house. "I want to thank you for all your help. You've been most kind."

"It's only what Mrs. Falcon pays me to do," Matthew answered casually. "You needn't thank me."

"I rather expected Mrs. Falcon to meet me when I arrived," Christy said, hurrying her words. "Will you tell her that I'm here?"

He laughed, but there was no pleasure in it as before. The sound coming short and harsh to his lips. "Don't worry. She knows you're here all right. When she wants you, she'll send for you."

With a brief nod he was gone, moving easily down the path and vaulting up into the wagon.

Walking to the door on legs that felt like matchsticks that might break at any moment, Christy called Jason into the house.

Standing there in the doorway, she followed with her eyes as Matthew's wagon bounced down the rutted road and was quickly swallowed up by the enveloping fog.

In spite of his dour manner, Christy couldn't help but feel a sense of loss. There was something strong and comforting about his presence, even though the man remained a complete enigma to her.

Now he was gone and she was completely alone, hemmed in by the failing light and threatened by the low kettle-drum rumble of thunder rolling in from the sea.

Three

AFTER closing the heavy oaken door, Christy drew the bolts and set about putting the house in order. Although musty and badly in need of a good cleaning, she found the cottage to be soundly constructed and comfortable enough.

It consisted of two floors. The lower was dominated by a large sitting room with a low-beamed ceiling and soot-blackened stone fireplace. There was a kitchen at the back which reminded Christy of nothing so much as the galley of a ship.

The kitchen turned out to be compact, yet primitive,

with a wood-burning stove and temperamental water pump that worked only occasionally—the water itself tasting slightly brackish.

The walls were lined with shelves and cupboards, complete with heavy crockery as well as pewter plates and drinking cups. While exploring a small pantry off the kitchen, Christy discovered a lovely hand-sewn damask tablecloth, a cache of old china, and a bottle of Madeira wine.

She was thoroughly amused at the thought of Mistress Cory—midwife of the moral little island—tippling to her heart's content with no one the wiser. There was, of course, the possibility that the wine had been used for medicinal purposes only. In either case the thought caused Christy to smile.

At the top of a narrow flight of stairs Christy found two bedrooms and a large storage chamber. She chose the larger of the bedrooms for herself.

The room was sparsely furnished with a hand-carved bureau, long low bench, and four-poster bed. The dormer windows commanded an easterly view of the marshes, one that she hoped would provide her with a lovely sunrise when the weather permitted.

Throughout the house the windows were mullioned and slightly frosted by the constant blowing of the sand off the dunes.

While putting her things away in the armoire, Christy came upon a large supply of hand-stitched linen sheets as well as several patchwork quilts and a goose-down comforter. For this she was grateful, feeling the chill of the coming night in the dying day.

In spite of herself Christy didn't feel entirely comfortable in the upstairs bedroom. She hurriedly finished her unpacking, anxious for the warmth of the downstairs fire and the company of Jason, who was at that moment eating a hearty dinner in the kitchen.

Her unease was caused by nothing in particular. It was a combination of things. Outside, the salmon sky had turned a dense gray and birds made soft rustling sounds as they sought shelter in the eaves.

An angry wind was on the rise, rapping at the windows and causing the old house to creak and groan. Glancing up, she noticed that the rafters above her head were festooned with cobwebs that wafted gently with each draft that seeped in through the cracks.

As quickly as possible she finished her work and made her way gratefully downstairs.

In the sitting room things were more cheerful. The firelight cast a muted golden glow over everything, softening an otherwise unfamiliar scene. Christy hummed bravely to herself as she moved about, adding the finishing touches and lighting the pewter candelabra. She was relieved to find that the woodbox was crammed full of driftwood, although in the faint light it appeared as smooth and white as old bones.

The room had a lived-in look to it that she found comforting. There was a circular oaken table with two caneback chairs, a scatter of colorful rag rugs, and a rocker placed directly in front of the hearth.

After having spent the afternoon unpacking, dusting, and setting the cottage to order, Christy began to experience a bone tiredness. Dropping exhausted into the rocking chair, she stared moodily into the flickering fire. Jason had curled up at the hearth and was soundly asleep.

For the first time she noticed a shotgun hanging on pegs over the mantle. The implications of its being displayed with such prominence caused Christy to shudder. She had never used a gun before and actually had a deadly fear of all firearms. She prayed silently that the time was long past since the shotgun had served any practical purpose.

Outside, the fog pressed close against the windows with gray, spongy fingers. The promise of rain had not yet materialized, although moisture hung heavy in the air. From where she sat Christy could look out and see the oaks, the moss hanging from their branches like ancient cobwebs. The weed-grown garden appeared lifeless, while barren stumps of rotting trees protruded from the oily black pond like talons.

On the small table beside her rocker Christy noticed two leather-bound volumes, both appearing to be quite old.

One was a Bible, while the other was entitled *Spells and Incantations,* the gold lettering almost entirely worn away.

Taking the Bible in her hands, Christy opened it and leafed through the closely scrawled pages at the front. They had been inscribed in many different hands and dated from 1625.

Briefly she scanned the curious entries. "Bridget Bishop. Meg Jenkins. Amity Cabot. Beth Calvert. Sarah Godwin." Here she paused, straining to read the scrawled note beside the last name.

She finally made it out to be some sort of poem or rhyme written in a cramped, unlettered hand.

> Light the flame and
> bright the fire;
> Let vengeance be mine
> as I desire.

It was signed, "Sarah Godwin. Bride of the hanging oak. 1732."

Following this cryptic and entirely puzzling entry, there was a lapse in time. The next signer was Leonora Dorn, who entered her name in a flowery script some sixty years later.

Christy followed the chronicle of names on down

through the decades until she came to the latest entry, dated fifty years before.

The last name to be entered was that of Eliza Cory—the quill pen having stabbed the page in a bold, slanting hand. Originally it had been followed by a more recent entry but the name had been scratched out with a single stroke of the pen. On closer inspection, however, Christy was able to make out the name to be "Jennifer Parrish."

Why that was Matthew's last name, she mused. Somehow, seeing it written there in a close, spidery scrawl left Christy slightly stunned. What possible connection could Matthew's mother—if that was who it was—have had with the cottage at Witch's Pond?

After staring at the signature for a long, wondering moment, she closed the Bible and replaced it on the table.

For some minutes she sat there listening to the hiss and crackle of the fire and wondering about the woman who had inhabited the cottage before her.

Matthew had indicated only that she had been the local midwife and was now dead. And what about the others? Equally puzzling was the strange reference to the "Bride of the hanging oak."

The only answer that suggested itself was that the women had successively acted as midwives to the local population, each inhabiting the cottage upon the death of the previous midwife.

It seemed incredible, of course, but no more so than what she had seen of the townspeople or for that matter the island itself. All of it was a throwback to another time, another century, the superstitions and ways of the past still lingering on strong and pervasive.

Why even the name of the house in which she sat—Witch's Pond—was enough to give one nightmares.

On the mantle the old clock slowly ticked off the passing seconds while the wind rattled the windows like china in an old cupboard.

Rising wearily to her feet, Christy went to the sideboard and poured herself a glass of Madeira, hoping to settle her frayed nerves. Then returning to her place by the fire, she gave in to her disappointment at not having been contacted by Iris Falcon.

Perhaps, she told herself, the woman was simply being thoughtful. Possibly she thought that Christy would be too exhausted after her long trip to receive visitors.

But then what had Matthew meant when he told her not to worry? That Iris would send for her when she wanted her. His tone had certainly implied something more, but just what she wasn't sure.

Christy's mind was growing numb with fatigue, refusing to function properly. Perhaps it was all a bad dream. Maybe she would soon awaken to find that she was back in her own familiar room in Boston. Soon she would have to go downstairs and help the cook with dinner.

For a brief moment Christy almost wished that it were true.

Realizing that her imagination would quickly run away with her if she didn't keep herself occupied, she decided to get out her knitting bag and occupy herself that way.

She had brought it along knowing that in the coming months she would have plenty of time to knit. Before leaving Boston Christy had signed a contract with the Falcons' lawyer agreeing to remain on the island for at least twelve months. To insure that she did, one half of her salary was to be held back pending completion of the contract.

With a deep sigh Christy steeled herself against the thought of winter at the pond. Considering the severity of the weather, she decided it was probably wisest to finish knitting the heavy scarf she had started some two years previously and had never yet had the time to finish.

Now here she was. Miles from civilization and without so much as a telephone. Taking the stony welcome she had received into account, Falcon's Island might as well be peopled by Martians. Hadn't Matthew in so many words warned her to stay away from the town altogether.

Nor did it seem likely that old Robin out in the stable would do her much good in the way of transportation. She had never even been near a mule before, much less hitch one up to a wagon and then drive it into town.

Perhaps, Christy thought, Iris could arrange to give her the use of a horse instead. She would like nothing better than to spend her idle hours riding in the mountains or out along the beach when the weather permitted.

She loved to ride and the thought cheered her somewhat as she set about her knitting with more enthusiasm.

As she sat there counting the stitches on her needles, Christy became terribly aware of every sound. The rain had commenced in earnest now, the water pouring from the eaves while the wind howled mournfully about the house.

Summoning all her powers of concentration, Christy began to knit, plying the long ivory needles in and out of the yellow yarn with obvious skill. She worked slowly at first and then, as habit began to reassert itself, with more assurance.

Gradually she became more involved with her work. Deftly she wove the yellow yarn into the pale blue and then intersected it at intervals with a soft apple green. The needles began clicking together more rapidly, moving along in their preordained pattern without pause.

From time to time Christy would glance apprehensively at the solidly locked door, taking some assurance from the sight of the bolt which she had earlier slid into place.

As the minutes slipped endlessly by, the house began to grow quiet and the stillness itself began to unnerve her far more than the fury of the storm had previously done.

The storm appeared to have died down briefly, the thunder quelling its angry clamor and the rain abating to barely a drizzle.

The clock striking six caused her to start from her chair. As she sat there listening, Christy felt the lonely impact of each dulcimer chime until at last the room was immersed in silence once again.

A hush seemed to have fallen over everything; her busy needles fell still and silent in her hands as she listened desperately for the sounds that had by now become so familiar.

Christy could no longer hear even the surf, which had whispered off on the edge of her consciousness ever since her arrival earlier that day. Nothing. Complete stillness.

A full minute passed. Another. And then another.

Then in the distance she heard the barely audible roll of thunder and breathed a sigh of relief. Her nerves were obviously getting the better of her. Instead of hearing things she was failing to hear them. A nice twist.

Staring moodily into the merrily crackling fire, she sat transfixed. Christy dreaded the coming night, deciding on impulse that she would sleep downstairs when the time came. The thought of climbing that narrow flight of stairs to the chill upper rooms was simply more than she could contemplate.

Then she was struck by a frightening realization. Eventually she would have to use the upstairs bed. The bed of a dead woman. Christy's skin tingled as she sat there contemplating her plight. Her fears began to mushroom and expand, moving in through the twilight as silently as moths on the wing.

She held out her hands before the flames, grateful for the warmth and companionship of the fire that flickered brightly for a moment longer and then died abruptly for no apparent reason.

Stunned, disbelieving, Christy sat staring with horrified eyes at the blackened logs. Then, as if an invisible hand were at work in the room, the candles in the pewter candelabra glowed brightly for an instant longer and went out.

The room was plunged into total darkness. Deep, black, and all pervading.

Thrusting her needles into the ball of yarn with trembling hands, Christy laid her knitting aside and sat listening. Once again everything was perfectly still.

Gripping the arms of her chair she rose, peering into the inky blackness. Could she possibly be suffering from hallucinations or was there something in the room with her?

When nothing more took place to further arouse her suspicions, Christy decided to make her way into the kitchen and retrieve a box of matches and an additional supply of candles.

She heard Jason rouse himself from where he had been sleeping in front of the fire. He padded over to her side, his wiry hair brushing against her legs. Then he emitted a low, menacing growl.

Summoning all her courage, Christy took a tentative step forward and then another before stopping and holding her breath in ghastly anticipation.

There was something or someone in the room with her. She was sure of that now.

It was more than Jason's low, rumbling growl. More even than her own fearful imagination. She could actually hear breathing. This was followed within seconds by the floor creaking over near the staircase and a sound like the rustling of voluminous skirts.

"Is someone there?" Christy's voice sounded high pitched and unnatural. Not her voice at all.

"Who is it?" she called out again, this time in genuine alarm.

There was no response. Only the slow creaking of the floorboards and soft footfalls that seemed to be moving across the room, drawing nearer and nearer. At the same time the heavy breathing increased in tempo to a low, asthmatic wheeze.

As Christy strained to penetrate the darkness, she was

suddenly chilled to the bone by a draft of icy air. It seemed to pass over her like an errant wintery gust and was gone.

Before she could summon the breath to scream, the candelabra mysteriously took flame immediately followed by the fire, which was soon crackling merrily in the hearth.

As if commencing on cue, the rain began to pelt the windows and the wind to sigh mournfully through the eaves once again.

Everything was exactly as it was, the room warm and cozy, pewter plates gleaming dully from the shelves, the old china clock tick-tocking away the seconds as if nothing had happened.

Yet it had. She knew that it had. No. It couldn't have been entirely her imagination since Jason had heard it—whatever it was—as well. Even now he was skulking beneath the table, his shoe-button eyes wary and alarmed.

Moving as if she were walking on eggs, Christy crossed to where she had first heard what sounded like footfalls and stood at the foot of the stairs.

Nothing. No sign whatsoever of an intruder. Only an old rag rug woven in many colors and adding a homey, comfortable aspect to the room.

Not quite knowing what possessed her to do so, Christy bent down and lifted the rug. She drew back in shock and surprise.

Underneath—on the rough plank flooring scoured bone white by the previous tenant—she discovered an ugly rust-colored stain.

With a gasp of recognition Christy drew back, her hands flying to her mouth.

It was dried blood.

Four

CHRISTY stood staring down at the pool of dried blood upon the rough planking. She could scarcely believe her eyes.

Trying desperately to get a grip on her mounting hysteria, she reasoned that it could very well have been the result of an accident. Someone could have fallen, and the most likely candidate was Mistress Cory.

If that were so, it could possibly explain her death. After all, the stairs were steep and narrow, probably difficult for an old woman to manage. It would have been so easy for her to have slipped and plunged to the bottom.

Christy's flesh crawled at the thought of the ghastly accident, if indeed that was what had taken place.

Of course there was also the possibility that the woman had not been killed instantly. How dreadful it would have been to lay injured in the lonely cottage and know that no one would discover her in time.

But what of the fire, the candles being snuffed out, and the sound of heavy breathing? Jason, who was only now creeping out from beneath the table with his tail drooping, had been as frightened as she. It couldn't have been entirely her imagination.

At that moment another sound intruded upon her thoughts. The roll of carriage wheels on the gravel drive leading up to the house.

Rushing to the windows, Christy saw a gleaming black

brougham pull up to the gate drawn by twin sorrels, their coats darkening in the rain.

A spare figure jumped down from the driver's seat and strode briskly toward the cottage. The man was almost entirely concealed beneath a billowing cloak, his sallow face barely visible through a cowled slit. Long before he reached the porch, Jason began barking frantically, his wiry coat bristling along the entire length of his body.

A fist banged loudly on the door. Once, and then again. Christy stood frozen with indecision. She was totally unable to act, to move, or even to think rationally. So much had happened in such a short space of time.

Who could the man be, she wondered? What could he want with her?

Then, experiencing a flood of relief, she realized that it must be someone sent by Mrs. Falcon.

Hurrying to the door, she threw it open only to be met by a gaunt and sinister figure scowling darkly at her from beneath beetled brows.

The man was tall and slightly hunched, his eyes burning with an unhealthy glitter in his stubbled face. His arms were long and simian and when he threw back the cowl of his cloak, a greasy tangle of long black hair tumbled almost to his shoulders.

"Miss Iris sent me to fetch you up to the great house," he rasped, appearing not to be entirely happy with his appointed task.

Christy smiled her relief, taking courage from the sound of another human voice. "I'm afraid I wasn't expecting visitors, Mr ——?"

"Scully, ma'am. Eustace Scully." For a moment his red-rimmed eyes played over her from head to foot until she felt a hot blush rise to her cheeks.

"I'm the caretaker up at Falcon's Eyrie."

"Would you like to come inside and wait for me?" she offered, not quite knowing what else to say.

"No, ma'am," he responded tartly, at the same time re-treating several steps backward as if anxious to be quit of the house. "I'll be waiting for you in the carriage. But best stir yourself. Mrs. Falcon don't like to be kept waiting."

After preparing Jason a snug bed in a box beside the fire, Christy dressed quickly in a tweed skirt, sweater, and low-heeled shoes. She decided against wearing any make-up, and after brushing her hair, tied it back casually with a blue ribbon. Then, donning a scarf and waterproof trench coat, she left the house and allowed Scully to help her up into the closed brougham.

Falcon's Eyrie was located between Witch's Pond and the town of Pirate's Cove, the drive consuming less than twenty minutes. The carriage rolled along the rutted roads with the rain beating an endless tattoo on the roof and streaming down the windows.

In spite of the storm and the jolting, rocking carriage, Christy felt comfortable enough, safe and warm, tucked beneath a thick woolen lap robe. Her previous fatigue had evaporated with the expectation of meeting the Falcon family. To this single purpose she had made the long and difficult journey to the island.

As the road began to grow steeper and more winding, Christy realized with a heightened sense of anticipation that they must be nearing the house on the cliffs. She re-called her first view of it early that morning, and Mat-thew's words echoed in her mind.

"There it is. Up there where they can keep an eye on everything that goes on down below."

As she sought once again to comprehend the strange nature of the man, the carriage came to an abrupt, jolting halt and Scully's pale face appeared in the driver's win-dow.

Sliding it open with a spidery hand, he peered in at her, a faint smile tracing his thin lips. "Sorry, miss. You'll have to walk the rest of the way up to the house. A tree's fallen across the road and it'll take some time to clear it away."

In spite of his fawning manner Christy couldn't help but feel that Scully was not entirely displeased at the prospect of her setting out alone in the dark and dismal night.

Still, she decided, it was better than being out there alone with him, and it appeared that she had no other choice.

Alighting from the carriage, Christy missed the step and sank up to her ankles in a puddle. Fortunately she had remembered to wear rubber rain boots, although her stockings were thoroughly splattered with mud. The weather being what it was, she feared that she was going to look a fright by the time she reached the house, but it simply couldn't be helped.

Without a word Scully appeared around the front of the carriage and pointed off into the slanting curtain of rain.

Christy was barely able to make out a road passing between large stone gateposts, each of them topped by a marble falcon.

"You'll find the great house directly up the drive," he grinned. "Not much of a walk for a healthy young lass like yourself."

At her look of dismay his smile turned obscene, his face splitting into a leer that exposed rotting stumps of broken teeth.

Anxious to be away from him, Christy started out at a brisk walk, making her way carefully around the fallen tree and fording a virtual torrent of water cutting diagonally across the road.

The drive to Falcon's Eyrie wound away before her, twisting and turning, almost totally obscured in places by pockets of drifting mist. It proved to be narrow and unkempt, a bower of trees forming a dark cathedral-like vault overhead.

The woods on either side crowded dark and uncon-

trolled to the borders of the drive, the mountain beeches
reaching out with white, tortured limbs that reminded her
of nothing so much as the bleached bones of skeletons.

Christy hurried her steps unable to escape the eerie sensation that something or someone was off there in the
darkness watching her every move, waiting for just the
right moment to lunge out at her.

It was probably just her nerves, she told herself as she
ducked her head to avoid the flailing branches that reached
out with leafy spectral fingers. God knows she had reason
enough to imagine the worst.

She had walked along for some twenty minutes before
the thought occurred to her that she must have lost her
way, somehow getting off on one of the many side paths
that led from the main drive. Struggling over the gnarled
roots that crisscrossed the path like sleeping snakes, Christy skirted a muddy ditch and peered into the choked wilderness for some sign of habitation.

Nothing. She was alone with the storm and the night.
For a moment she paused, wondering whether or not she
would be better off to try and retrace her steps. Then out
of the corner of her eye she caught sight of something that
sent a chill of cold, unreasoning fear coursing through her
veins.

It appeared to be some kind of animal. A dog. Sleek
and ghostly white, it crouched in the undergrowth at a
short distance, watching her every move.

Christy began to run, aware that the animal was keeping deliberately abreast of her—hunching low as he made
his way through the thick cover of underbrush. She surmised that he must have been following her for some
time, as his tongue was lolling from his muzzle, his eyes
were glinting red in the faint light.

Concentrating on the treacherous path before her,
Christy wondered if her eyes could possibly be playing

tricks on her. Then after stealing another apprehensive look, she saw that indeed she was not imagining things.

It was a dog, and there were more of them trailing along even deeper in the woods like ghostly shades of the first. Two . . . three . . . a whole pack of them loping through the thick and dripping undergrowth.

As the hopelessness of her situation dawned upon her, she experienced a stab of panic, an uneasy quickening that could not be entirely controlled.

Christy was plunging headlong through the trees now, with trailing vines and branches tearing at her face and clothes. Up ahead the lead animal had reached the top of a small rise, and throwing back his head, he bayed morosely to the sky. A spine-tingling howl of primeval terror. The mournful dirge was picked up by another and yet another further off in the woods, until their voices seemed to converge from every direction.

Forking off on another path, Christy thought for a moment that she had been able to evade her pursuers. Almost desperate with fear she crouched in the protective crook of a great white oak, listening to the animals as they crashed through the woods behind her. With a sinking heart she saw them bound into the clearing, their deep growls rattling in their throats.

As she watched, they fanned out about her, baring their teeth and surrounding her on all sides.

In one last frantic bid for freedom Christy raced across the clearing, stumbled downhill through a thicket of jack pine, and broke out of the trees onto a wide, grassy lawn.

At that moment a flash of lightning illuminated the mansion barely two hundred yards from where she stood.

With her heart fluttering wildly in her breast, she stumbled across the manicured lawn toward the lighted windows glimmering like beacons in the stormy night. She could tell from the sounds of crackling brush behind her that the dogs were still in hot pursuit.

When she was within a hundred feet of the stairs leading up to the broad terrace, she heard a sharp, piercing
whistle from behind her. Spinning about, she found that
the animals had melted away into the night just as mysteriously as they had originally appeared.

By the time she reached the top of the steps, Christy
was completely out of breath. Hurrying across the tiles to
the great metal-studded door, she reached for the iron
knocker, only to have the door swing miraculously open
before her.

A figure stood outlined in the light spilling out from the
hallway. It was a woman standing severely erect and
dressed in a shapeless black gown that fell to the floor.
The face was lean and ageless, the skin drawn taut over
prominent cheekbones. The lips were thin, forming a firm
line beneath a long, beaked nose.

Still it was the eyes that dominated the face. Regarding
Christy cooly from beneath heavy, straight brows, they
were sharp and as black as obsidian arrowheads.

Standing aside, the woman beckoned her into the house.

"Welcome to Falcon's Eyrie, Miss Randolph. I am Mrs.
Fears, the housekeeper."

As Christy stepped gratefully into the foyer, Mrs. Fears
eyed her bedraggled appearance with some distaste. "It's
unfortunate that you were forced to come out in such
weather," she said in a voice that was etched with condescension. "Scully was instructed to bring you directly to
the door. I see that as usual he has managed to disobey
orders."

"It wasn't really his fault," Christy said, gasping for
breath. "A tree had fallen across the drive. I had to walk
from the main road."

As soon as the words were out of her mouth, Christy regretted having spoken them. Why was she defending Scully, who had so obviously enjoyed the position he had
placed her in? Considering the whistle she heard on escap-

ing from the dogs, it seemed entirely possible that he was even responsible for the fright the ghostly dogs had given her.

Mrs. Fears nodded skeptically, but as Christy stepped into the light her face registered a look of shocked recognition. It lasted an instant only, her face going immediately blank.

"Here. Let me take your coat," she offered, attempting to cover the awkward moment.

Christy permitted the woman to help her out of her coat, only to find to her great dismay that her skirt was sopping. She was further distressed to discover that in spite of having worn a scarf, her hair was moist and bedraggled as well.

What terrible luck, she thought miserably as she stooped to remove her rubber rain shoes. But there was certainly nothing she could do about her appearance now.

"Will you please accompany me, Miss Randolph," Mrs. Fears instructed in a voice completely without tone or expression.

Christy followed her across the foyer and into the great lower hall with its inlaid parquet flooring, dark Victorian furniture, and—overall—a depthless, brooding silence.

Pausing in front of ornate double doors on the far side, the woman knocked twice and swung them open. "Miss Christina Randolph has arrived," she announced to the room at large. Then stepping back, she allowed Christy to pass inside.

Christy entered what she assumed to be the library, the double doors closing noiselessly behind her. The room in which she found herself was spacious and grand with polished mahogany walls, richly patterned Oriental rugs and art objects of obvious worth.

In spite of the elegant furnishings it was a comfortable room with leather-bound books lining the walls to the ceiling and a scatter of overstuffed chairs grouped around the marble fireplace.

All was still and silent, the only sounds being the crackling of the fire and the wind rattling the French windows, which were heavily draped against the storm.

There was an old, quiet smell to the library. The kind of closed, musty odor that Christy associated with art galleries and museums. The thousands of ornate volumes, paintings darkened with age, and dusty, faded tapestries only served to reinforce the impression.

Christy had been so taken up with the room and its rich decor that she failed to notice the figure of a man slumped in one of the oversize leather chairs.

"Good evening, Miss Randolph," he said, rising heavily to his feet. "I am Willard Falcon."

"How do you do," she stammered, taken completely off guard. Moving forward, she offered her hand and was immediately offended by the soft, spongy response of his limp grasp.

Willard Falcon was a man of approximately forty-five years. He was still attractive in a fleshy, well-fed manner, with the pouched eyes and mottled complexion generally associated with heavy drinkers.

As he stood there beaming down at her, he appeared to be made up of indeterminate grays and browns, with pale eyes, thinning hair the color of house mice, and a mouth that was far too soft for a man.

Christy couldn't help but feel that in some vague way he lacked substance. It was almost as if he had been partially erased.

"My wife will be joining us shortly," he said, motioning toward one of the chairs. "Won't you sit down and join me in a sherry?"

Christy did as he suggested, revolted by the strong smell of whisky flaming on his breath.

As she settled down on the edge of her chair, Willard

flashed her an ingratiating smile. "I trust you've had a pleasant journey," he beamed.

Considering the weather and the hardships she had been forced to endure it seemed a ridiculous question, one Christy didn't quite know how to answer without offending.

"Rather more a difficult one," she finally managed, forcing a smile. "The sea was quite rough."

"What a pity," Willard said, patting her hand. "Had I the power, I would have ordered up a perfectly glorious day for you to arrive on Falcon's Island."

Christy was by now nursing a growing dislike for the man. His manner was overindulgent and fawning, his smile false and unnatural.

"We so seldom have young and lively visitors here. I should have preferred for you to see us at our best," he concluded.

Christy managed to dredge up a pallid smile, instinctively distrusting his slick manner. She was no longer prepared to believe anything he had to say since he was so obviously a flatterer.

With a brief, self-satisfied chuckle, Willard crossed the room to a large, beautifully inlaid cabinet. Taking out two glasses, he proceeded to fill each from a cut glass decanter.

Returning to the fire, he leaned close and handed her one of the exquisite crystal goblets and raised his own in a toast. "Here's to our lovely new governess," he murmured, emptying half his drink in one gulp. "May your stay on Falcon's Island be a most memorable one."

Christy took a sip of her sherry and immediately experienced a warm, thawing sensation as it went down. She was still chilled to the bone from her long trek through the woods.

"Well now," her host exclaimed with hearty good cheer, "why don't you tell me how you managed to get so soaked?"

Christy related once again the story of having to walk from the main road and then added, "I'm afraid your dogs gave me quite a fright."

"Dogs?" Willard's eyes shuttered open in surprise. "But, my dear Miss Randolph, you couldn't possibly have run into any dogs."

"But I just saw them not twenty minutes ago," she stated flatly. "They chased me through the woods."

Willard cleared his throat and managed a careless laugh. "I'm afraid your imagination must have been playing tricks on you, my child. There are no dogs on this island."

"But there are," she insisted. "At least five or six. They looked to me like German shepherds. Surely you must have heard them baying just before I reached the house."

"I assure you, I heard absolutely nothing," Willard insisted in a snappish voice. Then softening his tone, "Nothing but the storm and the wind."

Christy could see that it was useless arguing with the man. He obviously didn't want to believe her story.

As she sat there wondering at his strange behavior, Willard walked to a glass case containing a magnificent stuffed bird. "Here you have one of the rare hooded falcons," he explained, obviously trying to change the subject. "My family brought the first ones to the island over four hundred years ago, although they are now completely extinct."

Still wondering at his refusal to accept her story, Christy nodded but said nothing. She continued to listen quietly as he went on at some length giving the bird's history on the island.

Returning to the inlaid cabinet, Willard refilled his glass, this time from a bottle of whisky. "You know, my dear," he said turning toward her once again, "the mind can play strange tricks." With an expressive shrug he went on to say, "A stormy night. A young woman lost in the woods on an isolated island."

At this point Willard's face broke into a jovial grin, his small, pouched eyes sparkling with amusement. "Why it has all the makings of a marvelous mystery thriller. All except for a plot, that is. . . ."

Willard sighed theatrically and returned to stand in front of the fire. "I fear we are quite a dull lot out here. Nothing exciting ever happens. We exist in a state of pastoral torpor that would bore a stone to tears."

His fat man's laugh bubbled forth. "Yes, my dear child. I'm very much afraid that it's going to prove quite tedious here for an attractive young woman such as yourself." His eyes narrowed and his voice grew intimate and familiar. "Surely you're used to a far more exciting life. A girl as lovely as yourself must have scores of young men friends."

Christy was immediately offended by his insinuating manner. There was a touch of ice in her voice as she replied, "I've been rather busy with my studies, Mr. Falcon. There really hasn't been much time for social life or . . . friends."

"Oh, come now," he coaxed. "I find that exceedingly hard to believe. You're young. Pretty. Obviously intelligent. Surely you must have at least one beau back in Boston."

Before she could formulate an appropriate reply, the doors swung open to admit a fashionably slim, late-thirtyish woman of better than medium height. She was dressed smartly in a floor-length hostess gown of pale-blue satin, her dark hair swirled high on her head in an elaborate coiffure of loops and swirls interlaced with ropes of pearls.

The face was arresting if not actually beautiful. A sculptor's study in planes and hollows, with prominent cheekbones and large hazel eyes that were lovely if overaccentuated with mascara and false eyelashes. The mouth was full, sensual, and overdrawn in the rouged bee-sting style of the thirties.

Extending one slim, heavily jeweled hand, the woman swept across the library to where Christy had risen uncertainly from her chair.

"My dear Miss Randolph," she enthused in a voice that was husky and slightly breathless, "how marvelous to have you here at last. I am Iris Falcon."

Five

THE cool, sophisticated Iris Falcon was anything but what Christy had expected. She was in fact slightly intimidated by the woman's grace and charm, feeling herself to be naive and awkward by comparison.

"Permit me to apologize for not being downstairs to welcome you on your arrival." Iris' smile remained gracious and constant, her face painted like an expensive doll's. "Amanda hasn't been feeling well this evening and I didn't feel I should leave her alone."

With catlike grace Iris began to circle about, her eyes shining in frank appraisal. Christy was reminded of a judge at a livestock exhibit, finding something piercing and not entirely pleasant in her hostess' rapt gaze.

"I'm afraid I got rather muddied in the storm," Christy offered, speaking for the first time. She was painfully aware of her disheveled appearance.

Iris seemed not to have heard her. "Yes," she said at last, "I think you'll do very nicely. Very nicely indeed."

Feeling embarrassed and uneasy, Christy said, "I have my transcripts and a letter of recommendation from the dean of my college if you'd like to see them."

Iris came back to the moment, rewarding her with a brilliant smile. "That won't be necessary. I'm sure your qualifications are completely in order."

For the first time she appeared to become aware of her husband's presence. Crossing to where he stood, she gave him a hard swift kiss on the cheek, which Christy couldn't help but feel was meant for her benefit alone.

"Now then," Iris exclaimed clasping her crimson-taloned fingers together. "I see that my husband has already seen to your drink." There was a hint of malice in her voice, even though her smile flashed automatically, exposing large perfectly shaped teeth.

"But that was to be expected. Willard is at his best when in the company of attractive, young women."

Rather than take offense, Willard laughed broadly and patted his wife's flawless cheek. "What my loving wife is trying to say, Miss Randolph, is that I'm not much good beyond the social level."

Iris threw him a cool, appraising glance and settled herself in one of the leather chairs, primly crossing her long legs. Then turning her full attention to Christy, she said, "Now tell me all about your journey. Did our Mr. Parrish manage to behave like a surly lout and bite your head off?"

"He was quite nice really, although I suppose in his own way he is a bit gruff."

"Rude would be more to the point," Iris responded. She then paused as if carefully selecting her next words. "Did Matthew say anything that you found out of the ordinary. Anything strange?"

"I'm afraid we didn't have much chance to talk." Christy related, "The sea was awfully rough."

Iris was clearly relieved, the worried little frown that

had furrowed her brow melting away. Once again she became expansive. "I wanted so much to be down at the dock to meet you on your arrival, my dear, but I've been so terribly busy of late.

"Ever since Willard's mother passed on the responsibility of administering the island has fallen on my shoulders." Flashing a withering glance in her husband's direction, she added, "Unfortunately Willard's no good at all in these matters. He's only interested in his arboretum and those ghastly tropical monsters he cultivates with such loving care."

"My wife has a tendency to minimize my interest in island affairs," Willard offered in his own defense. "But that's neither here nor there."

After taking a long pull from his drink, he shot his wife a look that was entirely undecipherable and returned to their previous topic. "What exactly did you think of Matthew?" he asked. "Do you consider him to be attractive?"

"He did seem to be very intelligent," she hedged.

Willard laughed, his tongue darting out to moisten his fleshy lips. "I'll grant you, he is that. While not too many people are aware of it, Matthew graduated *cum laude* from Harvard and has a master's degree in animal husbandry from one of the finest agricultural colleges in the country."

At the look of surprise that etched Christy's features, Iris cut in, "Matthew is brilliant, of course, but completely unsound. It's a pity that a man of his education can find nothing better to do than waste his life on this godforsaken island."

"Is his family native to the island?" Christy asked, wondering at the manner in which he was treated by the townspeople.

"Oh, my, yes," Iris informed her. "Matthew's family goes back to the earliest settlers. The first Parrish to come here was supposedly an English nobleman escaping the king's displeasure."

A tiny frown appeared and deepened, drawing a tiny crease between her eyebrows. "The Parrishes have always thought themselves better than the rest of the Falconers. In my opinion their insufferable pride was responsible for everything that happened to them."

As she spoke Iris had grown visibly angry, her mouth hard, the nostrils white and pinched. In response Willard shot his wife a warning glance that was not entirely lost on Christy.

"I'm afraid I don't understand," Christy responded, hoping that Iris would continue. "What exactly did happen?" In spite of herself she found that Matthew was a subject that interested her very much indeed.

"I'm sure you have no wish to be bored with our local squabbles," Iris said with a sharp staccato laugh that cut the air like a knife.

"Please, do go on," Christy begged. "I am interested— honestly I am."

"Well, there's not much to tell," Iris conceded. "Matthew's mother died when he was very young and he left the island while still a boy to join the merchant marine. Eventually he attended college on the mainland and finally found his way home about five years ago.

"It was a mistake for him to have come back," she stated bluntly. "The islanders don't want him here."

"Then why did he return?" Christy pursued.

"Oh, like so many young people nowadays, his head was filled with a lot of rubbish about improving the lot of the people who have lived here for centuries. Although he was determined to introduce them to modern methods of farming and agriculture, he got absolutely nowhere." Iris' bright, hard eyes sought Christy's as if to score her point. "You see, Matthew is an outcast on this island. He remains here only because I find his presence to be convenient."

Her harsh tone of voice abruptly ended the discussion and she moved swiftly on to another topic. "Now tell me, Miss Randolph, what did you think of the village?"

"Why . . . I suppose it was charming, but. . . ."

"But you were shocked to find that the people treated you like a leper. Isn't that it?"

Christy nodded, but said nothing.

Iris laughed once again, this time a sparkling, feminine laugh of genuine amusement. "Don't let it get you down, my dear child. I've lived on this island for seventeen years and they still treat me as if I were a scarlet woman. Personally I avoid the townspeople as much as possible. Mrs. Fears does all the shopping and Scully collects the rents from the tenant farmers."

She paused a moment before continuing. "You would do well to have as little contact as possible with those distasteful ingrates."

"Now, my dear," Willard broke in pointedly. "Don't you think that Miss Randolph would like to go upstairs and freshen up before dinner?"

"Why, yes. Yes, of course," Iris conceded. "Here I'm running on and you're all but exhausted. You must forgive me, Miss Randolph, but I so seldom have a chance for civilized conversation that I'm probably going to talk your ear off."

She laughed once again but this time it rang false. "One simply dies intellectually out here in the wilderness." Then with a glance at her diamond encrusted watch, "We'll dine at eight. That should give you time to run upstairs to your room and slip into something dry."

Christy rose obediently to her feet. As she did so, the doors swung open behind her and she was surprised to find the tall, gaunt figure of Mrs. Fears standing just outside in obvious anticipation.

"By the way, Miss Randolph," Iris said, uncoiling gracefully from her chair. "You must plan on spending the night with us. I wouldn't think of letting you return to the Pond in this storm."

As if to add emphasis to her statement, the house was shaken by a low rumble of thunder, and a renewed onslaught of rain pelted the French windows at the far end of the room.

"Fears will take you upstairs and find you something suitable to wear." By now Iris had taken her by the arm and was leading her toward the door. Once there, she took both her hands and allowed her eyes to run over Christy's figure from head to toe.

"A perfect size ten, I should say. Yes, indeed. I'm sure that everything will fit perfectly."

Christy went out into the hall in a daze. She was, to be sure, a perfect size ten. But what could Iris have meant when she said that "everything will fit perfectly"?

With Mrs. Fears preceding her across the hall, Christy was terribly aware of Iris standing like a sentinel in the doorway behind her. She could feel those penetrating hazel eyes burning into her back. What could she possibly be thinking, Christy wondered?

It was with some regret that she left the cheery warmth of the library fire. The great hall was chilly and drafty. Her heels rang out on the parquet floor and echoed to the frescoed ceiling high overhead.

Placing her hand on the balustrade, Christy proceeded up the staircase, the figure of Mrs. Fears mounting evenly just ahead of her. When the woman reached the upper landing, she turned and waited with folded hands.

Christy summoned a wan smile as she reached the top of the staircase, but it was not returned.

"Mrs. Falcon has instructed me to put you in Miss Victoria's room." Fears spoke in a voice that was as dead and dry as old leaves shifting in the wind. "If you will follow me this way, please."

They crossed the minstrel's gallery and passed along a broad, carpeted passage. Then turning left at the end of the hall, they climbed a short flight of stairs. At the top was a large oaken door, finely carved with smiling cupids and a delicate floral motif.

Mrs. Fears had gone ahead of her and after swinging the door open, stood aside, permitting her to enter first.

It was a beautiful room. The most beautiful room that Christy had ever seen or even imagined. A fire burned in the exquisite rose-quartz fireplace and the frescoed ceiling was like something out of a Roman basilica.

Clearly it was a woman's room. The walls were covered with rose-colored damask and the furnishings upholstered in matching tones of pink. From high above, a Venetian crystal chandelier cast its muted brilliance over all.

A great canopied bed with carved posts and lace hangings dominated from atop a low dais, even though the rest of the room was spacious and luxuriously furnished as well.

In spite of the faint scent emanating from a vase of perfect blood-red roses, the room smelled close and stuffy, as if it had been closed for some time.

A filmy nightgown, gossamer soft and the color of pale cherry blossoms, was folded on the lace pillow case. The letters "V. F." were stitched on the breast, and a pair of delicate silk slippers rested on a cushioned stool beside the bed.

"Who is Victoria?" Christy asked, her voice sounding strange and thin to her own ears.

Mrs. Fears moved into the room, her eyes dark and brooding in her ashen face. "She was Abigale Falcon's daughter," she related, "but now she's dead."

Christy began to move about the room, feeling as if she were a visitor in a museum of someone else's life. She drew her hand across the inlaid surface of the Chippendale escritoire, sat for a moment on the edge of the chaise longue, and finally came to a halt in front of the marble-topped dressing table.

It was cluttered with a selection of crystal perfume phials, cosmetic pots, and off to one side, a silver picture frame with the photograph missing.

As if reading her thoughts, Mrs. Fears drew close and said, "There used to be a picture of Victoria in that frame."

"Was she very beautiful?"

"Victoria Falcon was beautiful both inside and out," the woman volunteered fervently. "Everyone that ever met her worshiped the ground she walked on." After a pause she added, "There's a portrait of her down in the music room if you'd like to see what she looked like."

Terribly aware of Mrs. Fears's close scrutiny and feeling very much the intruder, Christy sat down and picked up one of the silver-backed brushes. As she did so, she noticed the fine dark hairs still clinging to the bristles. Strangely enough they were of exactly the same reddish brown shade as her own hair.

Christy began to brush her hair with short, attacking strokes. The face staring back at her in the mirror was wan and chalky, with faint dark smudges of exhaustion beneath the eyes.

Above her own reflection she could see the grim visage of Mrs. Fears, distant, fluid, and yet wearing a look of bitter resentment—almost hatred. As her eyes caught Christy's in the glass the woman quickly averted her gaze.

The porcelain clock on the mantle chimed seven. With a brief nod the housekeeper crossed to a door on the far side of the room and said, "Will you please follow me, Miss Randolph."

After giving her hair a few last strokes, Christy did as she asked, following her into what was obviously a spacious dressing room with tall wardrobe cabinets on every side.

As Mrs. Fears swung the doors wide on one of the cabinets, they were engulfed by the dark resiny smell of cedar wafting out into the room as pure and fresh as spring water.

Inside Christy viewed row upon row of protective clothing bags. Through the clear plastic covers she caught the shimmer of silver lamé, the muted softness of rose velvets, brocades, and a rainbow selection of filmy gowns and peignoirs. A second cabinet proved to be full of fur coats, and a third, casual day dresses and sportswear. The shelves above were stacked all the way to the ceiling with hatboxes.

Her attention was immediately drawn to a white satin wedding dress at the far end of the closet. Noticing her interest, Mrs. Fears unzipped the bag so that she might examine the dress more carefully. As Christy reached inside to touch the smooth eggshell satin, the vague scent of lemon verbena reached her nostrils. It seemed to hang on the air, even though slightly musty and faded by time.

"That was Victoria's wedding dress," the housekeeper said in a voice barely above a whisper. "She and the Senator were married in the National Cathedral in Washington."

Her words sparked an immediate recollection and Christy realized that Victoria Falcon had been someone of note.

Hers had been the wedding of the season some years back. All the society editors had called it the perfect match. A daughter of wealth and tradition marrying the Senator from Maine, whose family dated back to the American Revolution.

The pair seemed to have been ideally suited and Christy had often seen their names mentioned in the social columns during the ensuing years.

"Perhaps the yellow would be suitable," Mrs. Fears suggested, slipping a lovely yellow voile from its hanger and holding it up. The dress was simple, chic, and soft in color and texture. Christy had never owned a dress quite so lovely nor one so obviously expensive.

"Would you care to try it on before you decide?" the housekeeper questioned without inflection.

"That won't be necessary. I'm sure it'll do very nicely."

Going to another closet, Mrs. Fears selected a pair of linen pumps in a matching shade and then returned to the outer room to lay the things out on the bed.

After closing the wardrobe doors, Christy followed her into the bedroom, unable to shake off the feeling that she was intruding into another woman's life. Why had Iris put her in this particular room, she wondered? Surely there must have been others in the huge house that would have been more suitable.

"Are you feeling unwell?" Mrs. Fears asked with a glancing appraisal.

Christy made an attempt to smile, but her face felt wooden and stiff. "I'm fine, thank you. Just a little tired."

"Then unless there's something more you require, I'll be getting back downstairs." Without waiting for a reply, the woman turned and started for the door.

"Oh, Mrs. Fears," Christy called after her.

She turned around, her face a blank mask.

"How did Victoria Falcon die?"

Slowly Mrs. Fears retraced her steps until she was once more standing by the bed. Bending down, she picked up the slippers and held them lovingly in her hands. When she spoke, her voice was barely above a whisper. "Victoria was the loveliest of all the Falcon women."

With infinite tenderness she ran the tips of her fingers over the delicate arch of one slipper, her dark eyes suddenly misty with recollection. "She was always gay. Always laughing."

The housekeeper turned and moved like an automaton to the dressing table to pick up the brush Christy had only recently been using. "I used to stand behind her every night and brush her hair until it hung down her back in long silky coils."

She raised her eyes to meet Christy's. "You see, I was her nurse. With her ever since she was a tiny baby. Victoria was like a daughter to me."

"Her death must have come as a terrible shock," Christy murmured, sympathizing with the woman's anguish. Mrs. Fears appeared not to have heard, her eyes looking beyond the moment—beyond that particular time and place.

"Victoria wasn't in love with Luther Holland," she said slowly. "There was someone else. Someone here on the island." Her eyes came up to meet Christy's. "You see, Miss Randolph, Abigale was wrong. Victoria belonged here . . . on Falcon's Island."

As the woman spoke, Christy was struck by the strange and violent intimacy honing her voice. Although she had just used her name, it was as if Christy were not even in the room with her.

"But if she wasn't in love with him," Christy asked, "why did she marry Senator Holland?"

Mrs. Fears sighed deeply before answering, her hands tightly clasped together. "Abigale was used to having her own way and Victoria would have done anything to please her mother."

The fingers of the clasped hands tightened, the knuckles whitening. "And there was another reason." Crossing the room to where Christy stood, she regarded her levelly. "You see, the man Victoria was in love with was her cousin."

The two women stood staring at one another. It was several moments before Christy spoke, her throat as dry as straw. "You still haven't answered my question, Mrs. Fears. How was it that Victoria died?"

"Are you sure you want to know?" she asked, her voice completely devoid of emotion.

Christy nodded mutely, and the woman began to speak in a low, almost inaudible voice.

"It happened in early spring. Victoria had brought Amanda to the island to spend several weeks with Abigale. On the last night of her visit—the last night she was to spend on earth—the entire family dined together. They argued as usual. The two of them, Iris and Victoria, never had any use for one another.

"The Senator arrived late. Just after dinner. He hated Falcon's Island and seldom visited. But on that particular evening he had sailed into the harbor on his schooner, and he and Victoria planned to return to the mainland together that same evening."

Mrs. Fears' voice had taken on a soft, mesmeric quality and Christy found that she was hanging on every word she spoke.

"I begged her not to go," the housekeeper continued, "but she laughed and called me a foolish old woman." Then with a shuddering sigh she added, "She wouldn't listen. She just wouldn't listen.

"They never found Senator Holland's body," Mrs. Fears concluded. "But Victoria's was washed up on the island where she belonged." Turning her head like an ancient snake presiding over a lost treasure, she nodded toward the heavily draped windows—toward the sea booming in the distance.

"When they found her down there on the rocks, she had been in the water for over a week. Her lovely body was battered and torn beyond recognition." The woman's voice had dropped steadily in pitch and was by now barely audible. "Her beautiful face had been destroyed . . . eaten away by the fish and the things of the deep."

Mrs. Fears's hands, which had been clasped fervently before her, now fell limply to her sides. "I knew when Victoria left here that night that I should never see her again. A storm was blowing up and there had been portents—omens that bode ill to the entire Falcon family."

"What a terrible accident," Christy gasped, wondering if the woman had not become a bit mad with her grief.

Mrs. Fears regarded her solemnly, a secret inscrutable look coming into her eyes.

"Accident, Miss Randolph? I'm not so sure that it was an accident."

Six

AFTER lounging in a hot bath and dressing carefully, Christy applied a minimum of make-up and turned once in front of the mirror.

She was pleased with what she saw. The yellow dress exactly suited her, both clinging and flowing about her slim figure. In addition the color was in perfect harmony with her dark hair and creamy complexion.

Leaving her room, she proceeded down the steps and along the wide corridor to the minstrel's gallery. Catching herself tiptoeing along the passage, Christy was forced to smile at her own timidity. She was acting as if she were in some vast and reverential edifice full of an unseen religious presence.

Everything was very still and silent except for the demented howl of the wind outside and the rush of rain flailing the windows in torrents.

When Christy reached the top of the grand staircase, she paused, catching the hum and murmur of conversation drifting up from the dining room, which was directly off the lower hall. As she stood there listening, the voices grew louder: Iris, strident and accusing; Willard's, interjecting occasionally in a sullen monotone.

The loving couple must have come down already and were waiting for her appearance, she mused wryly. Still for some reason Christy could not entirely fathom, she wasn't looking forward to her first meal at Falcon's Eyrie.

The feeling that had been with her ever since stepping across the threshold of Victoria's bedroom had grown in intensity since donning the dead woman's clothing. Christy could not seem to shake the eerie sensation that she had intruded into someone else's life. That she herself was an imposter.

A board creaked at the far end of the hall. She spun about only to find that the passage behind her was empty . . . nothing.

The house slumbered fitfully, brooding and uneasy with the storm. Lightning flashed. High above her head the light pierced the stained glass dome and bathed the paneled walls and Corinthian columns with an eerie roseate glow that was somehow surrealistic.

As she stood there dreading her ultimate descent, a current of chill air swept along the hallway as if someone had opened a door or a window farther down the passage. When it failed to abate, Christy turned from the stairs, crossed the minstrel's gallery, and started down a passage lit only by a single muted fixture at the far end.

The paintings hanging along the walls were uniformly dark and murky with age. Without exception they were all of men and women dressed in the costumes of other years, other eras—obviously family portraits.

The subjects were mostly men on horseback with Falcon's Eyrie in the background. Women, all of them quite regal and lovely, were pictured as well in various poses about the house and grounds, often with their children grouped about them.

How strange, Christy thought. Each one of those innocent cherubic faces had eventually born children of their own, grown old, and were now moldering beneath the earth. The thought caused her to shudder.

At the far end of the hallway Christy could now see that one of the windows had blown open. The curtains were billowing like ghostly winding sheets, alternately being sucked out into the night and then billowing inward before each fresh gust of wind.

Approaching the open window, Christy could hear the sea in full concert with the storm, a soft sinister hissing sound coupled with the thunderous roar of the breakers as they hurled themselves upon the rocks at the foot of the cliffs.

Then she heard something else—something quite apart from the storm and the sea.

At first she had thought it to be the wind, but gradually the siren sound rose in a sweet, melodious voice calling out, "Victoria . . . Vic . . . tor . . . ia. . . ."

Christy remained perfectly still, scarcely daring to breathe.

Then it came again, this time soaring off in a high sweet contralto, repeating the name again and again in a haunting drawn-out lament.

A full minute passed, and then another as she stood there listening. The voice had stopped . . . or had it? Perhaps it had been the wind coupled with her imagination after all.

Hurrying on to the end of the passage, she stood for a moment before the open window, allowing the full force of the gale to rush over her. Then leaning out into the night, she grasped the handles and tried to draw the double windows inward.

Outside, the storm continued to rage. Where the cliffs dropped sharply to the sea below, she could see the surf tumbling madly over the rocks that lay broken and scattered in the boiling white water. A sudden sharp splintered crash of lightning illuminated everything with a sickly yellow light just as a lusty gust of wind tried to rip the windows from her hands.

Exercising all her strength, Christy was finally able to draw them shut and slip the bolts into place.

"There," she breathed. That was that. Glancing nervously down at her watch, she saw that it was several minutes before the appointed dinner hour of eight o'clock. Turning about, she retraced her steps along the hall, only to stop abruptly in front of a painting depicting a handsome young woman with dark tresses, a firm jaw line, and creamy porcelain skin.

The painting was life size and looked as if the subject might at any moment step down out of the ornate gilt frame and greet her.

Christy was held transfixed by the eyes—strangely hollow in the dimness of the hall, yet gleaming with life and intensity. As she drew close, they appeared to follow her every movement.

The grandfather's clock struck the hour farther down the hall, causing Christy to glance in that direction. For a full eight strokes the deep mellow chiming filled the passage. She was late. Iris and Willard would be wondering what had happened to her, if not actually angry at her lack of punctuality.

Turning back to the portrait that had so captivated her only moments before, she found that the eyes were now entirely blank. Devoid of life and spark.

Before her Christy saw a handsome if somewhat granite-like countenance from out of the past, but nothing more.

Entirely puzzled, she glanced down at the small bronze plaque beneath the canvas, trying to make out the name. It read, "ABIGALE FALCON 1917."

The doors of the dining room were open as Christy rushed down the stairs and across the great hall. Drawing on a smile that felt wooden and unnatural, she took a deep breath and entered, causing Iris to break off in the middle of a harsh tirade directed at her husband Willard.

At the sight of Christy an engaging smile suffused her face. "Well, here you are at last," she offered. "We thought that perhaps you had gotten lost."

Willard rose unsteadily to his feet and circled the table to hold Christy's chair. After she had been seated, he returned to his place on his wife's left.

"You look very lovely," Iris complimented. "The yellow is absolutely perfect on you."

Then turning toward her husband, she said, "Don't you think that Christine looks lovely, darling?"

"Ravishing, my dear. Simply ravishing," he responded, the glittering eyes and slack mouth revealing the sincerity of his words.

"What a treat it is for us to have a pretty face to look at," Iris continued, clasping her hands beneath her chin. "My husband and I get positively bored to stone with nothing to look at but one another, night after night." She gave a gay little laugh. "Don't we, darling?"

A sharp glance at Willard revealed him to be staring intently at Christy. The admiring look was unmistakable.

Turning back to their guest, Iris spoke once more, a hint of malice etching her voice. "You appear to have made quite a conquest, Miss Randolph. The laird of the manor has obviously found you comely and very much to his liking. What a pity that this dinner is not taking place some fifty years ago. At that time it was the prerogative of the male heir of Falcon's Island to take any woman he found attractive to the manorial bed chamber."

Christy smiled uneasily, refusing to be drawn into the verbal tug of war between her host and hostess.

The dining room was large and lofty, running the entire width of the house. Across from Christy stood a hand-carved mahogany sideboard gleaming with silver and crystal. A score of highly polished high-backed chairs surrounded the oval table bearing two double-branched candelabra, in which tall beeswax candles burned with a steady golden flame.

The three of them were grouped about one end of the table with Iris presiding at the head. Two serving girls dressed in somber black stood waiting to serve them with downcast eyes. They appeared to be nervous and watchful, as if anxious to anticipate the wants of the diners.

The meal began with oxtail soup, and one of the girls circled the table to fill their glasses with a dark red wine.

Willard had obviously been drinking steadily since Christy had seen him last and by now he appeared to be quite tipsy. His speech was slightly slurred, his eyes puffy and bloodshot.

As Christy began to spoon her soup carefully, she became painfully aware of the veiled glances he kept shooting her way. It was more than his drunken admiration that offended her. There was something furtive and almost obscene in the pale, squinting eyes. Something she found quite frightening.

Increasing her discomfort was the fact that Iris, in her queenly omniscient way, missed none of it.

Even so it was a very special dinner. Christy had never before dined in such state. For the first time in her life she was glad that her mother had insisted on teaching her perfect etiquette so that she was entirely familiar with the wide array of fine Georgian silver surrounding her plate. As the meal progressed, she wondered what her mother—a woman of taste and delicate sensitivity—would have thought of the situation in which she now found herself.

Iris for her part made a genuine effort to put Christy at ease, her light musical voice running on in animated brittle chatter. In her elegant polished way she asked about Boston, the latest fashions, and the opera season, all subjects which Christy felt woefully inadequate to discuss.

Gradually she began to relax, and by the time the main course was served the conversation had become easier and more congenial.

Christy found herself talking freely about her life and family background for the first time. She spoke of her mother, a gentle artistic invalid, who had given piano lessons in order to provide for her daughter's education.

As she talked on, the memories began to slide more easily through her mind. Once again Christy pictured her mother seated at the old upright piano with her dark hair and luminous eyes, her long, tapering fingers moving gracefully over the keys.

Experiencing a sadness as sharp as pain, she recalled as well the vase of white lilacs that always rested on top of the piano, their lovely scent filling their small rented house with a wistful, poignant smell.

Iris appeared to be even more interested as she described her life with the Lacy family. She had gone to live with them upon her mother's death, when she was just fourteen.

Christy answered her hostess' questions willingly, even though they ranged from the sympathetic to the purely inquisitive.

"I hope the Lacys won't be overly concerned if they don't hear from you regularly," Iris commented as Christy came to the end of her recitation. "The mail out here is so irregular and I shouldn't want them to worry unnecessarily."

"I'm sure they won't," Christy murmured, feeling the painful ache of truth in her statement. "Aunt Ellen was very much against my accepting this position. She warned me that if I choose to do so, I would not be welcomed back."

The look exchanged by Iris and Willard was not entirely lost on Christy even though it was furtive, split second, and totally incomprehensible.

As the meal progressed, Christy found herself thoroughly enjoying the deliciously prepared food that arrived in course after course. She found Iris to be an excellent hostess and witty and charming in her own sophisticated fashion.

Christy was fascinated as well by the opulence of her surroundings. The fine table silver, the slim-stemmed crystal glasses, and the dinner service of the finest Meissen— all of it combined with the elegantly appointed dining room and Iris' sympathetic interest to make her feel somehow special, singled out by fate to be there on that particular evening.

"I do hope you'll be comfortable out at the Pond," Iris said as dessert was placed before them. "It must seem a bit lonely at first, but I'm sure you'll get used to it in time."

Christy nodded and forced a smile of assurance she scarcely felt. For an instant she considered relating what had taken place that very evening but quickly decided against it. Surely a woman as sophisticated as Iris Falcon would think her a fool if she launched into a tale about candles snuffing out for no reason and a ghostly presence in the house.

Iris deliberately kept her eyes on her dessert as she proceeded to another subject. "Willard tells me you thought you were followed by dogs on the way up here this evening."

Christy simply nodded, having just taken a mouthful of crusty French cobbler.

"Of course I don't doubt that you think you saw them," Iris went on, choosing her words carefully. "But let me assure you that it would have been quite impossible. You see, there are simply no dogs on this island, as I'm sure my husband must have told you."

"Well, there's at least one," Christy retorted.

Iris glanced up sharply, her hazel eyes challenging the statement.

"You see, I brought my own dog Jason with me from Boston," Christy concluded with a smile.

"Well. . . ." Iris faltered. "How nice. I'm sure he'll provide excellent company for you."

Feeling suddenly uncomfortable with what was obviously a very touchy subject, Christy pointed out a lovely golden chalice displayed in an illuminated glass case across the room. "What a lovely cup," she exclaimed.

"Yes, isn't it?" Iris agreed, seeming willing enough to change the subject. "It's really quite rare. Twelfth century, so I've been told. It was aboard a treasure galleon bound for Spain when it was raided by the celebrated Captain Kidd."

"How on earth did it manage to get here?" Christy asked, remembering vaguely something Matthew had said about the island being a repository for pirates' treasure.

"Captain Kidd was a frequent visitor to Falcon's Island," Willard volunteered, pinching the stem of his wine glass between two fingers. "Legend has it that he left a secret cache of treasure here that has never been found. It's supposed to be guarded by an ancient and very powerful curse."

The switch in subject to Falcon's Island appeared to have wrought a sudden change in the man. He was at once interested, speaking lucidly and well on the topic.

"And the cup?" Christy pursued. "Was it found here on the island?"

"We have Willard's mother, Abigale, to thank for that discovery," Iris commented, a twisted smile animating her vermilion lips. "Some years ago Abigale discovered a small wooden cask containing the cup, some gold doubloons, and a few semiprecious jewels of no particular worth. The local islanders believed that there was a map giving the location of the main treasure as well, but that's most likely just a local myth."

"How fascinating," Christy exclaimed.

"Well, if it's true," Iris concluded sourly, "Abigale took the secret to her grave with her. She had a firm belief that wealth corrupts and consequently left us entirely without temptation."

Her nostrils flared and her eyes sparked with green fire. "We have Abigale to thank for the fact that the Falcons are now land poor gentry with scarcely a kopek to our illustrious name."

Christy looked up to find Willard glaring at his wife. For an instant she actually thought she saw a look of pure hatred igniting his usually pallid eyes.

"My wife and mother never got on well," he offered by way of explanation. "Mother thought Iris extravagant and wasteful. The greatest of sins according to her Victorian thinking."

"Your mother was a vicious, senile old woman," Iris shot back. "We are well rid of her."

Willard was so taken aback by the swiftness and violence of his wife's verbal attack that he upset his wine glass with a clumsy motion of his hand.

They all sat transfixed as the deep red wine spread like a bloodstain on the white damask cloth.

"I think you've had quite enough to drink," Iris stated coldly, interrupting the enlarging silence that had fallen over the table.

A taut, explosive look came into her husband's eyes, a look that Christy found quite frightening. She wouldn't have been surprised if at any moment the gold-edged dinner plates were smashed along with the empty crystal goblet he held clenched in his hand.

Christy could feel the tension building between the two of them. Hoping to ease the situation, she turned to Iris and said, "I hope you don't mind my asking a rather personal question regarding your niece."

Iris was immediately solicitous. "Of course not, my dear. Anything at all."

"How has the child adjusted to the loss of her father and mother? It must have been terribly difficult for her, considering that she lost her grandmother as well."

A hush fell over the table. For a moment there wasn't a sound in the room except the faint metallic clink of silver on china as Willard began eating once again.

After a brief moment's hesitation, Iris' eyes came up to meet Christy's. "I'm afraid she hasn't adjusted well at all. But then . . . you shall soon see that for yourself. You see, Amanda has escaped into a fantasy world of her own making."

Iris' hands fluttered helplessly into her lap. "But then, what can one expect? She's known nothing but tragedy throughout her short life."

After taking a sip of her wine, Iris sighed deeply and went on to say, "You see, Miss Randolph, the marriage between her mother and the Senator was not a happy one. It was of course a perfect match from a social standpoint. The Senator was the son of one of the oldest families in the state. He had everything. Wealth, sophistication. . . ." She spread her hands expressively. "But alas, Victoria was a headstrong girl. She only married him because . . . well, the story is not a pretty one so I'll spare you the details."

"It must have been terribly difficult for the child," Christy suggested sympathetically. She didn't pursue the subject, recalling Mrs. Fears's claim that Victoria had been in love with her cousin.

"Frankly, Miss Randolph, I was hoping that having you here would help Amanda. You see, she's a very lonely child. There's no one of her own age to play with and, of course, we're terribly isolated out here. That's why I wanted someone who was proficient in art, music . . . things that will afford the child new interests."

The conversation drifted on for awhile, the two of them discussing Christy's plans for Amanda's studies and proposing a weekly schedule of lessons.

When coffee was served, Christy turned to Willard, who had been drinking in silence for some time, and said, "I understand that Falcon's Island has quite a colorful history. I hope to learn all about it while I'm here. From what I've read your ancestors must have been fascinating people."

Her interest once again sparked an immediate response. "Yes, indeed. The Falcons were one of the first families to come to the New World," Willard stated proudly. "The island was bestowed upon us in 1624 by Charles I of England. It was the first such manorial grant in the New World and is the only one left today that is still entirely intact."

"Darling," Iris interrupted with ill-concealed impatience, "I'm sure our guest is just being polite." Then turning to Christy she continued, "Once you get him started on the subject of his forebears, there'll be no shutting him up."

Willard paid no attention. He was now leaning forward in his chair, his elbows planted squarely on the table. "The first Falcon to come to America was a soldier of fortune named Rufus Falcon. He came to trade with the Indians, learned their language, and eventually carved an empire out of the wilderness.

"As the years passed, the family acquired wealth in the spice trade, and at one period in history the town of Pirate's Cove was used to outfit vessels that trafficked between here and the Orient as traders."

"Is it true that the islanders now living here are all de-

scendants of the original settlers?" Christy asked, becoming more and more fascinated with his account.

"Indeed, yes," he responded expansively. "They were
all middle Europeans fleeing the Catholic Inquisition. In
fact they had some rather peculiar religious beliefs. . . ."
Here he paused, glancing cautiously at his wife before
going on. "Many of which they retain to this very day."

While her husband was speaking, Iris had extracted a
long oval cigarette from the gold case lying beside her
plate and inserted it in an ivory holder. She had been
keeping pace with her husband's drinking and when she
broke into the conversation, her speech was thick with
wine and sarcasm.

"What Willard is trying to say is that our native islanders believe in the dark spirits—the occult." Iris paused,
allowing her words to have their maximum effect.

Then fixing Christy with a look of chilling intensity, she
asked, "Do you believe in ghosts, Miss Randolph?"

"I'm not really sure whether I do or not," Christy responded. "Do you?"

Before answering, Iris lit her cigarette with a flick of a
tiny golden lighter and exhaled a spiraling film of smoke
that hung in a soft cloud above her head. "Yes," she said
in a low voice. "I believe in ghosts, or spirits, if you will.
You see, I know that they exist . . . that they have power."

Her almond-shaped eyes grew bright and hard, appearing to see beyond the room. "The spirits of the dead are
very much with us here on this island. They always have
been."

Christy blanched at her words, recalling in vivid detail
the incident at Witch's Cottage earlier that afternoon.

"Oh, don't be alarmed," Iris reassured her with a trace
of a smile. "I'm not raving. It's simply a fact. Falcon's Island is haunted. Just remember that as long as you remain
under my protection you are safe.

"You see, my dear, the spirits cannot prevail if there

lives one man or woman strong enough to defy anything that might choose to return from the grave. I keep the spirits that inhabit this island at bay by the sheer force of my will."

Iris' voice dropped to a husky purr. "They are there outside these walls at this very moment, creeping close to the windows to peer inside or hovering near the threshold, hoping that I will let down my guard so they might gain entrance."

She closed her eyes and her head fell back as if she had fallen into a trance. Still her voice droned on in that same mesmeric purr. "Let them come. Let them try what they will; it is all to no avail. I am the stronger. I have the power. Where I am, they shall never pass."

Iris lapsed into silence, leaving Christy stunned by her declaration. She had spoken fiercely, bitterly, heated with the wine and filled with a deep sense of her omnipotence.

Could she be drunk, Christy wondered . . . mad? Or was she simply speaking the truth?

She continued to gaze at her hostess in open astonishment, seeing in Iris a new dimension, another side to her many-faceted character. A stronger, fiercer, and more imperious woman, yet altogether fascinating. Even so, at that particular moment she found her awesome and a little frightening.

There was a sharp rap on the door that brought them all back to the moment. Iris broke out of her trancelike state with a shake of her head, her eyes shuttering open as if she were returning from another world altogether. "Come in," she called out.

Mrs. Fears entered the room accompanied by a flaxen-haired child with a plain round face and great china-blue eyes. She was dressed in a trailing pink nightgown and robe.

The child appeared wan and frightened, her eyes darting back and forth between her aunt, her uncle, and settling finally on Christy. For an instant something flashed across her small face. A look that Christy could not define and one that quickly melted away. Strangely enough it reminded her of the look that Matthew had given her when they first met that same morning.

"Come in, Amanda, darling," Iris called, waving her cigarette like a conjuring rod. "Miss Randolph has come all the way from Boston to be your governess. Won't you show her how glad you are that she's here?"

Obediently Amanda crossed on soft slippered feet to where Christy sat. Stopping a few steps away, she offered a tentative curtsy, although her eyes remained downcast.

Christy's heart went out to her immediately. Slipping from her chair, she dropped to her knees and drew the child into her arms. Beneath the woolen robe Amanda was painfully thin, her tiny hands fluttering against Christy's breast like frightened birds.

"Dear Amanda," Christy whispered into her shining hair. "I just know that you and I are going to be the very best of friends."

While completely docile in her arms, Amanda did not respond, although her eyes shuttered open to peer deeply into Christy's.

As they knelt together, there was a shattering crash of lightning that shook the house to its very foundations. The crystal chandelier overhead swayed, dimmed, and then went out altogether, leaving the room lighted only by the two candelabra.

In her fright Amanda had snuggled close into Christy's arms and was whimpering softly. For an instant Iris' face turned to stone, a small muscle twitching spasmodically in her right cheek.

Why she's actually terrified, Christy realized, her fascination at the woman's unexpected reaction stilling her own fears.

The flicker of stark terror lasted for only an instant.

Then once again Iris was cool, calm, and totally in control.

"Do you think there's damage?" Willard demanded in a stricken tone of voice, his features melting with apprehension.

Getting slowly to her feet, Iris took one of the candelabra in hand and turned to face her husband. "The best way to find out is to go and see. Wouldn't you agree, my love?"

Seven

IRIS led the way out into the hall with Willard shambling reluctantly along behind. Christy, with Amanda in her arms, brought up the rear.

After pausing for a moment to listen, they started off across the great darkened hall drawn by the tinkling sound of glass falling and shattering somewhere off in the west wing of the house.

Dazed and completely unnerved by this new turn of events, Christy followed Iris' lead through the myriad twistings and turnings of the lower halls. It was more her fear of being left behind rather than her curiosity that impelled her to do so.

At last Iris paused beside a large door. She threw it open to expose a large solarium with glass-enclosed walls and peaked gazebo roof.

The four of them crowded inside the doorway, staring at the wreckage about them in mute disbelief.

It appeared that lightning had struck the roof, shattering yards of glass and all but obliterating a marble statue that had once stood in the center of the flagstone flooring.

Outside, the wind still stalked the night. Torrents of rain poured in through the shattered ceiling, turning the tropical hothouse trees and flowers into a rain wet jungle smelling pungently of earth and decay.

"The statue's been completely destroyed," Willard gasped.

The statue of which he spoke had once been life-size and of pale Carrara marble of such quality and texture that it actually appeared to breathe. Apparently it had been fragmented by a single bolt of lightning.

While parts of the arms, legs, and torso were visible, strewn about the soft, green moss, nothing of the original form was left intact, the torso itself having been shattered into a thousand fragments.

There was something bewildering, even shocking about the scene of destruction amid that vivid lushness of foliage. Great blood-red poincianas towered far above their heads. The waxen blooms of heliconia reared up like the heads of prehistoric lizards and bobbed and nodded in the wind.

Golden trumpet flowers, looking like nothing so much as great bells about to toll, hung down from bamboo poles. They intermingled with great fern trees and massive stalks of tropical flowers—all violently arrayed in many hues of yellow, purple, and red.

Toward the back of the solarium were row upon row of banana and breadfruit trees, their shadowy forms suggesting contorted human bodies with arms flailing the wind.

As the rain continued to pour in through the open roof, the room became suffused with the sweet, dark smell of Madagascar jasmine, the delicate scent of the flowers mingling with the rich wet smell of the moist earth.

Standing there clutching Amanda to her, Christy was

reminded of a scene out of time. A prehistoric age of giant fern forests, where living creatures had flippers and scaly skins. Involuntarily she shuddered. Then for the first time she noticed the footprint.

As the others clustered about the remains of the statue she took a step closer, perfectly prepared to witness the footprint of some giant reptilian creature.

It was with some relief that she recognized it not as reptilian but as very much a human print, the booted footprint of a large man.

She noticed as well a portion of the statue's head that was lying close beside her feet. One eye, the finely chiseled nose and chin, was still perfectly intact. Staring down at it in the flickering golden light of the candelabra, she was struck by a sense of vague familiarity. Something elusive she could not quite put her finger on.

Looking up, she saw that Iris had followed her glance. "Christina, darling," she said in a silky voice. "Would you be good enough to take Amanda upstairs and put her to bed? You'll find her room on the other side of the minstrel's gallery. I'm afraid she'll take a chill if she remains here any longer."

Christy turned toward the doorway only to be confronted by the dark spectral figure of Mrs. Fears holding a candle aloft in her hand. A ghostly wisp of a smile traced her lips and her eyes glittered with an eerie triumphant light.

Accepting the candle proffered by the housekeeper, they left the solarium. Holding tightly to Amanda's small hand, she then retraced her steps to the great hall and climbed the staircase.

As they passed the portrait of Abigale Falcon on the upper floor, Christy lifted the guttering flame aloft only to find the eyes dull and lifeless, revealing nothing of their previous life and intensity. Could she have imagined the entire episode, she wondered?

They moved on down the hall, Christy's mind spinning

and confused by the events of the evening. She was lost in a labyrinth of her unquiet thoughts, unable to sort the real from the imagined.

"My room's over there," Amanda informed her, drawing Christy across the hall and into a lovely nursery, where a small night light was burning on the bureau.

The room was inhabited by a friendly scatter of dolls, which seemed to occupy every possible nook and cranny. Some of them were seated on shelves while the more exotic specimens reposed in glass cases along the far wall. The dolls ranged from antique to modern and were of every size and nationality.

Scattered about the room were doll houses, trunks of dolls' clothes, and shelves of miniature booties for miniature feet. Christy noticed as well an antique cabinet containing fragile china figurines, all of which appeared to be quite old and of great value.

Presiding over them all in a child's highchair was a loose-limbed rag doll with blue button eyes and hair of carrot-red yarn.

Christy helped Amanda out of her robe, and after plumping up her pillows, tucked her into the large, canopied bed. She was concerned by the fact that the child was still trembling, fearing that she might have taken a chill in the drafty solarium.

Amanda's face which had been pale before, was by now a chalky white and her teeth chattered with cold. Pulling her close, Christy rocked her gently back and forth until a rosy blush began to return to her cheeks.

"There now," she whispered, kissing Amanda on the forehead. "You go to sleep, and tomorrow morning I'm going to give you your first piano lesson."

"Please don't leave me," the child begged.

"I won't be far away," Christy promised. "Your Aunt Iris has invited me to stay the night."

This appeared to satisfy the child who yawned and

snuggled deeper beneath the thick goose-down quilt. Christy attempted to place several of the dolls beneath the covers with her but Amanda querulously pushed them away. "I want the Red Witch," she pouted.

At Christy's blank stare Amanda pointed toward the rag doll seated in the highchair.

Getting up, Christy crossed the room, retrieved the doll, and placed it in the child's arms. The sight of it coaxed a contented smile to her lips.

"Why do you call her the Red Witch?" she asked, wondering why such an obviously homemade doll would appeal to a child with such a glorious selection at hand.

"Because the Witch gave her to me," Amanda responded sleepily, cuddling the doll in her arms. "It's a magic doll and she told me to keep her always."

Taken slightly aback by her statement, Christy examined the doll more closely, recognizing with a sense of shock that the dress was made from the same homespun material as the curtains of her own cottage.

Since Amanda appeared to be growing drowsy, Christy decided that it was best not to ask her any further questions. "Good night, darling—and sweet dreams," she whispered, squeezing her small hand and tiptoeing from the nursery.

Returning to her room, she became terribly aware of the storm, which continued to batter the exterior of the house. The hallways were full of drafts and ancient creaking noises and Christy had the feeling of being in an old ship abandoned on a storm-tossed sea.

Even so she was glad that she didn't have to return to the Pond in such weather.

Back in her room once again, Christy found that she was still too troubled by the events of the day to sleep. She began to pace up and down, the past twenty-four hours coiling through her mind, accompanied by fears and uncertainties as intangible as the wind.

It seemed an eternity since she had left Boston instead of just a single day. There were so many questions left unanswered. So many answers that were either completely false or at the very least distorted.

The fire had burned to embers in the grate. Feeling suddenly chill, she crossed to the hearth and stood there chafing her hands together. She listened as the grandfather's clock struck farther down the hall, tolling the hour like a heart reluctant to beat.

On the final stroke of twelve there was a light tap on the door.

"Come in," she called.

Mrs. Fears entered, bearing a goblet on a silver tray. "Mrs. Falcon asked me to bring this up to you," she said, her face totally without expression. "She thought you might have difficulty in sleeping."

Crossing to where Christy stood in front of the fire, she proffered the tray. Taking the goblet in her hand, Christy took a sip and found the taste to be pleasant, warming, and spicy. "What is it?" she asked.

"Hot mulled wine," Fears related. "The Falcons often drink it during the cold months to drive off the chill."

For a moment Christy regarded the tall, spare woman standing before her like a living shadow. "Mrs. Fears," she said at last, "I'd like to ask you about the statue. Who posed for it?"

"Why Miss Victoria did," the housekeeper answered. "It was done by one of the finest sculptors in the country. He completed it just before her engagement to the Senator was announced."

At that moment the far-off sound of a dog baying came to their ears. The two women regarded one another for an instant, before Fears crossed to the windows, pulled back the drapes, and opened the shutters.

"She'll be walking the cliffs tonight," she said in a strange, murmurous voice. Then with a quick movement of her hands she reached to unlatch the double windows, throwing them wide to the night.

"Who are you talking about?" Christy asked, puzzled by her declaration. At the same time she was elated that someone besides herself had heard the mysterious dogs. They did exist. She knew that now, no matter what Iris and Willard might say.

Fears turned, beckoning her forward with her thin, almost waxen hand. "Why . . . Mistress Cory of course. The Witch of Falcon's Island. By Iris Falcon's order she was never buried, and her spirit can find no repose."

Christy gasped audibly, once again recalling her strange experience at the cottage.

"Don't be afraid," Fears whispered, her eyes black pits in her white face. "It's vengeance against those who took her life she's after. She won't do any harm to you unless. . . ." The words drifted off as the woman turned once again to peer out into the night.

"I'm afraid I don't understand," Christy said, coming over to stand beside her. "Are you saying that Mistress Cory, the midwife, really was a witch?"

"Aye. Indeed she was. Just as all the midwives have been for over four hundred years. A witch with the powers of Satan's anointed as well as the compassion of the angels.

"It has been over two centuries since this island was without a witch." The housekeeper shook her head and a dark knowing look stole into her eyes. "Ever since the hanging of Sarah Godwin."

"Hanging," Christy repeated almost stupidly. She vividly recalled the name from the Bible and the inscription, "Bride of the hanging oak."

Mrs. Fears nodded sagely. "Strung her up, they did. It was during the Salem witchcraft trials. We had a preacher here then. As evil, dark hearted a man as you'd ever wish

to see. He threatened the people with fire, brimstone, and
eternal damnation if they didn't hang Sarah Godwin.

"He finally drove them to it," she concluded, "and we
have all lived to regret that dark day."

As Fears related the story, Christy had visions of the
boy with the withered arm and recalled Matthew's scoffing
story of the witch taking vengeance on those responsible
for her death.

Then as if reading her thoughts, Fears interjected,
"Sarah Godwin took her revenge and does so to this very
day." A dry, rasping laugh escaped her lips. "Aye, that she
did, and Mistress Cory shall do as well. Those responsible for her death will pay in blood before that score is settled."

The dog howled once again. Only this time the sound
was closer, being picked up by others, who whelped and
bayed in spine chilling unison.

The storm had slackened considerably, the wind and
rain dying away to be replaced by a ragged veil of mist
rolling up from the sea.

Christy shivered with the cold and a sudden attack of
dizziness. She clutched the window ledge as wave after
wave of giddiness washed over her.

"Don't be afraid," Fears whispered. "You're quite safe
here."

Once again Christy heard the sharp whistle. The same
one she had heard earlier that evening. As she watched, a
pale, canine form emerged from the white wall of fog only
to be followed by another and yet another. The dogs were
trailed by a man carrying a gun beneath his arm, a man
she immediately recognized by his rolling seaman's gait.

It was Matthew.

She was stunned at the sight of him. So they were his
dogs after all. And what of the footprint in the moss
downstairs? Had he also destroyed the statue and then

broken the glass to make it appear that lightning had been the cause?

Perhaps it was a brief flash of candlelight that attracted her attention to the east wing of the house. She wasn't sure. It could have been that or the slight movement of the drapes hanging at one of the windows on the second floor. Whatever it was, Christy now saw the figure of a woman standing in front of the windows and peering out into the night.

The candle dimmed as the woman drew back, but not before Christy recognized her to be Iris Falcon.

Wondering if Mrs. Fears had seen her and the dogs as well, she turned, but found the room empty.

The housekeeper had slipped away as silently as a shadow into water.

Eight

CHRISTY lay in the high-posted bed staring off into nothingness.

What could it all mean: Matthew . . . the dogs, Iris' strange behavior, and Willard's fawning, unpleasant interest? The aura of danger in the house was so thick and persistent that she felt as if she were being suffocated.

She began to grow drowsy, her blood coursing sluggishly through her veins and her mind refusing to function properly. Perhaps she was exaggerating the things that had taken place because of her deep, ingrained fatigue.

The events of the day were indeed becoming confused

in her mind. Distorted. The people she had encountered as well as their words and actions looming all out of proportion to the actual events.

Shadows cast by the dying firelight moved in grotesque patterns across the ceiling—fluttering at times like hovering wings. As the fire dwindled to coals, they seemed to close in to engulf her. Christy closed her eyes reluctantly, allowing herself to be dragged down into unconsciousness.

She fell immediately into a deep and fitful sleep, shot through with nightmares and visions, some familiar, others entirely strange.

There were sounds in the dark world she now inhabited. The hushed murmur of voices. A whisper of satin. A prisoner of dreams. Christy found herself back at the Lacy home in Boston, dressing for a great ball. It was to be her debut, and downstairs they were all waiting for her to make her appearance.

For a moment she savored the feeling of being loved, admired. The center of all attention.

Practiced hands prepared her for the occasion, arranging her hair and slipping a gown of the palest eggshell satin over her head. This then was what it was like to be young and beautiful—a beloved daughter of wealth and lineage.

She was attended by a retinue of faceless phantoms, and in the flurry of expectation, neither knew nor cared who they might be. They worked silently, and at last Christy stood alone in the center of the room. She was ready.

From somewhere the disjointed sounds of an orchestra tuning up began to penetrate the confines of the chamber. Her pulse quickened. The ball, she thought with mounting excitement. She would have to hurry. They would all be waiting for her downstairs to make her entrance.

Christy moved gracefully to the full-length pier glass for one last turn, only to pause and draw back in surprise.

Slowly the mirrored surface began to change color,

shifting from clear silver through all the colors of the spectrum. It was a dazzling display and she remained transfixed, unable to take her eyes from the brilliantly flashing surface.

Something inside was beginning to take shape. The mirror was suddenly blinding to look upon, as if a thousand-watt spotlight had been trained on its reflective surface.

As she stood staring in utter fascination, a strange cloudy substance began to take form, evolving slowly into the recognizable figure of a woman. At the same time the sweet, cloying scent of lemon verbena which she had previously noticed had suddenly become overpowering.

Then she heard it.

Laughter. A sparkling crescendo of rich female laughter rippling out in the room like the tinkle of startled bells. It echoed back and forth, light, frothy, bouncing and reverberating from the paneled walls.

Strangely enough Christy felt no fear. Instead she drew closer, trying to recognize the reflection which was still little more than a drifting blue-white haze. Mesmerized, she continued to watch as it swirled out of the mirrored surface and gathered together in a curling mass to hang suspended before her.

By now she could see that it was indeed a woman, a woman not dissimilar in appearance from herself. The eyes, however, appeared to be larger, darker, the mouth fuller and more sensual. Hanging to her creamy shoulders, the woman's hair was a dark cloud that perfectly framed her face.

For a moment Christy thought that she must be staring at a mirrored reflection of herself, and yet it was not quite herself.

Confused, she hurried her face into a pleasant smile. The smile she received in return was slow, enticing—the smile of a temptress. Not her own familiar, open smile at all.

Once again the laughter sparkled forth, mocking and thoroughly self-possessed. The lips were slightly parted, the chin was tilting upward as the sound died away like a song abruptly ended.

As graceful as a dancer whose substance might drift away at any moment and disperse to the winds, the figure began to move toward her as if in slow motion. The white satin gown clung and flowed about the body like an avalanche of filmy white snow.

Christy experienced a sudden icy draft. Her perfect calm shattered as the chill intensified. Her blood ceased to flow in her veins, her heart refused to beat. All that moved was the misty apparition, trailing loosely toward her like seaweed drifting under water. The laughter began again and rose steadily in pitch and volume.

Like icy tentacles, the first vaporous wisps touched her breast . . . then her face and shoulders, enveloping her body like a monstrous cobweb. It continued to swirl about her, filling her nose, her mouth, smothering her until she gasped for breath.

Then all was still. The mirror reflected a single figure, a beautiful young woman dressed completely in white.

The door opened behind her and someone appeared at the threshold, dark, shrouded, a woman Christy dimly recognized as her Aunt Ellen. The figure beckoned, drawing her forward with a spectral hand.

The ball, Christy remembered. Yes, the ball. They must be waiting for her downstairs.

Feeling that she was beyond her own volition, Christy drifted off toward the door, completely weightless, her feet seeming not to even touch the floor. It was almost as if she were being drawn along magnetically.

As she moved along the outer corridor, the murmur and hum of voices began to grow louder, becoming a solid wall of noise by the time she reached the minstrel's gallery.

Down below, the great hall was a sea of elegantly

gowned women escorted by men in black ties and tails. The orchestra was playing "Musetta's Waltz" from *La Boheme* and the dancing couples became splashes of brilliant color as they whirled about the floor.

It was the most elaborate affair imaginable, with ostrich plumes dancing and the women's gowns sparkling with embroidered jet and jewels beneath the glittering crystal chandeliers.

Liveried servants flashed about bearing trays of champagne, while beyond the terrace windows hundreds of rockets painted the night sky with pinwheels and spiraling cascades of shimmering color.

The great hall itself was lavishly strung with garlands and swags of flowers, while long, snowy buffet tables shone with silver and gold platters containing mountains of delicacies.

As Christy hovered uncertainly at the top of the grand staircase, the sound of drums echoed out in the hall and the orchestra broke into a rousing fanfare.

Below, heads began to turn, bodies twist and rotate—all eyes suddenly fixed to the head of the staircase . . . on her. There was a rising chorus of voices, a sea of admiring faces, and the blinding spectacle of flashing jewels shooting light points off across the walls and ceiling.

Then with a frightening suddenness everything became perfectly still.

As the silence lengthened and deepened, Christy managed a frozen smile, entirely bewildered by the sudden pall that had fallen over the assemblage. She waited vainly for the applause, the cheering voices, but nothing happened. No one even moved, their faces turning hard, cold, and stony, the hundreds of glittering eyes narrowing with malice and ill-concealed dislike.

Then before her horrified eyes the chandeliers dimmed and the figures began to melt away, evaporating into the gathering darkness like so many phantom shades.

It was as if the vast shadowed emptiness of the great hall had swallowed them up, and there was nothing left but a gaping void of blackness, a bottomless pit that seemed to be drawing her out . . . beyond. But where? To whom?

She heard the same ghostly laughter ripple out once again, echoing in the emptiness. Pure. Melodic. Faintly mocking. Then gradually it faded away to blend with the wind and the ancient settling sounds of the house.

A wave of dizziness swept over her and she grasped the newel post for support, clinging tightly for a moment as the stairway, the hall, and the house itself spun crazily about her.

The sensation quickly passed and after recovering herself, she started down. Yes. Of course. It was all perfectly clear now. Her mother was waiting for her.

Her dear, long-suffering mother, who had wanted so much for her daughter to have the best of everything and had tried so hard to make the wish come true.

The railing was a ribbon of ice beneath her fingers, the stairs themselves were a dark and twisting tunnel of shadows stretching away to infinity and threatening to swallow her up with each and every step.

Upon reaching the lower hall, Christy was met once again by that sparkling crescendo of laughter rippling and echoing through the halls. It seemed to be drawing her away, leading her off across the empty hall and along a darkened passage she had failed to notice before.

Christy's heart was pumping wildly now, her steps quickening. She had to find her mother, find the woman who had left her so lost and alone in the world so many years before.

At last she stopped before a door, knowing that her mother was inside. She could almost feel her presence close and tangible.

Reaching out, Christy found the handle chill to the

touch. Turning it slowly, she swung the door open, crossed the threshold, and entered a large, dimly lit room.

For a moment she paused, allowing her eyes time to adjust to the faint light.

A fire had burned low in the grate, illuminating the walls with a mellow, moving light. The room itself was elegant enough to be the bedchamber of a queen, even though most of it lay obscured by shadow.

At the far end stood a vast canopied bed with drawn side curtains of a gauzy translucent material. On either side burned two giant silver candelabra—each bearing a single large candle of fragrant beeswax.

Slowly Christy made her way to the bed. She was unable to see distinctly but it was clear that someone—a woman—lay behind the draperies.

"Mother," she whispered, her voice sounding hollow and unreal to her ears.

Reaching out a hand trembling with expectation, she drew back the curtains and peered down into the face of a complete stranger.

The woman was old, her bone-white hair fanning out on the pillow about her ruined face. Her breathing was hoarse and labored, the mouth hanging slack. The eye sockets were dark and cavernous, the eyes closed.

Christy felt the bitter tears of disappointment spring to her eyes and choked off a little sob.

The woman stirred at the sound and moaned softly. Her clawlike fingers crept out to clutch at Christy's hand with the chill grip of death.

Christy watched in utter fascination as the woman's eyelids fluttered open, although the staring eyes remained milky and unfocused. She attempted to pull away, but there was amazing strength in the old woman's grip. Their eyes caught and held, the stranger's pupils growing large and disbelieving. The bloodless lips moved slowly, but no words came.

The dream was growing far too real; her senses were clearing. The awareness was deepening as well that something was quite wrong. As the notion dawned that perhaps it was not a dream at all, something moved behind her, and she heard the unmistakable creak of the floorboards. Someone was in the room with them, someone very real and somehow menacing.

From the bed the old woman was whispering now in a low, indistinct voice. "I'm so sorry," she murmured. "Please forgive me, Victoria. I'm so terribly sorry."

Great tears filled the rheumy eyes, spilled over, and ran down the withered cheeks, the skin was as crumpled and lined as old tissue paper.

"But I'm not Victoria," Christy stated, suddenly coming to herself. "I'm. . . ."

The woman's eyes widened in horror and Christy caught a flash of silver descending in the faint light. This was followed by the sharp bite of steel on her bare arm. At the same moment strong hands appeared out of nowhere to draw her back and back until the room closed in about her with a soft, velvety blackness.

It was just past nine when Christy awoke the following morning.

Her mind felt blunt and slow, her body heavy and listless. As she lay there, bits and pieces of the previous night's dream stirred restlessly just on the edge of consciousness.

She squeezed her eyes shut for a few seconds more, hoping to eradicate the nightmare from which she had so gratefully awakened, that strange, smothering dream in which she had been both herself and yet someone else entirely.

With a deep sigh she slid from bed and was relieved to find sunlight streaming through the louvered shutters, falling in warm, slanting frames of light on the wine-red carpet.

The previous night's dream seemed to fade with the light of the new day. The storm and her deep-rooted fatigue must have combined to produce the strange and haunting nightmare, she concluded.

Now with the room blooming with light it all seemed so terribly far away. The grand ball, her hopeless search for her mother, and the old woman who had called her Victoria. It was all nothing but a product of fatigue and her overworked imagination.

While steaming in a long hot bath, Christy noticed a red, slightly swollen area on her upper arm. It throbbed painfully as she probed it with her fingers and she was puzzled as to the cause.

Most likely, she surmised, it was nothing more than a mosquito bite received while making her way through the woods on the previous night. Without another thought she put it from her mind.

Hoping to still a throbbing and persistent headache, she searched through the medicine cabinet for something to give her relief. Finding a bottle of aspirin, she quickly popped two into her mouth and swallowed them with a glass of water.

Feeling somewhat better, Christy returned to the bedroom. The drapes had been pulled back and the shutters opened wide. The sunlight splashed in and she heard the happy trill of birdsong from the yew trees just outside her windows.

The waking sounds of morning came to her as well from inside the house. The scurrying footsteps of the maids hurrying along the corridor penetrated the heavy oaken door while the chiming of the grandfather's clock marked the hour in the minstrel's gallery. Then at a distance Amanda's shrill childish voice.

Clothes had been laid out on the bed and Christy

dressed quickly in a tweed skirt, ruffled linen blouse, and a cashmere sweater of the palest petal blue. Once again she was amazed at how perfectly Victoria Falcon's clothes fit her.

Seating herself at the dressing table, Christy arranged her hair with a few deft strokes of the brush and then tied it back casually with a ribbon. Although she ordinarily wore litttle or no make-up, she slipped the top off a lipstick and outlined her pale lips, rubbing some of the faint, rose coloring into her pallid cheeks as well.

As she entered the dining room a few minutes later, Iris glanced up and graced her with a dazzling smile. "Why good morning, Christine, darling."

Christy hurried her face into a smile and took the same place she had at dinner the night before.

"Although we generally rise at eight," Iris proceeded in a genial voice, "I instructed Fears to let you sleep late this morning. You had such an exhausting day of it yesterday that I thought you needed the rest."

Iris had already finished her breakfast and was just starting her coffee. She was dressed in suede jodhpurs, a blouse with full, starched sleeves, and a tightly cut bolero jacket.

Sitting there at the head of the table in her regal, high-backed chair, she looked very much the sportswoman and lady of the manor.

Still, in the harsh winter sunlight that poured in through the dining room windows, she did not appear to be quite as young as she had the night before. Her hair—pulled back in a sleek bun—was not nearly so flattering and a fine tapestry of lines furrowed her aristocratic brow.

In spite of the expert application of make-up Christy couldn't help but notice the crow's-feet that fanned out from the corners of her eyes as well as the slight hardness about the mouth.

"Do help yourself to whatever you wish," Iris instructed

with a wave of her hand toward the carved mahogany sideboard. "Breakfast is a casual affair." Then flashing one of her expansive, mechanical smiles, "Still I think you'll manage to find enough nourishment to keep you going . . . at least until lunch."

Christy found the magnificence of the breakfast selection a bit intimidating. The twin silver urns contained both tea and coffee, while hot dishes of eggs, kidneys, and even fish were kept warm above small gas burners.

There was in addition a large basket of fruit, a platter of cold cuts, freshly baked scones, and a wide variety of jams and jellies, all of which, Iris informed her, were grown and preserved on the island.

Although Christy wasn't in the least hungry, she helped herself to a small portion of scrambled eggs, a hot buttered scone, and several thick slices of ham.

As she returned to the table bearing her plate, Iris replaced her coffee cup in its saucer and glanced up. "Did you sleep well, my dear?"

"Not very," Christy admitted with candor. "The wine you sent up was delicious but it seemed to give me a terrible headache as well as the strangest dream I've ever had."

Iris' green eyes clouded with concern. "Oh, dear. I'm so terribly sorry. We all drink it during the winter months. I believe it has a mild sedative effect. Something the local Indians used to make from the bark of the hemlock."

The sounds of hammering and distant voices drifted in through the open doors of the dining room.

"That's Willard," Iris informed her, extracting one of her long oval cigarettes from the gold case beside her plate. "He had some workmen come up from the village early this morning to repair the damage to the solarium."

"Does that happen often?" Christy asked. "I mean . . . has lightning been known to strike here before?"

"Not that I know of," Iris responded easily. "Just one

of those freak accidents, I suppose. The sort of thing that happens once in a lifetime."

She lit her cigarette, inhaled deeply, and leaned back to regard Christy through a rising cloud of blue smoke. "If I were as superstitious as the local people, I'd say that it was an ill omen of some sort."

"But you said last night that you did believe in spirits," Christy retorted.

"I'm afraid that must have been the wine talking," Iris offered smoothly. "There's nothing on this island living or dead that can frighten me."

Then with an obvious desire to change the subject, she went on, "I'm afraid I'm going to be tied up with estate matters this morning. It's a bloody nuisance but at least it keeps my mind occupied. In any case I'm sure that you and Amanda can get started off on your own. After lunch I'll take you on a tour of the gardens. Just the two of us."

"That would be nice," Christy responded without much conviction. She was anxious to get back to the Pond, having left Jason alone overnight.

Iris glanced down at her watch and frowned. "Mrs. Fears will bring Amanda down in about thirty minutes. That should give you time to finish your breakfast and relax for a few minutes."

Rising to her feet, she retrieved her riding crop from the snowy linen cloth. "The music room is just across the hall. I'm sure you'll find everything there to your satisfaction."

Iris remained where she was, absently drawing the leather crop across the palm of her hand. "There is one thing more," she said, her brow furrowing. "I'm not sure how Amanda will react at first. You see, it was Victoria's favorite room and Abigale had it closed after her death." Then almost as an afterthought she added, "The child's mother was a fine musician, you know. She studied for several years in Vienna, hoping to become a concert pianist."

Christy could not take her eyes from the short but lethal-looking leather whip, or the slender but practiced hand that wielded it with such familiarity.

"If you need anything," Iris concluded, striding to the door, "simply ring for Fears. The old dragon may be a bit surly, but she's entirely competent."

Then touching the riding crop to her temple in a brief salute, Iris turned on her heel and left the room.

Nine

AFTER finishing a leisurely breakfast and relaxing over two cups of strong black coffee, Christy crossed to the music room and threw the double doors wide.

It was a lovely spacious room with large windows that looked out across the lawns to the sea beyond.

The tasteful feminine touch was unmistakable, the Louis Quinze furniture selected with care, every piece as fragile and lovely as an exquisite work of art.

There was in addition a large golden harp, a spinet piano, and along the far wall illuminated glass cases containing rare musical instruments. Most intriguing to Christy was a collection of small fiddles. They were the kind that had been played by dancing masters in the eighteenth and nineteenth centuries.

On top of the spinet was a large china vase of wisteria —the fragile scent of the blossoms faintly elusive on the still morning air.

Sitting down at the piano, Christy began to browse

through the music that was still in place above the keyboard. Bach, Chopin, and Brahms had all been obvious favorites of Victoria's. She noticed as well that the scores were signed in a delicate, slanting hand, the name "Victoria Falcon" inscribed boldly across the face of each piece as if to assert her mastery over the composition.

Allowing her fingers to float lightly over the keys, Christy began to play, but quickly discovered that the instrument was badly out of tune. Obviously it hadn't been played or properly tuned since Victoria's untimely death almost a year before.

With her fingers traveling across the ivory keys, Christy allowed her emotions to pour out into the music as she moved easily through the lovely harmonies of Brahms.

For some inexplicable reason tears began to gather at her eyelids, spill over, and run down her cheeks. Suddenly she felt terribly lost and alone. Even the excitement of being on her own at last had dimmed, although she had been on Falcon's Island for barely twenty-four hours.

She played on and on, allowing her doubts and confusion to find voice in the music. At last she could bear it no longer and her hands crashed down on the keyboard in a loud, banging discord.

Feeling utterly lost and full with despair, Christy dropped her face into her hands and gave way to tears.

Some moments later she felt strong hands upon her shoulders and heard a sympathetic male voice close behind her.

"There, there now, young lady. It couldn't possibly be as bad as all that."

Acutely embarrassed, Christy looked up to find Willard Falcon peering down at her, his face creased with concern.

Drawing herself up, she brushed at her eyes with a hasty movement of her hand and attempted to pull herself together.

For his part Willard immediately reached into his coat

pocket and produced a white silk handkerchief. "Take this," he offered in a coaxing voice, "and dry those pretty eyes of yours."

"I'm terribly sorry to behave like such a fool," Christy apologized in a muffled voice. "I suppose I'm just having a bad case of nerves."

Willard sat down beside her on the piano bench and took her hand in both his own with a fatherly comforting gesture.

"Think nothing of it, my dear Miss Randolph. It's only natural that you should be feeling homesick. After all you've come a long distance and left all your loved ones behind."

A small, worried frown blurred his features. "I'm afraid that my wife and I are partially to blame as well. We've given you little enough cause since your arrival to think that you've done the right thing."

"You've been very kind," Christy insisted, dabbing at her reddened eyes. "It's just that. . . ."

There was the sound of shrill childish laughter echoing in the great hall. This was followed by eager running footsteps. Then the doors to the music room burst open to admit Amanda. Her plain round face was flushed with pleasure and to Christy's immense surprise Jason was frisking happily about her legs.

With a sharp bark he sat up and tilted his head to one side, begging Amanda to throw the ball she held tantalizingly aloft.

"Oh, Christy," she said running over to the piano. "Jason and I have been playing out on the lawn. Every time I throw the ball he runs after it and brings it back to me."

Patting Jason fondly on the head, Christy glanced questioningly at Willard, who was gazing at her with a gentle, pleased smile. "I was afraid you'd be worried about leaving your little dog alone for so long, and so I sent a man down to bring him up to the house first thing this morning."

Christy smiled her thanks, thinking that she must have indeed misread the man the night before. His overattentive manner was most probably motivated by a genuine desire to put her entirely at her ease.

With another sharp bark Jason grabbed the hem of Amanda's dress in his teeth and began pulling in short, excited tugs as the child held up the ball and laughed with open delight.

"It looks as if you've found a real friend," Christy beamed. She was thoroughly enjoying the happiness that illuminated the small, drawn face for the first time.

"Do you really think that Jason likes me?" the child demanded with earnest concern. "He won't go away, will he —not like all the others?" Her eyes sought Christy's for confirmation. "I want so much for both of you to stay."

There was something so poignant in the childish plea that Christy felt like breaking into tears once again. Having lost everyone that she loved, Amanda was obviously starved for affection and Christy's heart ached for her. It was something she herself understood only too well.

"Jason adores you, darling," she said softly, "and both of us are going to stay right here on Falcon's Island for just as long as you want us to.

"Now then," she said assuming a more businesslike tone of voice. "We have work to do." With a snap of her fingers, Christy ordered Jason to lie down. He complied immediately, seeking out a warm spot on the rug where the sunlight fell in through the wide expanse of diamond-paned windows.

Willard rose to his feet and hoisted Amanda up on the piano bench next to her teacher. "Well, I'd better let you two get on with your lessons. Far be it from me to hold up the development of a budding concert pianist."

With a genial wave he was gone from the room, closing the doors behind him..

"Do you really think I can learn to play?" Amanda asked, her bright blue eyes anxiously searching Christy's face.

"That depends entirely on how good a student you are," she replied.

The child wiggled with excitement, her homely face almost pretty with expectation.

"Now place your hands on the keyboard and try and follow everything that I do."

With infinite patience Christy began to play a simple five-finger exercise, allowing ample time for Amanda's small fingers to follow her lead.

Appearing to be genuinely absorbed, Amanda picked out the notes with amazing ease, making a minimum of mistakes and exercising an unexpectedly light and musical touch. Soon they were playing a tune together and it was obvious to Christy that Amanda displayed a genuine talent as well as a very sensitive ear for music.

Suddenly she stopped and looked up into Christy's face. "Will you teach me to play "Musetta's Waltz" when I learn to play better?" she asked.

Christy could only stare down at her in stunned amazement. "Musetta's Waltz." That was the tune that the orchestra had been playing during her dream of the night before.

"Why . . . of course. But why do you want to learn that particular tune?"

"Because it was my mother's favorite," Amanda replied, returning her attention to the keyboard.

As she continued to practice, Christy got up from the piano and began to move about the room. From time to time she reached out to touch things she liked with a gentle appreciative hand: a rare porcelain figurine that she recognized immediately as a Sèvres; a carved ivory scrimshaw, yellowed and mottled with age. These and other things quickly took on a close and personal meaning.

Stopping beside a fragment of fine Greek statuary mounted on a marble pedestal, she allowed her fingers to play over the perfect contours, thoroughly enjoying the exquisite feel of the living stone.

Thoughts of Victoria Falcon were very much with her, just as they had been ever since the previous evening. The music room, like the bedroom upstairs, was ripe with a sense of the other woman's possession, a possession that had not dimmed with the passage of time.

There was still the feeling that she had just stepped out the door, her presence still hanging on the air like the heady scent of her favorite lemon verbena perfume. Even the child seated at the piano, while lacking her mother's reported classic beauty, had inherited her sensitive nature and musical ability.

Christy paused by the windows and stood staring out at the day. What a lonely child Amanda was. So lost and defenseless in the great house. So without the love she so desperately needed if she was ever to mature. Christy knew only too well what the loss of a beloved parent could mean to a child, especially one as sensitive as Amanda.

A hurrying cloud crossed the sun. The sea changed color before her eyes, going from a pale wintery green to dark viridian with frothy whitecaps dancing over the water. By listening hard she could hear the sound of the surf breaking on the rocks at the foot of the cliffs.

Still the sound held none of the menace of the previous evening, none of the orchestrated horror of the storm, the sea, and the night. Standing there enveloped in the warmth and the peace of the lovely music room, it all seemed somehow to be very far away, almost as if it had never happened.

Moving back toward the piano, Christy paused before a

painting that was notable only because it was so terribly out of place.

It was the portrait of a man possessed of the typical Falcon face. The same careless good looks, loose mouth, and aristocratic nose. The only real difference between Willard and his forebear was the long drooping mustaches that had been common to men of substance during the first quarter of the century.

The tarnished nameplate on the ornate gilt frame read, "Sebastian Falcon."

The picture proved to be a puzzle. By every measure it was an undistinguished piece of work. Christy knew instinctively that with her exquisite taste Victoria would never have chosen it to hang in the music room.

On closer inspection she noticed the discoloration of the surrounding wall. The painting had obviously been recently exchanged for one that had previously hung in that same spot.

Then Christy remembered. Mrs. Fears had mentioned that a painting of Victoria was hanging in the music room, and yet this was the only painting in evidence.

At the piano Amanda had begun to grow weary, her small inexperienced fingers stumbling occasionally over the keys. Even so she continued to persevere, having mastered several of the more difficult scales as well as the simple tune that Christy had taught her.

"I think that's enough for today," Christy called, thoroughly pleased with her pupil's progress.

Amanda looked up, a spark of triumph lighting her blue eyes. "When will I be able to play as well as my mother did?" she asked.

"It takes a long time and lots of hard work to become a fine pianist. Your mother started when she was still a small girl, just like you're doing now."

Disappointment starched Amanda's features and for a moment Christy thought that she was going to cry. Hurry-

ing over to her side, she cupped the small face in one hand
and drew her close. "Everything worth having in life re-
quires a great deal of hard work," she said softly. "Otherwise we wouldn't appreciate the things we work to get."

Then, in a firmer voice, "By the way, darling, do you
happen to remember if there was a picture of your mother
hanging in this room?"

Amanda nodded, her eyes traveling instantly to the
painting of Sebastian Falcon. She did not appear surprised
to find that Victoria's portrait was missing. "It used to
hang there," she said in a small, subdued voice. "But Aunt
Iris had it taken away."

"Was there some reason that your aunt wanted it replaced?" Christy asked, trying to sound as casual as possible. It seemed strange indeed that Victoria's photograph
had been removed from the silver frame in her bedroom
and that her portrait should be missing now as well.

With an apprehensive glance over her shoulder Amanda placed her finger to her lips, slipped from the piano
bench, and tiptoed to the door. For a moment she stood
listening before opening the door and beckoning Christy
to follow.

She did so, and after taking the child's hand, the two of
them moved out into the great empty hall, shutting the
door silently behind them.

The house was submerged in a deathlike midmorning
silence. Nothing stirred. Glancing down at her wrist
watch, Christy saw that it was going on half past eleven.

Just as they had reached the far side of the hall, there
was the sound of approaching footsteps accompanied by
loud argumentative voices. Pausing to listen, Christy made
out the unmistakable click of Iris' heels coming along the
outer foyer.

As the voices grew louder, Amanda pulled her into the
shadowy niche beneath the staircase, her eyes great with
sudden fear.

Micronite filter.
Mild, smooth taste.
For all the right reasons.
Kent.

© Lorillard 19

America's quality cigarette.
King Size or Deluxe 100's.

While thoroughly puzzled, Christy followed along, not quite knowing what else to do. Still, she pondered, if Iris should happen to walk past their hiding place, she might easily discover them, and what on earth was she going to think?

Huddling there in the dusty dimness, she regretted letting Amanda draw her into one of her childish fantasies. Should Iris discover them crouching there beneath the stairs, she would appear a perfect fool.

The footsteps stopped abruptly upon reaching the hall and a heated exchange followed. The voices were low and indistinct. Unable to contain her curiosity, Christy crept forward and peered out.

Iris was standing with Scully, her riding crop slapping restlessly back and forth against her thigh. At that moment she looked very hard and grim.

"You're a fool, Scully. The girl should never have been permitted to start out alone through the woods. Why she might have been killed or at the very least badly mauled by those dogs."

"I wouldn't worry about that one," Scully countered with a sullen scowl. "She's not the little bit of fluff you might think. If you ask me ——

"But I'm not asking you," Iris snapped. "And your opinions are of absolutely no interest to me. I want those dogs found and destroyed. And furthermore, if Matthew Parrish comes up here again sticking his nose into my business. . . ."

They began moving once again and although Christy tried to catch the words, Iris' voice had become muffled.

So Iris had lied. She had known about the dogs all along. And Matthew? What was his role in all this? Why was he poking into Iris' affairs as she claimed?

By now Amanda had drawn Christy from their hiding place and led her off into one of the dimly lit side passages leading along the east wing.

Christy had not realized that the house was so vast. She felt as if she were traveling through a maze. After several twists and turns she knew that were she called upon to do so, she would be entirely unable to find her own way back to the main hall.

Close beside her, Amanda clutched her hand fiercely, becoming more withdrawn and apprehensive with each step they took.

As they traversed the corridors, Christy peered off into the rooms opening on either side. Those with open doors were all steeped in darkness, heavy draperies pulled against the day. Shadowy forms bulked up beneath ghostly dust covers and the musty air had the dry, unused smell of a tomb.

By now they had proceeded to the back regions of the house. Furniture was sparse and threadbare with dust standing thick along the wainscoting. Obviously there was something to Iris' claim of the night before, that the Falcons had come upon hard times.

In spite of her practical nature Christy found it depressing to think of the noble Falcons living with the slow deterioration of Falcon's Eyrie, forced to keep up only the outward pretense of their former high station.

By this time they had arrived at the foot of a narrow flight of stairs and began to climb. The floral wallpaper was faded and peeling from the walls, while the steps themselves were covered with a frayed Oriental carpet runner.

The stairs creaked loudly as they climbed and Christy was forced to hold tight to the railing and pay strict attention to where she placed her feet. Upon reaching the upper landing, they turned into a wide hall both shabbier and darker than the lower passage. It was only faintly lit, the dingy window at the far end being blinded by cobwebs.

Christy pulled her sweater more closely about her

shoulders to ward off the icy chill that seemed to hold the empty hallway in its grip.

At the far end Amanda stopped before a door and looked up with a serious, set face. "In there," was all she would say.

Trying the handle, Christy found the door to be securely locked. How frustrating, she thought. Although she had said practically nothing since leaving the music room, Amanda obviously had an important reason for bringing her there.

Then Christy had an idea. Pulling a metal barette from the child's blond hair, she straightened it out and inserted the wire into the old-fashioned keyhole. Carefully she began working her hand back and forth until she heard a faint click and felt something give.

Convinced that she was now on the threshold of success, she continued to jiggle the wire up and down and was quickly rewarded by two more clicks as the lock sprung.

With infinite care she opened the door and stepped cautiously inside the room, which was only dimly lit.

The inner chamber slumbered in a musty, brooding silence, while roseate patches of light filtered in through the moth-eaten draperies. Feeling her way along the wall, Christy managed to locate the light switch and flicked it on.

A chandelier flared overhead, exposing a large room with a ragtag assortment of furniture, most of it swathed in yellowed dust covers.

The walls were hung with a variety of murky paintings as well as tapestries faded and worn with age. The collection of furniture stacked about in haphazard fashion comprised an exotic mixture of styles and periods. Obviously they had stumbled upon a repository for furnishings no longer of any use in the rest of the mansion.

Slipping past her like a shadow, Amanda went over to

an oblong frame leaning against a stack of wooden packing crates. With a quick tug she pulled the cover away.

The exposed portrait depicted a striking young woman with flowing dark tresses, creamy skin, and fine patrician features. It was life size and looked to Christy as if the subject might at any moment step down from the canvas and cross the room to greet them.

"That's my mother," Amanda whispered in a stricken voice bordering on tears.

Feeling suddenly weak in the knees, Christy reached out a shaking hand to steady herself against a nearby chair.

Victoria's face was as lovely as anything she might have imagined. Her curling dark hair provided the perfect frame and the lips were slightly parted in a mocking half smile.

But it was not just the remarkable resemblance that the woman in the portrait bore to herself that had shaken her so completely.

It was Victoria's gown, the same gown that she had worn in her dream of the previous night.

Ten

LUNCHEON that day was an uncomfortable affair. Christy ate little, brooding and puzzling over her discovery of the morning.

For some reason she could not fathom she had been deliberately brought to the island because of the resemblance she bore to Victoria Falcon. It was now clear why Iris had demanded current photographs when considering her qualifications for the job.

Her scheme—whatever lay behind it—had obviously succeeded far beyond her expectations. Not only was Christy similar in appearance to Victoria, but she bore almost a perfect likeness. She was nearly the same height and weight and was able to wear the dead woman's clothes as if they were her own.

If Iris was aware of her preoccupation, she gave no sign. Instead she kept up a brittle patter of conversation, discussing her prize Arabian stallion, her gardens, and the general affairs of the estate.

Willard for his part continued to be exceptionally polite and considerate. He drank sparingly of the wine and exhibited little of the churlishness that had so offended Christy the night before.

Amanda was brought in by Mrs. Fears for dessert, and when the housekeeper took her back upstairs for her nap, Iris commented that she had never before seen the child in such a happy state.

Christy, while pleased with Amanda's progress, conceded that most of the credit belonged to Jason. During the morning Amanda and the dog had become steadfast friends.

After lunch was over, Iris invited Christy to go for a walk as promised. Before setting out she dispatched one of the servant girls upstairs for warm coats, even though the day was surprisingly mild and breezy for so late in the year.

After bundling up warmly, they walked out onto the terrace and proceeded down the steps to the well-tended lawns with Jason bounding on ahead of them. Everything had been washed clean by the storm and the air had the precise clarity of fresh spring water.

The flower beds on which Iris lavished such loving care

were a shambles. Leaves had been cast up in piles and the carefully laid out gardens were strewn with broken branches and puddles of muddy water. The flowers themselves—mostly of the hardy, late-blooming variety—had been beaten to earth, their sodden petals scattering the ground. Those few that had managed to survive spilled out onto the gravel paths, ragged and drowned looking.

Iris stooped to gather a stray blossom here and there, making a small bouquet as she went along.

"Let's go this way," she said, striding out toward the thick growth of forest fringing the drive. "I have some place special I want to show to you. It's a spot I often visit when I need to be alone."

As Iris plunged into the woods ahead of her, Christy turned to look back at the house. She couldn't escape the feeling that their movements were being closely scrutinized.

The sun, having passed the zenith, was reflected in the diamond-paned windows and smoke curled lazily from several of the brick chimneys. All appeared to be perfectly peaceful and serene. Christy could almost picture Mrs. Fears moving from room to room in her dark, sweeping gown, touching flame to the logs in the various fireplaces.

Was it her eyes that Christy felt upon them or Willard's? The feeling grew in intensity and just as she was about to turn and follow Iris into the woods, a curtain moved in an upstairs window to reveal a blurred face. It was a face that Christy did not recognize.

"Are you coming?" Iris called out.

Dismissing the mysterious face as most likely that of a servant, Christy hurried her steps in order to catch up.

They had entered the woods at precisely the spot where she had escaped the dogs the night before. As the chill of the deepening shadows fell upon her, a rush of dark memory came flooding back.

Could it have been only the previous evening that she

had first approached Falcon's Eyrie? So much had happened since, that it seemed as if she had been on the island for ages.

As they trudged along, the ground underfoot became spongy with wet pine needles, while the bright noonday sun barely filtered down through the leafy canopy overhead. From the dense undergrowth nearby came the ratchet-like screech of a squirrel.

Following the same narrow path that Christy had trodden with such fear and trepidation, they made their way through an ever deepening forest of beech, alder, and pine.

Iris set the pace and the two of them moved along briskly, breathing deeply of the resin-scented air. In the branches above their heads starlings chirped and sang, uttering their plaintive melodies with a clear flutelike purity.

Ahead Christy could hear the rush of a brook. By the time they reached the cascading stream they found that Jason was already there ahead of them, lapping up the clear water in big, thirsty gulps.

"Let's rest here for awhile," Iris suggested, dropping down on a fallen log.

Nearly out of breath after their brisk walk, Christy was only too glad to comply, settling gratefully on the mossy bank a short distance away.

It was Iris who first broke the silence that had deepened between them. "I've noticed that you seem to be rather preoccupied, my dear. Is anything the matter?"

It was a moment before Christy answered. "Yes, there is," she confessed at last. Then summoning her courage, she told of discovering Victoria's portrait. Her recital ended with Christy saying, "To be perfectly blunt, Mrs. Falcon, I'd like to know the real reason you asked me here."

Iris appeared pale and strained, although she kept her eyes level, staring into Christy's own. "I suppose it was wrong of me to hide my true motives," she started out in a tentative voice. "Of course you were bound to find out in time."

Here she paused to pluck a sprig of sweet bay from a nearby bush, bruising the leaves between her slender fingers. "Please don't judge me too harshly," she entreated with a long, imploring look. "You see . . . Willard and I have never been blessed with children and quite frankly, coping with a seven-year-old has entirely escaped me.

"I'm afraid we've done rather a poor job of being substitute parents since Victoria and the Senator passed on, alternating between spoiling the child rotten or being far too overprotective."

An anxious little frown played at the corners of her mouth and her eyes fell away.

"You see, Christine, Amanda was devastated when she lost her mother. I thought . . . oh, I know it sounds naive, but I had hoped that someone alike in age and general appearance might soften the loss. That was why I insisted on having you sign a one-year contract. I wanted to give Amanda the chance to know you and for you to come to know us as well."

Iris sighed deeply. "We had hoped—Willard and I—that you might want to stay on here. At least until Amanda is old enough to attend a private school on the mainland."

At that moment Christy felt genuinely sorry for the woman, feeling somehow guilty for distrusting her motives. Her explanation after all was perfectly logical. The deception appeared suddenly quite innocent since it had been in the best interests of the child.

As Christy sat there pondering Iris' words, the woman's face took on a masklike emptiness. "You see, Christine, Falcon's Island is a prison. We don't live here like normal human beings. We simply survive as best we can from year to year. Willard and I are tied to this rock like bond slaves, and to tell you the honest truth, I wish to God I'd never laid eyes on the place."

She cast a narrow sideways glance in Christy's direction almost as if she were reading her thoughts. "Of course you must be wondering why I married Willard in the first place. It must be plain to see that we're far from ideally mated."

Iris paused, adding a sprig of holly to the bouquet of flowers and greenery she had been gathering along the way.

"But you see, my husband wasn't always as you see him today." Her voice took on a light, wistful note. "Dull, selfish—a man who deadens his senses with liquor and has no interests beyond those ghastly tropical plants of his."

She shook her head sadly and a ghost of a smile traced her lips as if she were recalling quite a different man. "Back in the beginning, when I first met Willard, he was a very attractive man. The scion of a fine old family. As wealthy as a prince and a most attentive suitor.

"At least that was how I saw him." She sighed and dropped her eyes. "I was a romantic at heart and I suppose I succumbed to his charms rather too easily. By the time I realized that life with Willard was not at all the life I had envisioned for myself, it was too late.

"There was a time when I had ambitions . . . dreams. . . ." Her words trailed away as she continued to stare off into the lengthening shadows.

"What was it you wanted to be?" Christy asked, seeing the woman in an entirely new light.

Iris' laughter shattered the stillness of the glade like the sound of breaking glass. "An actress," she confessed, her large hazel eyes flashing with remembered ambition. "A Duse or a Bernhardt. Oh, I had such great plans.

"In those days I was young, pretty, and talented. There was so much I wanted to accomplish. So many exotic places I wanted to visit." Her hands fluttered helplessly into her lap. "And here I am. An unhappy, middle-aged woman. Childless. Trying desperately to pretend that my life has some meaning. That . . . it hasn't all passed me by."

When she looked up once again to meet Christy's eyes, her own carried an appeal for understanding, the pupils widening and darkening with emotion. "It hasn't been easy. No, not an easy life at all in spite of how it might appear on the surface."

"But surely if you and Willard haven't gotten along all these years why haven't you considered———"

"Divorce?" Iris filled in crisply. "That's quite out of the question. You see, I was taught as a young girl that we make our bargains with life and are bound to stick by them." She cocked her head to one side and stared at Christy with no change of expression. "It's old fashioned, I know, but that was how I was brought up and it's too late for me to change now.

"You see, my dear, Willard and I are ghosts inhabiting a feudal world. One that no longer exists. Willard, poor man, lives totally within the past. In his own private fantasy, if you will." Her voice took on a dramatic vocal flourish. "My husband sees himself as the last in a long line of gallant chevaliers and gracious ladies, all to the manner born and doomed to uphold the crumbling family traditions at any cost.

"Sometimes I think it's best that he can't actually see things as they really are. That he can't see the truth about the Falcon family."

Her voice dropped to a low, slightly husky pitch as she continued. "If the truth be known, the Falcon men were nothing but notorious adventurers. They came here and systematically slaughtered the friendly Indians in order to gain control of the island.

"The Falcon women for their part were their equal in every way. Violent, cruel, and dictatorial. Why even Willard's mother, Abigale, was responsible for the death of a local woman simply because her half brother Sebastian had the ill fortune to fall in love with her."

Christy's eyebrows shot up in surprise. Then it was true. The Falcons did have the power of life and death over the islanders, something she had not quite been able to accept.

"But that's barbarous," she exclaimed. "Why didn't Sebastian do something to stop it?"

"He was away when Abigale gave orders that the woman was to be stoned," Iris went on to relate. "By the time he returned, it was too late."

Her voice dropped even lower in pitch becoming intimate and slightly mysterious. "You see . . . the woman was one of the Chosen. Something of a holy woman, you might say, if the term can be applied to these pagans. In any case the villagers scarcely needed an excuse to take out their moral outrage on the poor creature."

"And her lover?" Christy asked in an equally hushed voice. "What of him?"

"Sebastian eventually killed himself," Iris informed her. "He leaped from the cliffs not too far from this very spot."

The gloom of the forest glade deepened as clouds massed and passed across the sun. Glancing up through the overhead branches, Christy could see that the sky had become marble colored, with dark keeled clouds scurrying in formation toward the horizon.

Involuntarily she shivered. The beauty of the day had died with the telling of the fearful story. Even so she continued to listen in utter fascination as Iris continued.

"Yes. Willard's illustrious ancestors were quite successful at most everything they put their hand to. They made a fortune in the slave trade and were equally proficient when they went into piracy during the seventeen hundreds.

"Don't look so surprised," Iris said. "While the Falcons didn't actually rob anyone, the pirate ships would put in here to be outfitted and supplied, services for which the Falcons of the day were amply rewarded."

The rich tones of her voice hardened and her words now carried a harsh, metallic ring. "Make no mistake about it. The world will probably be a far better place when the last of the Falcon line is lowered into the ground."

Her eyes narrowed and her mouth became a thin, hard line. "And that day, God help us . . . may not be too long in coming."

"Why, what on earth can you mean?" Christy asked, completely perplexed by her grim prediction.

"Simply that the alliance between the islanders and the Falcon family has always been an uneasy one. An alliance based on mutual distrust.

"Falcon's Eyrie was built not only to set off the pride and riches of the family. It was built as a fortress. A warning to all, that force would be met with force and fire with fire."

"I'm afraid I don't understand. You make it sound as if a war were being waged here."

"Nothing could be closer to the truth," Iris responded bitterly. "Willard and I are the last defenders. You see, when the last of the Falcons is dead, the island will revert to the islanders."

"Do you mean to imply that they might actually try and harm you?"

One of Iris' sharply penciled brows shot up and she emitted a harsh, derisive laugh. "That is precisely what I mean. There have been far too many unexplained deaths. We can never forget for a moment that we are surrounded by our mortal enemies. People who are capable of any savagery in order to be rid of us once and for all time.

"Why it's been common knowledge for years that they are praying us to death day and night with their vile satanic rites."

"But you have your retainers . . . surely they're loyal."

Iris regarded her patiently for a moment before answering. "The truth of the matter is that I can trust no one. I never close my eyes at night without thinking that I could very well be murdered in my bed before morning."

Christy's mind was spinning with all that Iris had confided to her. At that moment Jason returned from a run in the woods and in order to give herself a moment to think she bent to stroke his head. With a joyful bark he rolled over on his back, his tongue lolling from his mouth and his eyes bright.

"I wouldn't be telling you all this if I didn't think you were strong enough to bear it," Iris added almost as an afterthought. "But as long as you remain on this island you must be on your guard at all times. Both for your own sake and for Amanda's as well."

Christy nodded mutely, although at that moment she scarcely saw herself as being strong and capable as Iris chose to believe. She actually felt that she was riddled by fears and doubts that Iris' words only served to exaggerate.

Shielding her eyes, Iris looked up at the glowering sky. "Well it looks as if we might be getting some more rain," she observed, getting to her feet. "Shall we be getting along?"

Mounting the mossy bank of the stream, they continued along the narrow path. Iris took the lead once again, making occasional quicksilver movements with her hands as she plucked a bit of fern or a sprig of fire thorn to add to her leafy bouquet.

After several minutes of walking in silence they came to a place where the path branched off in two separate directions.

"That leads down to the village," Iris informed her, all the while keeping firmly to the left fork.

The sky was by now fully overcast, sullen and glowering, so changed from the earlier day. Even the songs of the birds carried a somber, worrisome note, as if the birds were fluttering toward shelter before the oncoming storm.

The woods finally began to thin out as they approached the cliffs, and after ducking through a tortured clump of cypress, Christy found herself standing on a rocky promontory high above the sea.

From that vantage point she could see the town of Pirate's Cove off to her right. It appeared further away than she had imagined, the tiny cottages scattered over the encircling hillsides like so many building blocks recently discarded by sleepy children.

Far in the distance thunderheads gathered and darkened on the horizon, the last rays of the dying sun flashing through openings in the dark layers of cloud, throwing translucent patches of light on the sea below.

Tasting the clean salt air, Christy breathed deeply and tried to erase the dizziness that high places always engendered. Making an effort to ignore the sheer abyss gaping before her, she allowed her eyes to drink in the rugged majesty of the coastline falling away on either side.

Far below their perch the surf battered the shore with a deep thundering roar. Hollow. Timeless. Like the rumbling of great stones rolling together in the primeval depths.

"It was from this very spot that Sebastian jumped," Iris shouted in order to be heard above the wind.

Overhead the gulls wheeled and dipped, hovering motionless for a space of time before careening off to swoop and cry out to one another. Their shrill, piercing voices sounded to Christy like nothing so much as broken sobs.

One by one Iris consigned her flowers to the wind and the sea. The breeze quickened, fast whipping them away to be lost in the swirling gray mist that was beginning to enshroud the cliffs.

Off in the distance Christy saw the figure of a man materialize from the soft, gray bank of fog that was moving slowly toward them. He walked with downcast eyes, his broad shoulders hunched against the rising wind. As he drew on she recognized him to be Matthew Parrish.

Iris had seen him as well and as Christy watched, a look of pure malignant hatred began to twist and distort her features.

Then as if suddenly aware of Christy's gaze, her face softened. "Come along," she said brightly. "I think we ought to be getting back to the house before the storm catches us out of doors."

Eleven

THE following weeks passed without event. Each morning Christy arrived at Falcon's Eyrie, usually remaining until late in the afternoon. After Amanda's lessons she lunched with Iris, who genuinely seemed to enjoy her company.

She continued to find the woman to be highly charming and intelligent, with an underlying strength that at times could be quite intimidating.

Willard, while consistently polite and friendly, was seldom in evidence and, according to his wife, spent all his time absorbed by his horticultural pursuits.

Sometimes Christy would feel his eyes lingering upon her during dinner, only to quickly fall away when she looked up. On several occasions he had invited her to visit him in the solarium but she could not bring herself to do so. Thoughts of that lush and sinister jungle under glass lingered on in her memory like an ugly nightmare in the mind of a child.

Amanda proved to be her greatest joy. The child was a natural talent, taking easily and quickly to both art and music. She was less successful in mastering her lessons but continued to make daily progress, attacking each subject with genuine interest and enthusiasm.

Only one thing continued to mar Christy's visits to Falcon's Eyrie. On those occasions when she stayed over-night—usually because of inclement weather—she was tormented by the same dream she had experienced on her first night in the house. Again and again it returned to haunt her with all its sinister implications.

As time passed, Christy even found that the cottage at Witch's Pond was not nearly as lonely and depressing a place as she had at first imagined. She actually came to enjoy the solitude, spending a great deal of her spare time reading and knitting, as well as taking long solitary walks along the beach.

As the days grew shorter and the long winter nights blacker and more all pervading, she gradually became ac-customed to the cadenced, trampling roar of the sea. It was always there—somewhere off in the back of her con-sciousness. Rhythmic. Relentless. As vital and alive as the pulse in human flesh.

Day by day the northeast wind became steadily more insistent, the pale December moon reflecting off the pond with a ghostly shimmer of light.

During the long evenings Christy huddled in front of the fireplace with Jason at her feet. The hearth fire had be-come an elemental presence, a household god to be nursed, coaxed, and fed as well as a welcome friend to warm the long empty hours of evening.

Viewed from her front windows, the beauty of the marshes was a continual delight. Great isles of tawny, burnt orange and smoldering mustard yellow, the tributary creeks running dark and still beneath a leaden wintery sky.

Most of all Christy looked forward to the sunset, her favorite time of day. It was then that the silver herons returned to the marshy high ground from the day's hunting along the beach.

The birds would stand on a single stilted leg dreaming throughout the night. Their heads were nestled beneath their dusky feathers to ward off the nightly mantle of frost that lent a stark, glacial purity to the entire marsh scene.

In time even Robin the mule proved to be a boon companion of sorts. He was a large, somnolent beast with a worn buckskin hide, mournful countenance, and long drooping ears. Although well fed, his ribs jutted out like old barrel staves and his neck was as long and gaunt as a camel's.

In spite of her aggressive determination to master him, Christy retained a certain awe of the animal. It had nothing to do with his manner, which was docile enough. Her fear was centered about his left eye, which was moonstruck and appeared to stare into her very soul, while the right remained placid and totally indifferent.

In spite of her misgivings, each morning Christy hitched Robin up to the rickety buckboard and started out for Falcon's Eyrie. The old mule seemed to enjoy the daily outing, stopping along the way to nibble at the sparse yellow grass while making the trip in his own good time.

Amanda loved the gaunt, gray beast and often begged to be taken on short rides about the estate after the day's lessons were over.

Robin exhibited another of his idiosyncrasies when returning to the Pond in the late afternoon. His steps would quicken into a brisk, measured trot as they neared the old windmill. Then when directly abreast of the ancient stone structure with its slowly turning sails, he would stop and, throwing back his great coffinlike head, bray to the sky.

Christy was unable to break him of the habit even though his baleful heehawing in that lonely, treeless place always served to unnerve her.

It was on an unusually mild Sunday afternoon in mid-December that everything changed.

The pallid, wintery sun—several hours from setting—rode the arch of the sky while a stiff breeze had swept it free of every wisp and tatter of cloud.

Christy was busying about the cottage when the distant barking of dogs came to her ears, the harsh, atonal clamor, traveling sharp and clear across the marshes.

Immediately Jason was at the door. The ruff rose at his neck and a low, menacing growl rattled deep in his throat, causing Christy's heart to pound in her breast. She had almost forgotten that first night and the stark terror of being pursued through the woods by those gaunt and ghostly animals.

Rushing to the door, she looked out just in time to see a young doe run out of the pitch pines on the far side of the pond. She recognized it immediately as the same delicate creature who came down to the pond to drink in the earliest dawn, accompanied by a larger doe and a buck with magnificent antlers.

As she watched with mounting concern, the dogs rushed out of the pines and pursued the frail animal into the chill and icy water.

She appeared to be confused, swimming this way and that before striking out for the far shore.

Barking and baring their teeth, the dogs set off around the perimeter of the pond in an effort to cut her off before she could reach the relative safety of the dense thicket on the opposite side.

Rushing back inside the house, Christy grabbed the shotgun from where it hung on the wall above the fireplace. With trembling fingers she slipped in two of the cartridges she had found earlier in a kitchen drawer.

As she once again emerged into the yard, she saw that the doe was staggering up out of the freezing water. For a moment the animal stood there among the tall mustard grass, looking about in a bewildered fashion before stumbling forward on her spindly, frozen legs.

The doe was obviously weak and terrified by the sight of the dogs closing in for the kill.

Raising the heavy gun to her shoulder, Christy took careful aim at the marauding curs, holding the lead dog in her sights. Then bracing herself against the backlash, she pulled the trigger.

There was a loud click, but nothing happened.

With an angry, frustrated sob she squeezed the trigger once again and was rewarded with nothing but an additional sharp, metallic click.

The dogs were almost on the doe by this time. Too weak to take flight, the frail creature had crouched down in the tall grass, remaining perfectly still.

The safety, Christy thought frantically. She had forgotten to take the safety off.

Quickly she slipped the bolt, all the while trying to keep the streaking dogs in her sights.

As they drew on, the doe panicked, broke cover, and ran—her eyes great with fear. She stumbled almost immediately and fell in a helpless sprawl upon the ground.

Bracing the gun against her shoulder once again, Christy swiveled about and fired, the resulting jolt knocking her to the ground. The shot went high and wild, missing her intended targets by several feet.

By this time the enraged dogs were upon the doe, the clamping, tearing jaws of the leader ripping at her throat, while the others clustered about with guttural snarls and low, threatening growls.

Struggling up to her knees, Christy fired a second time at the maddened pack. She managed to strike one in the rump without affecting the doe's fight for survival. In her heart she knew it was already too late.

The injured dog's howls rang out and the pack immediately scattered, leaving the russet body of the doe bloodied and broken upon the grass.

After making sure that the animal was indeed dead, Christy started back toward the house. She was completely shaken by what she had witnessed. The tears streaming down her cheeks were chill, her teeth chattering with shock and cold.

Most of all she was heartsick at her own impotence and the idea of the delicate and lovely creature enduring such a cruel fate before her very eyes.

By the time she reached the cottage she had begun to shake with an unreasoning fury. Matthew was responsible for what had taken place. They were his dogs. Dogs he allowed to rampage about the island—to terrorize and to kill.

Changing quickly into sturdy walking shoes, Christy slipped on a nylon parka and hastily tied a scarf about her head. She was determined to go to Matthew's house that very afternoon and confront him with what had taken place as well as his own responsibility in the affair.

Thinking that it would be faster to take the path through the marshes and along the cliffs, she left the cottage and started out at a brisk walk.

The afternoon was clear and chill, a strong easterly wind blowing in from the sea. Christy kept to the edge of the pond, making her way along a narrow path bordered with golden dune-rod and clumps of beach plum. Beyond the high dunes the sea remained unseen although its thundering reverberations gently shook the spongy earth beneath her feet.

As she progressed to the far side of the pond, the marsh grew dense and forbidding, tortured clumps of mangrove rising above her head to a height of ten to fifteen feet. The leaves were of a waxen bottle green, while the gnarled and twisted roots protruding from the oozy mud looked like writhing snakes.

A rank, unpleasant odor rose up from the twisting canals, and Christy found that the path had become elusive, dwindling several times almost to nothing.

She quickly began to regret not having hitched up Robin and taken the wagon to Matthew's instead of choosing to walk.

As she picked her way carefully along, myriads of reddish-brown crabs scuttled off with a dry rustling sound. Although they were not overly large, they had an unnerving way of lifting their pincers and challenging her briefly, before disappearing into the dense undergrowth.

Knowing that the pine woods could not be too far distant, Christy hurried her steps. On either side of the path strange forms of life Christy could not identify oozed and slid through the tall grass while swarms of insects buzzed incessantly about her head.

Shivering with cold and apprehension, Christy was alert to every sound. Her sudden anger had quickly turned to fear and she blanched and started as a loon cried off in the distance. To Christy it seemed a mournful dirge, warning of danger, loss, and despair.

At last the marsh was behind her and she entered the darkening pine forest that sloped gently upward toward Falcon's Eyrie. The pine needles underfoot were soft and spongy; the watery winter sunlight barely filtered down through the silvery green canopy overhead.

Christy hurried along the forest track, relieved to have left the dark and eerie marsh behind her. Still the path was seldom used and she was forced to choose her steps carefully, leaping nimbly over fallen branches and skirting muddy quagmires as she made her way toward the trail that led along the cliffs.

She had been walking for about twenty minutes when

she heard a rustling sound from somewhere behind her. Suddenly she had the creeping sensation that someone or something was following her.

Immediately Christy thought of the dogs. How stupid she had been to set off alone, knowing they were still on the loose. Although she hated the very thought of it, she had not even had the foresight to bring along the gun to insure protection.

From off to her right there was a sudden rush of quail, their wings flapping loudly as they mounted the sky. The occurrence only increased her apprehension, sending her running headlong up the trail.

Taken by her own sudden panic, Christy left the path and struck out through the drifts of dead leaves and fallen branches. At times she was forced to forage her way through patches of prickly elderberry and bend low in order to escape the trailing branches that caught and tore at her clothes.

As the trees began to thin out at last, she caught sight of the glimmering expanse of sea. She knew that she could not be too far from the path that Iris had pointed out, the path to Pirate's Cove.

It was then that she heard the rush of approaching footsteps from behind. A branch snapped nearby and Christy instantly froze, too petrified to move. Crouching down behind a moss-grown stump, she listened and was able to make out the distinct sound of footfalls coming in her direction.

"Who's there?" she called, thinking that since Falcon's Eyrie was nearby, it might possibly be someone from the house.

The footfalls stopped immediately, although by now Christy was sure she could hear the sound of labored breathing as well. Still she was unable to see anyone.

After calling out again and receiving no answer, she

started to run, breaking out of the woods and onto the narrow path that wound torturously along the cliffs.

Above the treetops she could see the turrets and chimneys of Falcon's Eyrie etched against a sere sky. Safety was close at hand and yet so very far away. She knew she couldn't possibly make it to the house with an unknown assailant hidden somewhere in between. No. Rather than reenter the forest she would continue on to Pirate's Cove. It was her only chance.

With her heart in her throat she made her way along the narrow path that was sometimes little more than a foot wide.

Close beside her the cliffs fell away in a sheer drop, the surf curling in to crash along the jagged rocks below with a loud, thundering roar.

Just ahead the path passed through a brief stand of hardy pines clinging to a rocky promontory, a spot Christy recognized as the same place that Sebastian Falcon had leaped to his death.

Beyond that the trail became a dizzying crisscross descent down the face of the cliffs to the town below and safety. Moving more cautiously now, Christy stepped into the underwater green shadow of the trees, only to have a figure loom up out of the undergrowth to block her path.

Her startled scream caught in her throat and died.

It was the boy she had seen that first day on the road. The boy with the withered arm.

"Oh, thank heavens, it's only you," she breathed, sinking down on the mossy bank.

The boy simply stood there regarding her solemnly, a look of dull misery dimming his eyes. He was shorter and thinner than she recalled, dressed in the same castoff clothing, with one arm hanging limply at his side.

"What's your name?" she asked after regaining her breath.

"Cain," he responded, dropping his eyes to the ground.

Christy's heart went out to him. As if he didn't have burdens enough to bear without having been given the name of a man damned for all eternity.

Summoning an encouraging smile, she said, "I don't like the name of Cain. If you don't mind, I'd prefer to call you Jeremy."

It was a name she had snatched from the air, but one that brought a glimmer of gratitude to the boy's eyes.

"Jeremy," he repeated, allowing it to roll off his tongue. The name seemed to please him, having a gentle, musical ring to it.

"Now then, Jeremy," she said getting to her feet once again. "I have to be getting along, but you're perfectly welcome to walk me into town, if you like."

A haunted look came over his face at the invitation. "Don't . . . go down there," he begged with an awkward stammer. "The village bodes ill for you. There's . . . danger."

"I'm afraid I don't understand," Christy replied in puzzlement. "What kind of danger?"

Jeremy scuffed his worn shoes and refused to meet her eyes. "There are those who would do ye harm," he intoned solemnly. "Elder Dawkins has spoken to the people against ye."

"But that's absurd," Christy responded indignantly. "I've done nothing wrong."

"Aye, but 'twas after you came that the millrace ran red with blood. The people of the village blame ye for bringing ill fortune to the island."

"How dare they?" Christy exploded. "They have no right." It seemed intolerable that she should be blamed for their primitive superstitions when she hadn't even visited the village since her arrival.

"Aye, so it is, Mistress," he pursued. "But all the same . . . there have been omens that bode not well. Yesterday the hooded falcon was sighted for the first time in many generations."

"The hooded falcon," Christy repeated remembering vaguely that Willard had once mentioned the bird to her as being extinct.

" 'Tis the bird of ill omen. Legend has it that if ever the falcon returns to the island, the people shall be driven from their homes." There was a stark plea in the boy's voice as he added, "I fear that they might do ye harm, Mistress. Pray, for your own good, do not go among them."

From their nesting places high on the cliffs the terns took sudden flight, as if some telepathic alarm had been spread among them.

As Christy turned to watch, they rose in silver clouds, streaming away to the south in a fugitive storm of wings.

"Look there," the boy cried, his voice shrill with warning.

Following his pointing finger with her eyes, Christy saw a great bird advancing through the heavens and growing larger and more menacing as it came. The bird had only just emerged from a plume of hovering cloud into the open blue sky and was sailing landward on wide, almost motionless wings.

"Why . . . it's the hooded falcon," she whispered, recognizing the dusky, brownish bird by its sleek white head and the wide sweep of the powerful wings.

As the falcon drew close to the cliffs, it seemed to hover motionless, riding the corridors of the wind with a lofty grace and majesty. The bright aerial eyes of the predatory hunter scanned the water below, ready to plummet seaward at any moment to grasp its wrything prey in a vice-like, taloned grip.

Then as Christy watched in utter fascination, the great bird screamed. Shrill. Piercing. The primitive cry went straight to her heart and caused her blood to run cold.

She remained mesmerized as the falcon rose on effort-
less wings and continued to climb the sky in the direction
of the central spine of mountains.

"It's come back," she gasped, turning to where Jeremy
had been standing beside her.

The path was empty, the boy having vanished without a
word or a sound.

It was late afternoon by the time Christy reached
Pirate's Cove. The smell of the sea filling her nostrils was
so sharp and pure that it made her a bit dizzy after her
long climb down the face of the cliffs.

It wasn't until she had crossed the bridge that she realized that the little town built on a crescent-shaped sweep
of bay and backed by low hills lay in total silence.

There was no one abroad. The houses were closed and
tightly shuttered, without even a wisp of smoke rising from
the brick chimneys.

As she walked along the street, the encroaching shadows of late afternoon fell in spreading pools beneath her
feet. Even the gulls appeared to have deserted the wharf.
Everything was shrouded in an uneasy and unnatural silence.

Passing the general store, she caught sight of a brief
flicker of life. A face appeared at the grimy window, although for an instant only. It was a woman's face—pale
and uncertain—peering out at her with hooded eyes and
then quickly retreating into the gloomy interior.

Somehow the brief and mysterious appearance caused
Christy to hurry her steps, anxious to be quit of the town.
There had been something so openly malevolent in the
woman's eyes. It was a look she could not entirely define
but one that managed to frighten her badly.

Once outside the town she had no trouble in locating
the path that ambled off among the dunes in the direction
of Matthew's cottage. Off to her right jade green breakers

rolled up onto the beach, their long sweeping arms reaching out with frothy tentacles to mark the high tide with bits of shell and seaweed.

At last the path disintegrated into trackless sand and ended abruptly at the edge of a high bluff.

From there she could see the beach stretching away until it disappeared around the headland on which Falcon's Eyrie was located.

It was completely deserted. No one. The only sign of human habitation was Matthew's shack standing far back among the dunes. It was protected by an encircling fence constructed entirely of driftwood. All of it as bleached and faded as the bones of prehistoric animals.

As Christy stood there trying to make up her mind on how best to approach him, a figure emerged from the shack, picked up an ax, and began to chop logs.

It was Matthew, splendidly built and shirtless in spite of the brisk wind blowing in from the sea. Standing naked to the waist, with his feet planted wide apart, he gathered his strength and brought the ax down with great force, slicing through each log with a single stroke.

The powerful symmetry of his body was beautiful to see and Christy continued to stand watching although he remained completely unaware of her presence.

Finished at last, Matthew took up an armload of the newly chopped logs and returned to the shack, closing the door behind him.

Now was the time, Christy decided. She would face him on his own home ground. Tell him to his face what his murderous dogs had accomplished that day.

She started toward the house only to stop abruptly before she had gone very far. For a moment she stood staring down at the sand before her.

The trail was well trodden, indented every few inches with perfect booted imprints. They were identical to the print she had seen that night in the moss of the solarium, easily recognized by the unusual crosshatching pattern.

So it was Matthew who had shattered the statue of Victoria Falcon. And if that were true, what else might he not be guilty of?

Christy's hands flew to her mouth as she recalled his ax flashing in the sunlight, the naked strength of those powerful shoulders that could rend a tree trunk in a single stroke.

Could it have been he as well who severed the head of Mistress Cory from her shoulders?

And the dogs. Why had they been out at the pond that day? Couldn't they have been meant for her instead of the hapless doe? After all he had set them on her that first night and from the way they had obeyed his whistle it was clear that he was completely in control of their movements.

Pulling her parka more closely about her to ward off the sudden chill, Christy turned and began to quickly retrace her steps toward town.

Twelve

BY the time Christy reached Pirate's Cove she was amazed to find that the townspeople had come out of hiding.

They stood in sullen clusters, their dark garb and sallow, suspicious faces rendering them an integral part of the gathering dusk.

As she passed along the street, they followed with their eyes, murmuring quietly among themselves. It was not until she had proceeded to the center of town that Christy glanced back to find that the villagers were falling in behind her, forming a hostile, silent procession.

She was even more alarmed to discover on closer inspection that many of them were carrying an evil-looking assortment of scythes, cudgels, and even large wooden cooking spoons.

There was a moment of silent panic. What could it all mean? Were they simply trying to frighten her out of town? For if that was their intent, they had certainly succeeded. Under the circumstances she was willing enough to leave just as fast as her feet would carry her.

Now more than ever she regretted not having brought the wagon. The distance between herself and the furthest reaches of town, while measured in yards, seemed an infinite and treacherous gulf that she was condemned to cross.

Oh, why hadn't she listened to Jeremy when he tried to warn her, she lamented regretfully?

As Christy drew near the bridge, a dark and threatening figure stepped out to block her path with raised arms. He was a tall man and spare, with the beard of a Biblical patriarch and a narrow craggy face dominated by a thin, high-bridged nose.

It was more than his dour countenance that caused Christy to stop abruptly. It was the fanatic zeal that burned in his eyes, igniting her forebodings into tiny brush fires of sheer panic.

From behind, the murmur of the crowd had grown to a low, menacing roar. There were cries of "Stone the vixen," and a rock sailed through the air to strike her painfully on the shoulder.

Reeling from the blow, Christy spun about only to have a portly, hard-featured woman give her a shove that sent her sprawling in the dusty road. Completely dazed she looked up to find herself surrounded by a ring of threatening faces.

"Stoning's too good for her," a man shouted, spitting in the dust at her feet.

"Aye, and right you are," the portly woman agreed, exposing the stumps of rotting teeth in a lurid grin. "But we have other ways of dealing with this Jezebel."

The crowd shouted their agreement, parting at the same time to make way for the man who had blocked Christy's way at the bridge.

Moving into the hostile circle that had by now gathered about her, he stared down at Christy with eyes that glowed like live coals.

"What say ye, Elder Dawkins?" a man demanded. "What shall be her fate?"

Pointing a long accusing finger, the man spoke in a voice that thundered above the general tumult. "Indeed the woman must be punished." He turned to a man standing beside him. "You, Jeb Dorn. Go and fetch a barrel of tar from the blacksmith's." Then to another, "And you, Goodwife Freely, bring us your finest down pillows for the feathering."

There was a sprinkling of excited agreement as those to whom he had addressed himself started off about their appointed tasks.

"Now," he intoned, "let us take the woman to the stocks."

Willing hands pulled Christy to her feet and in spite of her frantic struggle she was dragged along the street toward the dilapidated church.

Realizing at last that she was totally helpless and completely at their mercy, she began to cry, her body racked by long, shivery spasms.

This simply could not be happening. Not in twentieth-century America. Any moment now she would awaken and find that it was all a terrible dream.

It wasn't. At the western extremity of town a scaffold had been erected in the weed-grown yard of the church.

The fact that it was newly constructed caused Christy to gasp with even greater alarm. It was an exact replica of the ancient pillories that had been used in Salem during the infamous witchcraft trials and were still kept as tourist attractions.

"Make way . . . make way," Dawkins cried as they proceeded toward the scaffold. "I promise ye that the woman shall be set where all shall have fair sight of her."

At that moment a birdlike woman ran up and tore the scarf from her head, announcing in shrill tones, "Let her be seen for the harbinger of evil that she be."

Christy was sobbing openly now, the tears streaming down her cheeks to mingle with the caked dust. Her whole body began to tremble and her mouth opened and closed with dry, rasping convulsions. There was a dull, throbbing ache in her shoulder and she feared that those dragging her along might well pull her arms from their sockets in their zeal.

The sunset had by now become a fiery ball, the surrounding sky deepening to a smoky carmine. On the horizon purple-keeled clouds patrolled the sky like ancient triremes propelled into battle by billowing cumulous sails.

Each step became an agony. Ahead of her a scrambling crowd of eager, curious children ran before their elders, turning their heads to stare back into Christy's face.

There was no compassion in their eyes, and to her horror she saw one of them pick up a large rock and hurl it in her direction, striking her sharply on the temple.

Christy reeled back in pain and confusion, experiencing a piercing depth of sadness that children should take such glee in adding to her suffering.

Upon reaching the churchyard, she was dragged up the short flight of steps and forced to turn and face the milling throng. Behind her stood the grim pillory, a wood and iron contrivance built to cruelly confine a human head and wrists.

Dizzy with pain and despair, Christy looked out over a sea of raised fists and scornful angry faces. Was there no one among them who felt compassion, she agonized, not one who would speak out in her defense?

Above the bobbing heads she caught sight of a man wheeling a squeaking barrow bearing a cask of tar. Nearby, others prepared a flaming wood fire, piling on the logs until it was kindled into a roaring blaze.

Strong work-blackened hands lifted the heavy cask out of the barrow and poured it into an iron cauldron hanging on a tripod. At the same time others were busily ripping open the pillows provided by Mistress Freely and spreading a white blanket of feathers on the yellowed grass.

By now Christy was drifting in and out of consciousness. There were moments when the scene before her vanished completely and other moments when it glimmered indistinctively like a mass of imperfect images.

In her dazed state she relived random scenes from her past, most of them immaterial and totally unrelated to what was happening at that moment. Childhood quarrels of no particular importance with her cousin. The smell of new spring clover and the taste of fresh-baked corn bread.

Her mother's lovely liquid eyes appeared out of nowhere to haunt her, the lovely face materializing again and again like a hovering angel of mercy.

"Mother," she whispered, her lips barely moving. "Mother."

Then harsh reality intruded once again and she knew with certainty that this was not a nightmare from which she would soon awaken. The searing pain in her shoulder and the wavering sea of cold, stony faces told her that it was indeed all too real an experience. It was happening, and there was no one to save her.

Without further struggle she permitted herself to be firmly clasped in the stocks.

"She must be shorn like a sheep." It was a woman's voice shrilling out above the general outcry.

"Aye, Mistress Hibbens. Indeed she must," the crowd shouted in agreement.

Christy watched with dread as a thin, sharp-eyed woman mounted the scaffold brandishing a pair of shears in her hand. Circling behind the stocks, the woman grasped her long, dark hair, wrenching her head back against the wooden block with such force that it very nearly rendered Christy unconscious.

In her final moment of lucidity she became aware of the approaching thunder of horses' hooves.

Everything that happened after that, happened with such rapidity that Christy wasn't sure whether or not it was actually taking place or whether she was only imagining it.

The approaching horses drew into her range of vision and she gasped at the sight of Iris Falcon mounted on her magnificent Arabian stallion.

After experiencing a moment of total disbelief, she realized that the vision was real, although with the setting sun at her back Iris appeared more of an apparition than a reality.

Iris was costumed in a black velvet riding habit with a plumed hat drawn aslant on her head. She was followed at a short distance by Scully. He was armed with a shotgun, which at that moment was leveled at Elder Dawkins.

At the sight of her employer Christy experienced a feeling of almost unbelievable relief.

Without slackening her speed Iris plunged into the assemblage, the massive chest of her mount scattering people to the right and left. Not far from the scaffold itself she reined in sharply and sat surveying the faces massed before her with open disdain.

The smaller group surrounding the pillory continued to

stand their ground, the shears in Mistress Hibbens' hand remaining frozen above Christy's head.

Suddenly everything was very still, the only sound the snorting of the horses coupled with their harsh, labored breathing. It was obvious that they had been ridden hard and fast all the way from Falcon's Eyrie.

"Elder Dawkins," Iris called out, her voice sharp and commanding, her chin held at an imperious tilt. "I command you to release Miss Randolph immediately."

"This is none of your affair," the man retorted, moving to grasp the railing.

Down below, the iron cauldron bubbled and boiled over the roaring wood fire, throwing orange reflections on the faces of those gathered about.

"Indeed it is my affair," Iris responded with perfect calm. "And you shall answer to me for violating the hospitality of my house. This girl was brought to the island under my protection and if any harm comes to her the blame shall rest squarely upon your head."

The grim visaged man remained unintimidated as a wave of murmurous resentment swept the crowd.

Then to everyone's great surprise Iris dug in her spurs and the stallion reared up, his sharp forefeet pawing the air. On all sides people fell away, scrambling to get out of her path.

With a quick, practiced movement of her hand, Iris uncoiled a long bullwhip from her saddle and sent it singing over their heads to cut the shears from Mistress Hibbens' hand.

They clattered to the planking with a dull metallic sound and Christy breathed a deep sigh of relief.

"Now, Elder Dawkins," Iris continued in a cool, superior voice, "release the girl."

Dawkins remained immobile, standing tall and defiant before her. "You interfere in matters that are of no concern of yours, Mistress Falcon. You would do well to leave Pirate's Cove before ye too come to harm."

Their eyes met and dueled, Iris' sparking dangerously.

Turning to Scully, who had remained a few paces behind her, she gave a signal with her gloved hand.

In an instant he had driven his rearing, plunging mount through the crowd and dismounted at the foot of the scaffold. Then before Dawkins or the others could make a move to stop him, he leapt to the pillory and pressed the twin barrels of his shotgun to the head of Goodwife Hibbens.

"I am not loathe to exercise my right of execution," Iris called out in a high, deadly voice. "So do not tempt me. It is my judgment that Goodwife Hibbens is as guilty as yourself and I shall not hesitate to give the order to blow her head off if you resist me further."

Elder Dawkins blanched, glancing nervously at the terrified woman, who had dropped to her knees in a prayerful attitude. The gun barrel was pressed close to her temple by the leering Scully and she was beseeching Dawkins with her eyes.

"Indeed it is not only this woman who should be in the stocks," Dawkins thundered. "But yourself as well. You, Mistress Falcon, and all those who bear your name."

"Enough," Iris spat out. Then turning to Scully, she instructed, "I am going to count to five, Mr. Scully. If the good Elder Dawkins has not obeyed my command by the end of that count I want you to shoot the old woman dead."

Iris began to count slowly. "One . . . two . . . three. . . ."

On the count of four, Dawkins dropped his head in resignation. "The woman shall be freed as you demand," he rasped, at the same time indicating to two men that the prisoner should be released.

There was a scrape and clank of metal as the great wooden beam was lifted from Christy's neck and hands.

She made an effort to stand but found that her legs had turned to jelly beneath her.

Stumbling forward Christy braced herself against the railing for support, fearing she wouldn't be able to make it down the steps without help.

"And as for you, Elder Dawkins," Iris intoned, "I intend to see that you never have the audacity to violate the hospitality of my house again."

The man stood with head bowed, a bitter smile of resignation masking his face.

Recoiling her whip with the practiced hand of an expert, Iris pointed the stock toward the bridge. "I want you to run," she said, her eyes glittering triumphantly. "I want you to run for your very life."

For a brief instant blank fear whitened the man's eyes. Then drawing himself up to his full height, he descended the stairs and began walking slowly toward the bridge in direct contradiction of her order.

As Iris' whip sliced the air above his head, he broke into an uncertain jog, increasing his speed as he heard the stallion wheel about and start off in hot pursuit.

Iris circled wide toward the quay, galloping faster as Dawkins began dodging and zigzagging from side to side.

As the massive chest of the great white stallion bore down upon him, he looked back over his shoulder and shouted his defiance, his words drowned out by the horse's hooves exploding on the cobbles.

Just as Iris drew abreast he tripped and fell, the singing whip curling about his face several times and then unspooling rapidly as he rolled over and over on the ground.

A strangled scream broke from the man's throat, and Christy found herself grasping the railing of the scaffold until her knuckles turned white. Her fear and panic had eased but she found that she was none the less horrified by the unbelievable scene playing itself out before her.

Iris Falcon spurred her horse and drew off as Elder

Dawkins rose to his knees. His long, thin hands were clutching at his face. There was a low, communal moan at the sight of the blood streaming through his fingers and spilling down onto his coat, which had been sliced through in several places, revealing the lacerated flesh beneath.

"Now, my good man. I want you to get up once again and run back to the church," Iris instructed as she wheeled her mount around in the street. "I'll even give you the benefit of a head start."

There was a high-pitched wail from Mistress Hibbens, in spite of the fact that Scully's shotgun was still pressed hard against her temple.

"Have mercy, Mistress Falcon," she begged. "Please . . . have mercy."

Iris appeared to be completely deaf to her plea, and once again the deadly game commenced.

This time Elder Dawkins ran faster, his head low against his chest and his hands trying vainly to shield his face. Once again his pursuer gave him a leading start by cantering off to his left. Then spurring her horse, she began to close in and pick up speed as Dawkins sprinted for the safety of the churchyard.

Iris took her time at first, coming in at right angles to him and then swiftly cutting between her intended prey and the assembled crowd and forcing him to veer off.

For a moment it appeared that he might reach the steps of the general store in time. Christy hoped that he would, but Iris spurred on her horse and at the last moment passed directly in front of him, bringing down the whip with a loud crack along the entire length of his body.

The sheer force of the deadly blow threw Dawkins forward. As the stallion thundered past, he spun around only to be caught by the lash a second time. Bouncing off the passing horse's flank, he finally landed in a crumpled broken heap.

Christy found that she had been holding her breath for

some time. Her terror had been completely forgotten and she was shocked and sickened by what she had been forced to witness.

Without a backward glance Iris reined in her horse before the scaffold once again. This time the crowd willingly made way, their faces gray and strained with stark terror. Not a word was spoken, although Mistress Hibbens had begun to weep piteously.

"Scully," Iris commanded, "help Miss Randolph to your horse. I don't believe she can make it on her own."

Christy felt herself being led down the steps and lifted up on Scully's mount. By this time her brain had grown numb and her movements were beyond her control.

Scully mounted before her, wheeled about, and spurred his horse over to where the tautly erect figure of Iris Falcon sat astride her mount.

She was staring down at the body of Elder Dawkins, a cruel mandarin smile tracing her lips.

The unfortunate man lay on his back in the middle of the street, his face mangled beyond recognition. The eyes remained wide open, staring up blankly at the sky.

Christy was horrified to see that a portion of his upper lip had been severed completely by the whip, the proud, high-bridged nose smashed to a pulp. One eye was quickly swelling shut while the stumps of broken teeth protruded from his gaping mouth.

With infinite patience Iris recoiled her whip and fastened it to the side of her saddle. Then turning to face the huddled villagers, she said, "As Mistress of Falcon's Island I exercise my right of banishment. You have until high noon tomorrow to be off this island.

"Should any one of you choose to defy me in this matter, I give you fair warning. I will put your homes, your boats, and your fields to the torch and drive you into the sea with this." Her gloved hand came down to gently pat the whip at her side. Once again she smiled. "You would be wise not to tempt me."

A low moan swept the listening crowd. Women began to wail and sob while the men simply stared up at Iris with blank disbelief blotting their features.

Without another word Iris wheeled about and galloped off down the street. Following her lead, Scully dug in his spurs and started off in pursuit with a dazed Christy clinging helplessly behind him.

As they crossed over the bridge that she had once found to be so quaint, the world began to spin around her. Christy clung desperately to Scully's waist as the ringing in her ears became louder, the rhythm of her pulse galloping in perfect tandem to the horse's hooves scissoring the ground beneath them.

Then just as she feared she must lose her balance completely and fall to the ground, a grateful blackness closed in about her and she knew no more.

Thirteen

DURING the first forty-eight hours following her rescue Christy remained in a state of semicoma. She watched her troubled dreams steal by in procession while making no conscious effort to interrupt their sequence. Although terrifying and painful she knew somehow that they had to be expiated if she were ever to be free of them.

Again and again she relived the nightmare. Being dragged through the hostile village. The stoning. Her bitter humiliation as she was confined and tormented on the pillory. Then Iris' appearance, riding into town on her great white stallion like an avenging angel to deliver her from her tormentors.

Writhing and twisting in a fever of recollection, Christy saw the thin, singing lash rise in the air and come down across Elder Dawkins' face. Cutting, lacerating, brutalizing. Over and over she heard his screams and saw the gaping wounds—his vacant, staring eyes.

After that there was nothing but the blessed darkness closing in about her, a darkness she was reluctant to leave in her return to reality.

Late in the afternoon on the third day she awoke in the great canopied bed with the sound of her own screams still ringing in her ears.

A cool, reassuring hand was placed on her forehead and she realized that she was conscious at last, emerging slowly from a long, twisting tunnel of shadows.

The nightmare was over and a woman's voice was speaking to her, although at first the words failed to penetrate.

It was a strong voice, yet comforting. One that both commanded and gently cajoled. "Come now, Christine. Do try and rejoin the world of the living."

There was a murmur of hushed conversation in the room and then once again the voice spoke. "It's all right, dear . . . everything's all right now, but you must make an effort."

Christy's eyelids fluttered open to stare up into the serene face of Iris Falcon. Her questioning gaze was met by eyes that compelled her to return from the darkness.

A short distance behind her the figure of Mrs. Fears swam in and out of vision, staring down at her with a cold, impersonal expression masking her features.

Christy lay perfectly still, struggling to locate herself in time and space.

She allowed her mind to explore her injuries. By far the most severe pain was in her head, which still throbbed with a heavy, dull insistence. The rest of her body felt sore and abused—almost as if she had been beaten all over with a lead pipe.

"You're a very fortunate young woman," Iris was saying. "You've suffered only a minor concussion. As far as your other injuries go, they're mostly of a minor nature and will heal of their own accord within a few days."

Her large hazel eyes widened and darkened sympathetically. "Under the circumstances it could have been far worse. You do realize that, don't you?"

Christy accepted her words without emotion, trying to relate the woman gently stroking her forehead to the woman who had wielded the deadly whip with such authority.

Like illusive shadows, nightmare fragments of her ordeal and Iris' part in it came back to haunt her.

"What about . . . Elder Dawkins?" she asked in a quavering voice.

"I shouldn't concern myself about him if I were you," Iris said smoothly. "He received exactly what he had coming to him."

"And the townspeople . . . ?"

"Gone," she replied with a satisfied glint in her eyes. "We have the island entirely to ourselves now. That is of course except for the Jenkins family and Matthew Parrish.

"In fact you have Cain Jenkins to thank for your life. If he hadn't come up to the house to warn me that you were on your way to the village and there was likely to be trouble, I shouldn't have known."

Her dark eyebrows knit together with concern. "If Scully and I hadn't ridden into town, God knows what might have happened to you. Those superstitious fools were quite capable of cold-blooded murder."

Christy shook her head weakly and tried to speak, but the words wouldn't come.

"Now that you're feeling better," Iris commented, a shade of coolness tracing her voice, "just why was it you went into town in the first place?"

"I was on my way to see Matthew," Christy responded without thinking.

Iris regarded her with a flash of suspicion. "Well, you seem to have made quite an impression on that young man. He's been up to the house twice to find out how you were getting along. Personally, I haven't spoken to him, but according to Willard, he appeared to be quite distressed over what had taken place."

She continued to regard her beneath lowered lids. "And just why was it you wanted to see him?"

"I wanted to speak with Matthew about. . . ." Suddenly it dawned upon Christy that what she was about to say could be entirely damning, and she quickly swallowed her words.

From what Iris had said she must have been wrong about him. His visits to the house and his obvious concern over her well being were scarcely the acts of a man who had intended to harm her.

In any case there was no point in telling Iris about the incriminating boot print or the dogs. If she were to do so, Matthew was sure to be banished from the island just like the others.

"Well," Iris prodded. "Why was it you went there?"

"I wanted to ask him to pick up some things for me on his next trip to Land's End," Christy lied.

Iris was clearly relieved. "In the future give me a list of anything you might need and I'll see that he picks it up. The less you see of that man the better off you'll be." Then clasping Christy's hand with her long slender fingers, she said, "Trust me, dear. You must believe that I have only your best interests at heart."

When Christy awoke again many hours later, she felt decidedly better. While still weak and languorous, her only persistent physical discomforts were a slight headache and general aches and pains of no importance.

She lay in bed watching the flickering shadows from the fireplace dancing across the ceiling. Once again her thoughts turned to Iris and the part she had played in Pirate's Cove. On her earlier visit she had given no explanation of her open cruelty. Indeed her manner seemed to challenge any question Christy might have of her cold-blooded actions.

Trying to find some justification, she reasoned that perhaps it had been necessary for her to mete out justice with a firm hand. She was after all the center of her small island world with all the power and prerogatives of a queen.

Still Christy could not help but be appalled by the swiftness and fury of her retaliation even though she realized only too well that those same actions had only narrowly saved her from a dreadful fate, possibly even death.

She blinked hard, trying to keep back the tears. What had happened was entirely her fault and now she had no choice but to leave the island. The memory of what had taken place that day was simply too terrible to allow her to stay on.

Christy lay perfectly still, listening to the empty timeless sound of the grandfather's clock striking farther down the hall. It was twelve midnight and the chimes tolled the hour with a heavy, dull finality.

Yes. It was best that she leave as soon as possible.

The following morning Christy felt well enough to dress and go down to breakfast.

Iris appeared bright and cheerful, acting as if nothing had happened. As the meal commenced, no further mention was made of the terrible events in Pirate's Cove or the resulting departure of the islanders.

Confronted by Iris' determined good humor and her

rambling discourse on Amanda's progress in both music and painting, Christy didn't have the courage to speak of her decision to leave. Dinner that evening would be soon enough, she promised herself.

Over coffee Iris suggested that Christy take Amanda for a picnic outing, maintaining that a day out of doors would do both of them a world of good.

They approached the waterfall on horseback, riding through quiet, green avenues of pine, poplar, and white cedar. The surrounding woods looked stiff and brittle in their sparse winter foliage, the dull green monotony relieved here and there by clusters of red fire thorn and colorful holly berries.

"Can you hear it?" Amanda called back from atop her sorrel pony. "It isn't much further now."

The green cloak of forest grew thicker as they mounted a steep rise and passed beneath a stand of Atlantic white cedar, the trees so tall and closely set that they seemed to blot out the sky.

Christy lifted her head and tested the cool, precise air with her nostrils. She was feeling much better after the long pleasant ride from Falcon's Eyrie.

While the events of the past week were still very much with her, she had somehow managed to put them to the back of her consciousness. Even so the outing was only a brief respite, and soon she would be forced to tell Amanda that she was intent on leaving.

The sound of the water grew louder, a surging mysterious roar, changeless in rhythm and flowing like uninterrupted rain. As they drew closer to its source, the roar grew louder, escalating into a resonant thunder that seemed to be magnified by the forest's heavy silence about them.

At last they broke out of the woods and rode into a clearing surrounding the pool at the foot of the cataract.

Sitting there astride her horse, Christy allowed her eyes to travel upward. She was hypnotized by the spectacle she saw before her, a shining sunlit veil that threw up a delicate haze of spray and was intersected half way up by an opalescent rainbow.

They chose a lovely spot for their picnic. It lay on a mossy bank with the river rushing wildly alongside after spilling over the rocky rim of the pool.

Taking a blanket from the picnic hamper, Christy spread it on the ground and arranged their carefully packed picnic lunch upon it. Then they settled down to eat, both of them ravenous after their long morning's ride.

At first they spoke little, putting away quantities of sandwiches, fruit salad, and drinking several cups of steaming hot chocolate.

After lunch Amanda retrieved the rag doll she insisted on calling the Red Witch and held an impromptu tea party of her own beside the river. In the meantime Christy busied herself with putting the picnic things away, her mind entirely occupied by the declaration she intended to make at dinner that same evening.

Little by little a rhyme that Amanda kept repeating in a singsong voice began to penetrate her thoughts.

> Orbiting Jupiter, the new day's begun;
> Blue eyed is the child of the moon and the sun.

Turning about, she found Amanda rocking the rag doll back and forth in her arms and crooning the words over and over.

"Amanda," she called quietly, "where did you learn that?"

"The Red Witch taught it to me," the child responded, "on the day she gave me the doll in the woods."

Christy pondered her statement, wondering just how much of the encounter had been the child's imagination.

Still the doll's dress had been made from the same material as the curtains at Witch's Pond. There had to be some truth to the story.

In any case, she reasoned, what on earth was so strange about the local midwife making a doll for Amanda Falcon? It was probably the most natural thing in the world.

But what of the strange rhyme? Christy stared at the child rocking her doll and suddenly she realized something that had previously escaped her notice.

While the Falcons were uniformly dark eyed, Amanda's eyes were a bright china blue. Having recently viewed the color wedding pictures, Christy knew as well that her father, Senator Holland, was both dark haired and brown eyed.

To add to the mystery the button eyes on the doll were of the palest indigo, not unlike Amanda's own.

Orbiting Jupiter, the new day's begun;
Blue eyed is the child of the moon and the sun.

Amanda repeated the rhyme, rocking the doll lovingly in her arms. Then glancing over at Christy, her small face clouded and her mood changed abruptly. Scrambling to her feet, she ran over to where she was sitting and threw her arms about Christy's neck.

"Please don't ever get sick again," she whimpered softly. "I was so frightened."

"I'm much better now," Christy managed, feeling the stinging mist of sudden tears.

"Will you promise never to go away?" the child pleaded.

For a moment Christy was unable to speak, completely taken aback by Amanda's plea.

But of course Amanda was right. She couldn't possibly leave. At least not while the child needed her so. It would be needlessly cruel to abandon her just when she was making such progress. Why even the thought of abandoning her in the old mansion with Iris and Willard was enough to make Christy blush with shame at her own selfishness.

"Don't worry, dearest," she said, pulling Amanda close. "I won't leave you. I promise you that."

It was some time later. Christy had begun to doze, stretched out on the picnic blanket with the sun streaming down and warming her face and arms.

Faintly troubling and elusive, the words of Amanda's rhyme kept running through her mind. Somewhere, somehow they carried a meaning, which proved to be as intangible as the wind. What could the old woman have been trying to tell the child? Surely there had to be some special meaning—some hidden message.

"Come see what I've found," Amanda called out excitedly.

She had been playing by the pool, poking with a stick at the lazy brown-speckled trout that hovered motionless just beneath the surface of the water.

Getting to her feet, Christy joined her on an outcropping of rock where Amanda stood pointing her stick toward the center of the pool.

Something glinted brightly beneath the clear water, rippling golden in the sunlight. It was impossible to tell what it might be from that distance and Christy decided to wade out and investigate.

Slipping off her shoes and holding her skirt high, she stepped into the icy water and was quickly immersed to the knees. Beneath her feet the cold rocks were slippery; the icy water almost paralyzed her movements.

Above her head the falls were a rush of quicksilver pouring down through a deep, green tunnel. Sourceless. Endless. Drowning all sound with a primeval roar.

"What is it?" Amanda called, her voice barely audible.

Christy bent down and lifted a glimmering object from the water, then another and a third, which she found a short distance away. She held the chill metal disks in her hand, forgetting for a moment the water's paralyzing cold.

Then choosing her steps carefully, she made her way back to shore.

Amanda was ecstatic. "They look like coins," she exclaimed, taking the three gold pieces from Christy's hand.

"You're right," Christy informed her through chattering teeth. She had recognized them immediately to be golden doubloons by the face of the Spanish king stamped on one side. This was further confirmed by the barely visible date, 1612.

Although thoroughly elated by their discovery, Christy was puzzled by just what it might mean. Perhaps there was some truth to the stories of buried pirate treasure on the island. Her first inclination was to share the news of their find with Iris, but she immediately had second thoughts.

After the grisly events of Pirate's Cove she no longer entirely trusted the woman and quickly swore Amanda to secrecy. The child was only too happy to comply, thrilled by the shroud of secrecy surrounding their discovery.

Dusk was drawing on fast as they mounted their horses once again and started back down the mountainside. The shadows began to lengthen, plunging the surrounding woods into deep, pervading gloom.

They continued to follow the small, rushing river downstream, retreating farther and farther from the sound of the falls until they could hear them no longer.

Mile after mile they rode along, crossing the river many times at shallow fords. On several occasions they were forced to ascend to heights from where they could view the sea, only to plunge once again beneath the dense forest canopy.

As they rode along, Christy realized that for the first time in her life she experienced a genuine sense of belonging. Falcon's Island was surely the most lovely spot she had ever imagined and her truest emotions were in response to beauty.

She had been a fool to even think of leaving, of running away. Not just because of Amanda's need of her but because she felt a personal responsibility to the islanders themselves. It was up to her to see them reestablished in their homes.

It was true that they had mistreated her badly, but she would simply have to be big enough to forgive and forget. After all they were a superstitious and backward people who really didn't know any better.

In fact it almost seemed as if fate had deposited her on the island with a mission. She was after all a teacher and it was her moral obligation to enlighten the ignorant. Perhaps if she stayed, one day things would be quite different on the island.

By the time they reached the main road it was dusk and Christy was surprised to see two riders galloping toward them in the distance. As they drew closer, she saw that it was Willard Falcon accompanied by Scully.

They quickly drew abreast and reined in their mounts. "Well, how was your outing?" Willard inquired after tipping his hat.

"The falls were lovely," Christy enthused. "We had a marvelous day together." Then turning to Amanda she said, "Didn't we, darling?"

One glance at the child's rosy cheeks and shining eyes was enough to bear out the truth of her statement.

"That's wonderful," Willard responded. Then turning to address his companion, he said, "I think we're about through for the day, Scully. Why don't you ride back with Amanda while I accompany Miss Randolph."

With a short nod of agreement Scully slapped the rump of Amanda's pony. "Come along, young miss. I'll see you back to the house."

Christy watched in dismay as the two galloped off and were soon lost to view down the dusty road.

Clucking softly to her horse, she began riding slowly along, with Willard keeping pace at her side. "What brings you all the way out here?" she asked, in an attempt at casual conversation.

"Scully and I have been making a survey of the outlying farms. With no one to tend them, the fields are all going to seed."

"Mr. Falcon," Christy said, seeing her opening. "Why don't you try and talk your wife into letting the islanders return? After all . . . I wasn't hurt and——"

"How are you feeling, by the way?" Willard interrupted, deliberately trying to turn the conversation.

"Much better, thank you. But that isn't what I——"

"You experienced a terrible ordeal," he cut in once again. "It's lucky for you that Iris arrived in time."

Seeing that he was determined not to discuss the matter and that further argument would be futile, Christy lapsed into silence and willed the uncomfortable ride to be over.

They had proceeded for less than a mile when Willard suddenly seized the bridle of her horse and brought it to a halt. When he turned to face her, she noticed for the first time that he exhibited a waxen pallor, his features melting like paraffin. He did not appear to be a well man.

"I suppose my wife told you that Matthew Parrish was quite concerned over the state of your health."

Christy nodded, completely baffled both by his action and by the stricken tone of his voice.

"Is there something going on between the two of you?" he demanded.

"Why, whatever can you mean?"

At the wild, answering look in his eyes Christy experienced a stab of panic, an uneasy quickening that could not be entirely controlled.

His face seemed to be under two different spells, one

fawning and the other glowering with intimations of violence. "Come now, Miss Randolph. Why would a young woman like yourself visit a man's house unless——"

"Just what are you getting at?" she demanded, thoroughly shocked by the implication.

Willard was growing visibly more agitated. His mouth had become hard, the nostrils pinched and flaring with every breath. Seizing her roughly by the shoulders, he rasped, "I'll tell you what I'm getting at. You're in love with him, aren't you?"

"Why, Mr. Falcon," Christy managed, her throat tight and dry. "I can assure you that there is absolutely nothing between Matthew and me."

He appeared not to have heard. "I won't have it," he growled. "I tell you I simply won't stand for it."

His next move was to pull her roughly into his arms, his breath warm against her cheek as she turned her face away. Christy opened her mouth to scream but the sound froze in her throat as she realized the hopelessness of her situation.

They were alone on a country road on a nearly uninhabited island. Willard Falcon was still a strong man in spite of his dissipation. If he wished, he could easily overpower her and she wouldn't stand a chance of defending herself.

Willard was smiling down at her now with the adoring eyes of a worshipful but destructive child who could become violent at any moment.

His hands still clutched her shoulders in a steely determined grip. "Don't you see that I'm mad for you, Christy? That I have been from the first moment I laid eyes on you."

"Please. You're hurting me."

He released her then but regained his grip on the bridle, while raining passionate kisses on her cheeks and neck until she managed somehow to pull away.

As she did so his face changed immediately. To her growing dismay, she saw a warning look close over his features, which were slightly stunned and angry.

"I want you more than I've ever wanted anything before in my life," he grated between clenched teeth. "If it's Iris you're worried about—she need never know anything about us. Just permit me to love you. That's all I ask."

Trying desperately to maintain some semblance of calm, Christy forced a wooden smile to her lips and decided that it would be far wiser to play along. Reluctantly she allowed him to caress her hair, which hung in wild disorder about her shoulders.

"You're so beautiful," he murmured, letting her hair trickle through his fingers like dark, warm molasses.

Mustering her courage, Christy spoke in a strong, commanding voice. "Please . . . Mr. Falcon . . . Willard. You mustn't."

"I must have you," he said grasping her once again by the shoulders.

As he released the bridle, Christy saw her chance and seized upon it. Bringing back her arm, she swung her riding crop, catching him squarely across the face.

They grappled for the whip, but she managed to hang onto it long enough to strike her horse across the flanks and dig in her spurs before Willard ripped it from her grasp.

The animal reared up with a startled whinny and took off at a fast gallop with Christy still digging her heels into his sides.

While an experienced horsewoman, Christy was terrified to suddenly find herself riding at such speed, with her mount completely out of control. Even more frightening however was the thought of Willard catching up with her, and it was this thought alone which continued to spur her on.

Clinging for dear life, she allowed the bunched fury of

the horse to explode beneath her, making no attempt whatsoever to rein him in. Willingly she gave herself over to the galloping animal and the twenty-minute ride to Falcon's Eyrie passed in a terrifying few minutes.

Willard had quickly become a small speck in the distance, falling farther and farther behind. He had disappeared completely by the time Christy galloped through the stone pillars marking the entrance to the estate.

After dismounting at the stables and turning her lathered horse over to an astonished groom, Christy hurried toward the house.

She had already made up her mind to say nothing of what had taken place to Iris. To do so could only result in her immediate banishment from the island, and there was still much she had yet to accomplish.

Fourteen

PIRATE'S Cove was deserted and still as Christy rode through, with Robin's hooves making an empty clopping sound on the cobbled pavement.

Although the inhabitants had been absent for little more than a week, there were already signs of neglect and decay. Leaves stood in tattered mounds against the buildings and the sign over the smithy's had come loose and swayed and banged in the wind.

As the gathering shadows of late afternoon stretched across the road before her, Christy was filled with a deep-

ening sadness. The town appeared to be under a malign
spell. Empty, lonely, and forlorn.

From off in the west the dying sun threw soft relief
upon the surrounding hills, reflecting off the gently surging
waters of the bay. The restless murmur of the sea was answered by the quickening breeze sweeping down from the
high mountains.

"Banished," the wind seemed to sigh, kicking up the
dry leaves and sending them skittering crazily off across
the paving stones. "Banished forever."

The empty words echoed in Christy's mind like a half-
forgotten tune, suddenly, abruptly ended.

As she rode along atop the buckboard, she looked out
across the bay. It was now completely empty of the sturdy
fishing ketches that had appeared to be so picturesque
upon the day of her arrival.

How the people must despise her, she thought, recalling the exiled inhabitants. After all in their own superstitious way they honestly believed that it was she who had
brought their trouble upon them. She—the stranger who
had come unwanted into their midst.

And then there was Iris, that strange and violent
woman. Why had she been driven to take such drastic action? She actually seemed to have enjoyed the sadistic
punishment meted out to Elder Dawkins. And as if that
weren't enough, why had she sent the people from their
homes? Homes where their forebears had lived before
them for centuries.

Christy shuddered at the remembrance of that black
day. In her mind she now questioned that Iris was completely sane. Her mercurial moods seemed to change so
swiftly, her grace and charm depending entirely upon her
disposition and temper of the moment.

Next came the thought that continued to torment her
through the long sleepless nights. Had Iris banished the
villagers because of their ill treatment of her niece's gov-

erness—or had she yet another reason, a reason as yet unsuspected by Christy?

She was no longer sure of anything except her determination to return the people of the island to their rightful heritage.

Clucking softly to the plodding mule, Christy urged him on, hoping to put the empty village behind her as quickly as possible.

She was on her way to visit Matthew, not having seen him since that ill-fated day. Christy no longer felt that he was responsible for Mistress Cory's death nor did she believe that he deliberately sent his dogs to the Pond to ravage and kill.

If that were the case then why had he shown such concern over her condition as she lay in a coma? Concern so evident that it had sent Willard Falcon into a fit of jealousy that culminated in the unpleasant encounter the day of the picnic.

Although nothing had been said regarding what had taken place, Willard remained withdrawn and avoided her whenever possible.

No. Whatever Matthew was guilty of, Christy could no longer believe that he was a man who had brutally murdered a defenseless old woman. Of that she was now convinced.

When the rutted road ended abruptly at the top of the dunes, Christy left the buckboard and made her way down the path to Matthew's shack.

On reaching the door she knocked once but received no response. Christy knocked again, more forcefully this time.

There was a muffled crash from inside, followed by a hoarse male sibilance that could only have been a muttered curse. Then the door was flung wide to expose Matthew Parrish standing on the threshold.

He looked haggard and unwell, although he showed no visible signs of surprise at finding her there. For a long drawn-out moment he simply stood and stared, a vaguely amused glint in his bloodshot eyes.

Christy was shocked by his appearance. His hair was noticeably longer, unkempt, and a ragged fringe of beard stubbled his jaw.

With a derisive smile curling on his lips he stood back and bade her enter with a wide, sweeping gesture of one arm.

"Well, well, well. If it isn't the Devil's handmaiden," he offered in a mocking voice. "Please enter and make yourself at home among the flotsam and jetsam of my life."

Although thoroughly shaken by his drunken manner, Christy did as he suggested, sinking down on the edge of one of the rough wooden chairs.

"May I offer you a drink of whisky?" he asked, picking up a bottle and splashing his glass full.

Christy shook her head and glanced about her, stalling for time in order to regain her composure.

She was surprised to find that the cabin was quite comfortable in spite of the general disarray of clothing, fishing gear, and used crockery. The room had a presence all its own. Very male, careless, yet nonetheless comforting and extremely livable.

There was no ornamentation except for a faded daguerreotype hung over the bed. It depicted a young woman bearing a striking resemblance to Matthew. Her pose was stiff and highly formalized after the custom of the period.

Draping himself along the rough-hewn mantlepiece, with his back to the fire, Matthew fixed her with his piercing blue gaze and said, "Well now, Miss Randolph. What do you think of our cozy little island after your first and last encounter with the local inhabitants?"

Christy shook her head slowly. "I feel very badly over . . . over what happened. So much of it could have been avoided if I had listened to your warning."

He nodded solemnly and for a moment she thought that she detected a flash of sympathy on his craggy features. "I must admit I'm surprised to hear you say that," Matthew said gruffly. "Under the circumstances I think it's rather generous of you."

Then with renewed resentment kindling his eyes he added, "But you were at fault. I told you that if you came into town unescorted, something like that was bound to happen."

Christy nodded her head but said nothing further.

"Those poor fools," he went on. "They were so easily mislead by their ignorance . . . their superstition. When the millrace ran with blood they thought sure that all the fiends of hell were descending upon them to take vengeance."

"I . . . I heard about that," Christy started, only to be silenced by a wave of his hand.

"And did you hear as well that a score of cattle had been found with their throats slit—drained completely of blood? Or that hex signs had been painted on their doors while the villagers slept?"

She shook her head in disbelief. "Why, no. I didn't have any idea."

"Or did you know," he went on, "that the legendary hooded falcon was seen soaring over the village for the first time in over two hundred years on the day you decided to pay your visit?"

Matthew took a quick gulp of his drink and his voice turned deadly serious. "You see, Miss Randolph, the people had to blame someone for all these mysterious events and you were the most likely candidate."

"I feel so guilty about everything that's happened," Christy confessed with genuine sorrow, "so terribly sorry that all those people were driven from their homes because of me."

"That wasn't entirely your fault," he relented. "You

simply provided Iris with the excuse for doing what she had intended to do all along. Whether you know it or not you were only a very convenient pawn in her scheme."

"But why?" she asked in surprise.

Matthew shook his head. "I'm afraid I don't know the answer to that." Then switching to a different tack, he asked, "Why was it you did come into town that day? You were warned that the townspeople were beside themselves. You knew perfectly well how superstitious they were."

"I came to see you," she said simply.

"Me?" His thumb jabbed at his chest, his eyes blazing a bright, hard blue. "What could you possibly have wanted with me? After all I'm only a simple fisherman. An outcast."

She hesitated a moment and then looked into the fire, unwilling to meet his gaze. "It was about those murderous dogs of yours," she said in a tight, dry voice. "They attacked and killed a young doe near my house."

Christy's eyes quickly misted with tears, even though she had determined to remain as unemotional as possible. "I tried to stop them . . . but it was no use. It was horrible. They tore her. . . ." Here she faltered in her recitation, unable to continue.

For a long while Matthew said nothing. When he finally spoke, his voice was low and perfectly sober, his face creasing into a thorny scowl. "What makes you so sure that these mysterious dogs belong to me?"

Blinking back the tears, Christy looked at him squarely. "Oh, stop it, Matthew. I saw you prowling around up at Falcon's Eyrie that first night after I arrived. You know perfectly well that your dogs followed me through the woods.

"I don't know why you wanted to frighten me and frankly I don't care. But please . . . let's not pretend with one another any more. It's too late for that now."

With a soft grunt Matthew refilled his glass and began

hovering restless about the room, his hands plunged deep into the pockets of his baggy trousers.

"And if they were my dogs," he said at last, obviously testing her reaction, "what then?"

"Matthew," she said quietly. "I don't know and I don't care what you're up to. I assume you have your own reasons for what you're doing. But those dogs are vicious—dangerous. What if they should attack Amanda or me? Then how would you feel?"

He made a vague discouraged sound and shook his head in agreement. "You're right," he admitted at last. "I'll have to be more careful."

He stood looking down at her for a moment, a vein pulsing in the center of his forehead. "How much have you guessed?"

"I don't really know anything," she confessed, "other than the fact that it was you who smashed the statue of Victoria Falcon and tried to make it appear as if it had been done by lightning."

Matthew's eyebrows shot up in surprise as Christy went on to explain that she saw the boot print in the solarium and had matched it with those she had seen on the path.

"Have you said anything to Iris about this?" he demanded when she was through.

"Of course not," she reassured him. "I saw what she did to Elder Dawkins. She'd do the same to you if she knew the truth. Do you think I actually want to be left alone on this island with her?" Christy shook her head vigorously. "To tell you the truth, the woman is beginning to frighten me. I'm not at all sure she's entirely sane."

"Then why do you stay?"

"For two reasons," she responded. "Amanda needs me more than ever now, and I'm determined to see the people of Falcon's Island return."

For a moment Christy felt as if she were being consumed by his eyes. Then, lifting his glass in a toast, he drained it and offered her a curt bow. "I'm afraid I've been quite mistaken about you, Miss Randolph. It would appear that you're far more of a woman that I gave you credit for. Still," his eyes grew mocking once again, "a dead heroine isn't going to be much good to anyone."

"Don't toy with me, Matthew. If I'm to succeed, I'll need your help."

"There are still many things you don't understand, Miss——" he paused. "Or may I call you Christy? After all we are conspirators, in a manner of speaking.

"You see, Christy, Iris has no intention of permitting the islanders to return. It would interfere needlessly with her plans."

Christy stared at him, by now completely mystified.

"Oh, they'll come back eventually, I'll see to that, but not before a lot of things have changed here."

"Iris mentioned something about the island reverting to the people, once all the Falcons are dead," Christy suggested. "Is that what you're referring to?"

"Not exactly. You see, there's another clause in the original grant. It states that at least one member of the Falcon family must remain in residence on the island at all times in order to retain title." Matthew's broad shoulders shrugged expressively. "There are only three left. Iris, Willard, and Amanda. Given time I think I can bring about their departure."

"You mean to drive them off by playing on their fears," Christy guessed. "By making them feel that their lives are threatened."

"Precisely," Matthew retorted with some satisfaction. "Iris and Willard are as superstitious as the islanders, make no mistake about that. As for Amanda . . . well, she would be much better off on the mainland, where she could attend school and play with children her own age."

As Christy pondered her feelings about his proposition, Matthew downed the second half of his drink. Then tilting the bottle, he filled his glass once again. The alcohol was by now taking its effect, his speech becoming gradually more slurred and halting.

"I'm going to tell you a story," he said at last. "One that will quickly correct any idea you may have in that pretty head of yours that my motives are purely humanitarian. I assure you they are not. I want to drive the Falcons off this island for only one reason."

He regarded her steadily for a long moment before adding, "And that reason is revenge."

With Christy listening intently he continued. "Have you ever heard of the Chosen?"

"Why, yes. I think that Iris mentioned something about them. But I wasn't sure exactly what she meant by it."

"In that case I shall be only too glad to explain," he said dropping down on a bench by the fire.

"The dual practice of Christianity and paganism has been a tradition on this island ever since the first settlers arrived. Some say that they brought it with them from Europe when they were forced to leave the Protestant Reformation.

"In many ways it's very practical theology. You see, by worshiping both God and the Devil the people managed to offend neither. Of course," he continued with a shrug, "at the same time they were equally subject to the vengeance of both, so they very prudently walked a middle path.

"Until recently they always had a vicar as well as a local midwife well versed in the mysteries of sorcery. You might call them the two representatives of God and the Devil.

"I say until recently, because when the last vicar insisted that they give up all satanic practices, the people rebelled and sent him packing. Since that time no emissary of the Christian church has dared set foot on the island."

His voice fell silent and he turned to stare moodily into the fire. "Traditionally the local midwife was succeeded in her lifetime by a young girl chosen from the village. She was taken to live at Witch's Pond and taught all the lore of the forest, such as healing, birthing, and all the various spells and potions.

"Eventually of course she herself became the witch in residence upon the death of her teacher." At this point Matthew got up to put another log on the fire. He stood for a moment after doing so, rubbing his eyes hard as if struggling to clear away the whisky mist.

"My mother was the last of the Chosen," he said in a voice that was entirely devoid of expression. "And she was sent to her death by Abigale Falcon."

The room was perfectly still except for the crackling of the fire and the wash and whisper of the sea in the distance.

Christy was startled by his statement, not quite knowing what to say. "But why?" she implored.

When Matthew finally responded, his voice had a hard, grinding edge to it. "Because Abigale's half brother fell in love with her." He turned from the fire and looked directly into her eyes. "You see, Christy, Sebastian Falcon was my father."

"I think I'd like that drink now," Christy said in a shaky voice.

Matthew filled a glass and placed it on the table before her.

Then staring down into the amber depths of his drink, he sloshed the liquor around. "After I was born, Mistress Cory—good soul that she was—kept the two of us out at Witch's Pond. There was no longer any question of my mother succeeding her, as the position of midwife had always been reserved for women who had renounced the life of wives and mothers.

"Old Cory was kind to both of us, and God knows by then we hadn't a friend left on the island. The townspeople were outraged and the Falcon family felt that they had been completely disgraced by the incident."

"But your father," Christy interjected. "Couldn't he have done something to help?"

Matthew shook his head. "He wasn't a bad man," he said softly, "but like so many of the Falcon men he was a weakling. He was glad enough to go when Abigale sent him away on business. When he returned a month later, it was too late."

"What happened?"

"While Sebastian was gone, Abigale had my mother abducted from Witch's Pond and run through the streets of Pirate's Cove, where she was stoned by her own people." His eyes deepened into pools of pure pain as he stared up at the faded photograph hanging on the wall. "She was such a gentle woman," he said in a voice by now choked with emotion. "It was all so terribly senseless."

A surge of sadness and understanding swept over Christy as she watched his face in shadowed profile. She wanted to go to him, take him in her arms, and give him what comfort she could.

Instead she did nothing, remaining where she was in mute silence.

Matthew refused to meet her eyes as he began to speak once again. "My mother died very soon after that," he stated in a dull, aching voice. "Mistress Cory raised me until I was sixteen. Then I went away to sea."

When Christy was at last able to find her voice, she said, "But after all that happened here why did you choose to come back? I was told that you went to college and returned to try and make a better life for the people of this island. Those same people who . . . who killed your mother."

"What took place here over thirty-five years ago happened because of ignorance," he related in a deep, resonant voice. "In the beginning I blamed not the people themselves but the superstitions that brought about those terrible events."

He turned to face her. "I came back to Falcon's Island with forgiveness in my heart. I wanted to teach . . . to improve the lot of those who had destroyed my mother and ultimately drove my father to suicide. I was prepared to forgive both the Falcon family and the islanders as well. To forgive all those who shared in the guilt."

He shook his head slowly from side to side, his eyes glinting dully in the shadowy half light. "But they wouldn't give me a chance. In spite of everything I did they remained divided against themselves, both sides steeped in violence and hatred. As far as they were concerned I belonged neither to one side nor the other. The Falcons refused to recognize me as bearing their blood, and to the islanders I was a pariah—a man whose mother had sinned beyond redemption."

"But you stayed on?"

"Yes, I stayed." Matthew lurched to his feet and began striding back and forth in front of the fireplace. "I stayed on determined to have revenge. To free this island once and for all from the Falcon family and to force the islanders into the twentieth century whether they liked it or not."

The lines in his face grew fierce with resolve. "And believe me, Christy, I still intend to accomplish that mission."

After a moment of silence he sighed heavily a harsh uneven sound from deep within.

"I can't help but admire you," Christy said, the words sounding false and meaningless to her ears.

"You mean because I haven't run away from my past as you have," he countered.

Christy's immediate reaction was one of total surprise. How had he managed to read her so easily?

"It's all right," he added in a gentler voice. "I knew the first night I saw you. Perhaps I was so rude because I envied you the ability to put the past behind you—something I could never do."

Christy felt the sudden sting of tears and was forced to look away in order to control her emotions. Then almost as if it were not her voice at all, but that of a stranger, she began to speak.

She told him everything. About her life with the Lacys, and of her aunt's unbearable condescension. All about the frustration and unhappiness she had experienced while growing up as a poor, orphaned relation.

Matthew proved to be an attentive listener, drinking occasionally from his bottle, but never taking his eyes from her face or interrupting her recitation.

About twenty minutes later, when Christy had gotten it all out of her system, she felt as if a great weight had been lifted from her shoulders. Matthew remained silent and thoughtful, appearing completely absorbed by the intimate recital.

"Do you see now why I feel that I belong here?" she asked. "For the first time in my life I'm truly needed. I have a purpose."

When he failed to respond but simply continued to gaze at her, she turned away, unable to meet his eyes after exposing so much of herself, all that she had kept so carefully hidden for so many years.

The log Matthew had thrown into the fire had by now burned down. Grateful for something to do, Christy rose and added another, stabbing the embers into a blaze with a long metal poker.

When she was through, she went over to him and took a handkerchief from her pocket. Untying it, Christy removed the golden doubloons and placed them on the table, where they shone with a burnished golden luster. "I found these at the base of the waterfall while Amanda and I were on a picnic," she said by way of explanation.

Matthew leaned forward, interest sparking his eyes as

he took the coins in his hand and examined each in turn. At last he looked up, regarding her intently. "Have you shown these to anyone else?"

Christy shook her head.

"And Amanda?"

"I made her promise not to say anything."

Matthew appeared relieved as he tied the coins once again in the handkerchief and handed them back to her. "I want you to take these and hide them somewhere. And for God's sake don't say anything to Iris or anyone else about finding them. I want you to promise me that."

Christy nodded agreement. "Do you really think there could be hidden treasure up in those mountains?" she asked.

"It's possible," he admitted. "After all Abigale did find a buried cask some years ago. It's been rumored ever since that there was a map inside telling where the rest of the treasure was hidden."

"But if she knew where it was all along, why didn't she go in search of it herself?"

"Abigale was a strange woman," he observed without malice. "She distrusted her son, Willard, for being a weakling and never could stand Iris, who she thought was grasping and extravagant. The only one she ever really cared for was Victoria. But then. . . ." His words trailed off.

They stood staring at one another, the firelight climbing the walls and painting the rough planking with a flickering golden light.

"I . . . think I ought to be going," Christy said. "I want to get back to the Pond before dark."

"Yes. Yes, of course," he agreed, getting to his feet and accompanying her to the door.

They shook hands awkwardly and Christy left the house with Matthew standing in the doorway.

As she passed through the gate and started up the path through the dunes, she heard the sound of running footsteps and turned just in time to have him seize her by the shoulders and pull her close against his chest.

"Christy," he said, his blue eyes earnest and pleading, "it's not easy for me to ask forgiveness . . . but I'm truly sorry for the way I've treated you. I just assumed that you were like all the other women I've known. Empty. Self-ish."

The anguish drained from his voice and his sudden, unexpected smile showed a certain degree of boyish charm that Christy found terribly appealing.

"I'm not?" she questioned. She was deeply moved by his sincerity and didn't know quite how to react.

"Not at all," Matthew smiled down into her eyes. "You're not like anyone else in the world."

Then, his voice dropping to a low, resonant pitch, he added, "As far as I'm concerned you're a very special kind of girl. I want you to remember that."

Fifteen

CHRISTY was awakened by the harsh, dry rattle of sleet against her bedroom windows, accompanied by the fierce howling of the wind.

Earlier that same day she had been warned that one of the dreaded March storms was blowing up out of the Atlantic and was due to strike the island sometime that night.

Wrapping herself up warmly in a goose-down comforter, she lit the lamp, and getting out of bed, crossed the chill plank flooring to the garret windows.

The wintery desolation of the marsh appeared a thousand times more bleak and empty under the spell of the white storm flailing down from the sky. Blown landward by a fierce wind that swept in off the sea, the icy sleet fell as heavily as rain.

With sleep all but impossible, Christy slipped into a dressing gown, put on warm slippers, and went downstairs.

Fortunately she was well prepared for the storm, having brought in several baskets of firewood during the day. After building up the fire, she went into the kitchen, lit the primitive oil stove, and prepared a steaming mug of hot black coffee.

Then returning to the fire, she seated herself in the old rocker. Jason, who had been padding about at her heels, settled himself in his box near the fire and promptly went back to sleep.

Christy sat there sipping her coffee, rocking gently, and listening to the storm assaulting the cottage. The sleet seemed to come in short, fierce rushes, attacking the slate roof and rattling sharply against the windowpanes.

Six months had passed since her arrival. Six months in which the island had come to be her whole world, peopled only by those few who were left. Some of them she had grown to love. Others engendered only fear and distrust.

Matthew visited often now, and they spent many long winter evenings sitting together in front of the fire. Sometimes they played chess or worked crossword puzzles, while at other times they simply sat in silence, content in the sharing of one another's company.

Although Matthew revealed little of himself, Christy had gradually come to be extremely fond of him. She suspected as well that while his true feelings for her remained obscure, he cared for her more than he was willing to admit.

There had been other victories during her stay on the island besides gaining the love and trust of both Matthew and Amanda. Several times a week Christy would return to the cottage to find Jeremy waiting for her with some small gift. An exquisite sea shell. An arrowhead or a wooden whistle he had carved especially for her.

Although his progress remained slow, he was gradually learning to read and write. Christy hoped that eventually he would trust her enough to bring along his sister, Sarah, to join in their impromptu lessons.

The daily routine at Falcon's Eyrie remained much the same with one important difference. She no longer trusted Iris since the events at Pirate's Cove and avoided the half-mad Willard at every opportunity. He had grown noticeably more silent and withdrawn, and no mention had ever been made regarding his advances on the day of the picnic.

On the table beside her the kerosene lamp—its china shade painted with delicate rosebuds—cast a warm pool of yellow light. In spite of the storm raging outside she felt snug and peaceful inside the cottage. By now it had become her home and Christy thoroughly enjoyed her sense of ownership. On that particular night it reminded her of a sturdy ship carrying her to safety through a raging gale.

Her thoughts drifted back over the past two months to Christmas. It had been a bleak and dreary affair, celebrated only by a dinner at Falcon's Eyrie. Relations between Iris and Willard had been strained and Christy was relieved when it was over.

Amanda had been confined with a cold and Christmas Day had been spent reading beside her bed. Before retiring for the night to dream once again that terrible dream that had come to haunt both her waking and sleeping hours,

Iris had given her a tortoise-shell comb she claimed had once belonged to Victoria Falcon.

The day after Christmas Christy had visited Matthew to give him the muffler she had been in the process of knitting for so long. To her great surprise he had a present for her as well. It was a lovely piece of polished amber suspended on a fine gold chain.

Could she be falling in love with him, she asked herself? Or was it simply the enforced loneliness of life on the island? Admittedly she had never felt that way about any other man before meeting him.

Perhaps if he weren't so secretive and evasive, holding so much of himself in reserve. Whenever she delved too deeply into his feelings or his past she always felt a wall go up between them, one she was unable to breach no matter how hard she might try.

Not the least bit drowsy, Christy picked up the leather-bound volume she had found on the table her first day in the cottage. It was entitled *Spells and Incantations*. Settling herself more comfortably, she began to read, rocking slowly back and forth in front of the fire.

Idly she skimmed through the pages, reading of the legendary powers of warlocks, covens, witches, and their familiars. Much of it was slow going and difficult to understand because of the use of the old English dialect as well as the fact that the pages were tattered and worn with age.

Here and there she paused over a verse or spell that managed to capture her imagination: the "blood charm," which was guaranteed to catch and hold a lover; "Isis vengeance," a spell which promised to visit ruin and destruction on one's enemies. Most interesting, as well as extremely complicated, was the preparation of the "Coleopterous charm," which would guard one against all harm, if prepared properly in the full of the moon.

Before coming to Falcon's Island Christy would not have taken any of it seriously. But now after all the strange occurrences that had taken place, she was no longer entirely skeptical.

Perhaps there were such things as supernatural or spirit forces, she mused. Spirits of the dead who clung to their earthly surroundings to exact vengeance or carry out bloody vendettas against those who had wronged them in life.

Hadn't Mrs. Fears told her that first night that Mistress Cory would continue to stalk the island until such time as she had meted out punishment to those responsible for her death?

Turning at last to a page marked by the insertion of a pressed sprig of bay leaf, Christy began reading only to have her interest suddenly quickened.

The essay was entitled, "Satanic Habitation and the Vengeance of Witches."

Be it known that those who consort with Satan and do enter into compact with Him do give themselves up both body and Spirit in exchange for powers both in this life and beyond mortal habitation.

Henceforth they do assume whatever shape they so please accomplishing all manner of purpose both good and evil according to their desires.

Most fearful of the Witches supernatural powers be Her ableness to possess the mind or spirit of another so as that person shall be forced to do Her bidding or suffer Her vengeance.

Those who be in league with the Arch Fiend are full able to transform themselves into various shapes at will as well as to inflict harm on whomsoever they please and punish their enemies misdeeds according to their just deserts.

In the tract of time it oft passes that the Witch wereth odious and tedious to Her enemies and so despised and despited by them so as they nurseth a grudge of such nature as to put Her to death.

Woe betide that mortal who shall spill the blood of Satans annointed for it be their fate to suffer Her wrath unto their final day.

Let the tidings be spread abroad that the vengeance of Witches knows no bounds and those who raise their hand against Them shall be cursed for all time. Both they and their issue shall be visited by mischance, violence, and diseases of the mind that effect them strangelie. When the hand of death is visited upon these accursed it shall come in that way most painful and violent.

Be it known as well that in all Her works the annointed of Satan shall be aided in Her endeavors by those animal familiars known by the common name of Robin.

The last word seemed to jump out of the page before Christy's eyes, the name looming large and ominous before her.

As she sat there trying to make some sense out of what she had read, she realized that the storm had mounted in intensity. The throbbing rhythms of the sea were now at one with the elemental howling of the wind. The ocean had risen up out of the night to attack the dunes, hurling breaker after thundering breaker against the high sandy bluff that offered the only protection to the house and the marsh.

The cottage, being strongly built, stood solid as a rock, although the walls hummed and sang with the force of the gale. Christy was only too aware of the thundering vibrations in the wooden flooring—the foundations trembling incessantly with each fresh onslaught of the savage surf.

As she sat there deeply immersed in thought, the door was suddenly flung open with a loud, crashing bang. The angry wind swooped inside, fluttering the pages of the book in her lap and extinguishing the lamp.

Rising quickly to her feet, Christy crossed to where the door was banging wildly to and fro. For a moment she stood poised, allowing the full force of the gale to rush over her as she peered out into the night.

Streaming over the dunes, the storm howled and screamed with elemental fury. The islands in the marsh were by now completely white with fallen sleet and ice floes were forming and blocking the channels.

It was a scene of incredible desolation, the storm having become a thing of terror and violence.

Grasping the handle firmly, she threw her full weight against the door and finally managed to force it shut. By now thoroughly unnerved, Christy drew the latch and paused to catch her breath.

The room was as cold as a tomb and as she started forward to relight the lamp something caused her to stop and stare.

Nothing. Simply a shadow moving and then evaporating into nothingness. It must be her nerves, she thought. And yet the feeling persisted that she was no longer alone in the cottage.

Listening intently, she thought she heard the sound of slow, halting footsteps coming from the floor above. They seemed to be proceeding along the upstairs hall with a soft, measured tread.

Remaining rigid and still, Christy held her breath with mounting anxiety, her eyes glued to the murky dark at the top of the stairwell.

As she stood watching, the shadows congealed, and a figure began to materialize out of the darkness. It was not her imagination, she was sure of that. Separate from the demented howl of the wind she could now make out the sound of heavy, stertorous breathing. It was the same breathing she had heard on that first day, only this time she actually saw someone as well.

Gradually the figure took shape and began to slowly descend the stairs. It was clearly an old woman, shuffling, slow, her eyes peering myopically down into the room below as she carefully negotiated the steps one at a time.

She appeared to be totally unaware of Christy's presence, concentrating solely on making her way safely to the bottom of the stairs. A knit shawl was pulled about her hunched shoulders and she was wearing a long trailing nightgown. Her face had by now become clearly visible— pleasant if somewhat moon-shaped, with loose jowls and numerous chins.

From the corner of her eye Christy caught another movement off in the farthest reaches of the room. It was a second shadowy figure creeping stealthily forward one step at a time. As the old woman descended, it drew closer and closer, the two of them moving in slow motion, like ballet dancers exhibiting a slow, mesmeric grace.

The fire crackled and flared briefly and the second figure was caught in a chance shaft of light. Christy saw that it was a man, both masked and heavily cloaked, with only his hands visible.

In them he held an ax, which he lifted slowly above his head and held poised, ready to strike.

She wanted to scream, to cry out a warning, but she was frozen in time, unable even to breathe.

As the two figures drew closer and closer together, Christy realized that he intended to kill her. Somehow in some strange way she was seeing the recreation of Mistress Cory's death—or perhaps she was viewing the actual event with her own eyes.

At the foot of the steps the old woman appeared to sense another presence. Pausing with her hand grasping the newel post, she turned her head just in time to see the ax blade flash in the firelight. It fell swift and sure, burying itself in her neck.

It was a long, horrifying moment before her expression changed, the startled look dissolving slowly as the body deflated and crumpled heavily to the floor.

The head rolled free, turning over and over as the blood pulsed in spurts from the severed arteries. Christy, who had seen the features register the mortal blow, now watched in horror as the eyes rolled up in the head to catch her own with a look of pure vengeance. They remained fixed. Compelling. Sparking and glowing with a strange luminosity.

Then in a swirl of smoke the body of Mistress Cory began to fade, the cold vengeful light in her eyes growing dim as her body lost form and substance. There was one last blinking of something—a key that had been cupped in her hand. It fell to the floor, remaining as the only sign of the woman's passing. She was gone.

The harsh, unearthly laugh of the assassin rang out in the room. Before Christy's disbelieving eyes, he touched his finger to his lips as if miming the blowing out of a candle and then faded abruptly, taking a thief's farewell.

Sixteen

CHRISTY had no idea how long she remained frozen to the spot. Perhaps seconds or even minutes. It was Robin's frantic braying that at last brought her back to the world of the living. She was still numb with the horror of what she had witnessed, a faint patina of sweat sprouting over her entire body in spite of the icy chill.

As Robin's braying continued unabated, she crossed to the window and peered out into the night. At first she could see nothing but the driving white pellets of sleet and flailing branches as the trees whipped wildly about in the wind.

Then as she moved to one side, the light spilled out to illuminate the old mule standing directly in front of the house. Nodding his head and stomping his forefeet, he appeared to be gazing directly at her.

Christy was astounded not only by his strange behavior but by the fact that he was hitched up to the wagon. But how, she wondered? Who could have done it?

For a moment she stood mesmerized by that baleful moonstruck eye. Her emotions were in a turmoil, her practical good sense quickly losing ground to a strangely compelling desire. Robin was waiting for her.

As if hypnotized by that misty moonstruck eye, she returned to the fire and put on her fur-lined boots. After shrouding herself as well in a warm, hooded mackintosh, she returned to the front door.

When she opened it, the wind almost tore the door from her hands and it was with some difficulty that Christy finally managed to pull it shut behind her.

Robin was covered with sleet and sand, his buckskin hide now an eerie white, while his ears and muzzle were frosted with ice. As she made her way down the path, that milky eye she found so disturbing appeared to follow her every step. There was no let up in the furious braying as the mule stomped his feet and tossed his head as if anxious to be away.

Christy climbed up into the buckboard, but before she could seize the reins Robin took off at a brisk trot. She could do nothing but bow her head against the wind and cling tightly to the seat to avoid being swept out of the wagon altogether.

An invisible moon had risen behind the rushing sea of cloud, and some of its wan light fell upon the ravaged earth. The air was full of sleet hissing with a swift and terrible insistence. It pelted the dead barley grass to earth and ripped through the Spanish moss until it wafted from the trees like tattered funeral veils.

They bounced along the road with the sea hurling white water over the dunes behind them. When they reached the main road, Christy turned to find that the marsh had become an immense, flooded bay. As they gradually made their way inland, the wind lost some of its ferocity, although it still howled mournfully through the blinding white night.

It was a journey full of suspense. A headlong flight to nowhere, in which panic threatened to overtake her if she lost her momentum or paused to think rationally for even a moment.

Somehow it seemed to have been preordained—a space in time over which she had no control. Even so Christy experienced an enormous sense of relief when the wagon at last came to a jolting halt in a sheltering grove of tall locust trees.

Climbing down from the seat, she stared about her trying to get her bearings. On one side was a moving wall of forest, while farther up the hillside the lights of Falcon's Eyrie were just visible above the treetops.

Off to her right a vaguely outlined path mounted the hill to the old windmill.

Christy started out, her eyes fixed on those revolving sails, tattered and fluttering like pale flags in the winter's night. They turned slowly, in direct counterpoint to the bullying gusts of wind. She could hear them creaking as they rose and flashed in the moonlight, sailing skyward only to plummet earthward in the next rotation.

The path she followed was narrow and overgrown with dead grass and clumps of nettles that caught at the hem of her long cloak. Drawing close to the mill she could see that the windows were boarded up, giving the ancient stone structure a blank, blind look.

At last she reached the door and automatically inserted Mistress Cory's key, which ground in the rusty lock just as she had known it would. The door swung open and she hurried inside, turning to throw all her weight against the heavy paneling in order to close it behind her.

For a moment she stood gasping for breath, allowing her eyes to become accustomed to the faint light that emanated from cracks in the boarded up windows. Within seconds Christy was able to make out the general lay of the single large room as well as a rusty kerosene lantern hanging on a nail nearby.

Gratefully she extracted matches from the pocket of her cloak and lit it. The lantern spread a pool of pale light that illuminated the scene with a ghostly white radiance.

The mill was bleak and dusty with disuse, cluttered with old casks, ancient grinding machinery, and empty storage bins. Christy could see no sign of recent habitation, and cobwebs fluttered like silken threads from the time-mellowed beams overhead.

The sleet continued to patter on the roof and tap upon the boarded windows with unseen fingers. Holding the lantern aloft, Christy made out the sinister outlines of a long pine box mounted on sawhorses at the far side of the mill. Even before she began crossing the floor to view it more closely, she knew what she would find.

The inscription had been rudely burned into the wooden lid and read, "Here lie the mortal remains of Eleonora Cory and here she must remain being forbidden burial in hallowed ground by order of Iris Falcon Mistress of Falcon's Island." The inscription was followed by the year and date of her death.

The sound of the storm rattling the windows had suddenly become more threatening and Christy shivered at the chill nearness of death. She recalled all too vividly her vision of Mistress Cory's demise. As she died, she held in her hand the key that Christy now possessed. Could it have actually been left for her by the hand of a woman already beyond the world of mortal habitation?

With these thoughts spinning about in her brain Christy backed slowly away from the coffin, only to notice for the first time a door at the back of the mill.

She moved toward it on lagging feet, unable to rid herself of the odd, uneasy feeling that something lay behind it that she had no wish to see. She was almost sorry to find the door unlocked as she lifted the latch. It creaked open on rusty hinges.

On first inspection it appeared to be some sort of storage chamber stacked with various grinding stones, piles of canvas, and a dusty litter of little consequence. Then something caught her eye, its outlines long and sinister, rolled in a blood-stained rag rug. A rug not dissimilar from those scattered about the floors of her own cottage.

Placing the lamp on top of a nearby barrel, she began to unwrap the dismal-looking parcel with fingers that refused to work properly.

She gasped audibly as a long, evil-looking ax was revealed to her, the blade rusting and smeared with dried blood. There was no doubt in her mind that it was the same dreadful instrument that had dispatched Mistress Cory with such speed and precision.

Carved deeply into the stout handle were the initials "E.S."

"Eustace Scully," Christy murmured, her voice barely above a whisper. Slowly the naked horror of his monstrous act began to take hold in her mind and she opened her mouth to scream, only to have her voice overridden by a blood-curdling shriek.

The sound echoed out in the mill, seeming to come from somewhere above her. Grabbing the lantern, Christy lurched backward and edged carefully out of the storage room, slamming the door behind her.

So Scully was the murderer. She might have suspected as much, never having trusted the man. But why? What possible motive could he have had?

Once again the wild shriek ripped the night, chilling her to the bone. Fighting the immediate urge to run from the mill as quickly as her legs would carry her, she stood listening, straining to hear some further sound.

In her hand the lantern trembled and glowed intermittently as an icy draft passed through the mill like a sigh.

Then she heard it again, this time sounding almost inhuman in its piercing anguish. It seemed to be coming from above and Christy made her way warily toward the spiral staircase in the center of the mill.

Slowly she began climbing upward, sliding her hand along the rough wooden railing as she went. Shivering uncontrollably, she pulled her cloak more closely about her to ward off the bitter cold that gripped the building with an icy hand.

The stairs were broken and rotted through in places and it was necessary to cling tightly to the railing and pay strict attention to where she placed her feet. At that moment she longed desperately for the cozy warmth of her own cottage with its cheery fire. What was she doing here? Why had she been compelled to come?

When at last she reached the upper floor, Christy found that she was standing in a spacious attic only barely illuminated by her lantern and the moonshine spilling in through a single dormer window.

The floorboards creaked ominously beneath her feet as she crept forward to peer into the shadowed far reaches of the room. She started visibly as the light caught a pair of yellow eyes staring out at her from the dark. There was something not quite human about them, something positively demoniac.

Before she could gather her senses enough to flee, the creature shrieked once again and spread a pair of great wings, fluttering them restlessly as if anxious to be off the perch to which it was securely tethered.

It was a hooded falcon. She could see that clearly now as she lifted her lamp higher. Most likely, she thought, it was the same great bird she had seen flying above the cliffs on the day she met Jeremy.

This too must be Scully's work. It had been he who released the bird hoping to play on the superstitious fears of the villagers. He had obviously wanted to drive them to—to what, she wondered bleakly? What could his motive possibly have been?

Drawing closer, she discovered the usual gear of the practiced falconer. A thick leather glove and a mask for the bird to wear when he was not in flight. Scattered on the floor were the bones of small animals and rodents. Obviously someone came there to feed the bird on a regular basis.

As she proceeded with her investigation, the bird watched her with sharp yellow eyes, its wedge-shaped head swiveling about to follow her every move.

It was in fact the falcon who warned her that someone was coming. Cocking his head sharply to the left, he appeared to be listening intently. Christy listened as well, and was quickly able to make out the sound of approaching horse's hooves far in the distance.

Someone was riding toward the mill and that someone was most likely Scully.

Turning on her heel, Christy made her way hastily back down the stairs only to hover indecisively, wondering what to do next. Scully would surely kill her if he were to discover her there, but where could she possibly go? Where could she hide?

It was then that she noticed the dusty outlines of what appeared to be a trap door beneath her feet. With a shaking hand she reached down and tugged at the ring. To her dismay the door refused to budge.

Breaking out in a cold sweat as the sound of the approaching rider grew closer, Christy straddled the door and drew upward with all her strength. Slowly it began to open, exposing a yawning square of blackness beneath.

Blowing out her lantern, she placed her foot on the first step and began descending on legs that had suddenly turned to jelly beneath her. When she reached the lower level, Christy reached up and pulled hard, lowering the door as quietly as possible above her head.

It was pitch black inside what she could only assume was a basement. Although the air was stale, damp, and musty, she felt momentarily safe and sheltered—out of harm's way. Then crouching there in the total darkness, a horrifying thought came to mind.

Her footprints on the dusty floor overhead. Surely they would be noticeable and would lead Scully directly to her hiding place. Although the chance of his not seeing them was slim, she prayed silently, hoping against hope that she would be spared.

There was nothing to do now but wait. She was trapped. Crouching back as far as possible against the stone wall, Christy tried to still the wild beating of her heart.

The bloody ax she had found upstairs flashed briefly in her mind, bringing her almost to the edge of hysteria. She was going to die. Here in this cold, bleak basement, with no one to know of her passing.

There was a splintery, scraping sound from above as the door of the mill was thrust open. This was followed by slow, halting footsteps on the flooring overhead. Suddenly there was a loud banging noise as if Scully had stumbled over a box or cask, and Christy held her breath in ghastly anticipation of what was to happen next.

The footsteps continued to move about, only to halt at last, directly above her head. After a moment of complete silence the trap door was wrenched up and a piercing beam of light plumbed the depths of the cellar.

Christy remained pinned to the wall as booted feet appeared and began slowly descending the stairs. Inch by painful inch the legs and then the arms became visible. To her horror she saw that a gun was held in one of the black gloved hands.

Unable to stand the strain any longer, Christy screamed. A long wail of utter terror that echoed through the basement, repeating again and again against the damp stone walls.

The torch swung around in a wide swift arc to catch her in a blinding pool of white light. Falling to her knees Christy began sobbing piteously, too frightened to even contemplate what might happen next.

"Christine," a voice cried out. "What on earth are you doing here?"

It was Iris, sounding entirely bewildered at the sight of her governess crouching among the debris of centuries and sobbing in abject terror.

Unable to believe her ears, Christy looked up to find Iris standing half way down the stairs wearing her familiar riding habit.

Hurriedly she descended the remaining steps and crossed the floor to Christy's side. Taking her by both hands, she drew her up and helped her gently back up the staircase.

Moments later Christy found herself seated on an empty keg while Iris soothed and comforted her with soft words and tender hands. "There, there, my dear. It's all right now. No one's going to harm you."

Then by way of explaining her own presence, she told

Christy of being unable to sleep and seeing lights in the old mill from her bedroom window.

"I thought it was Scully," Christy gasped, dabbing at her swollen eyes with the lace handkerchief Iris had given her. I was afraid he was going to murder me."

"But, my dear child," Iris exclaimed with some surprise, "why on earth should he want to do that?"

In a slow, halting voice Chrristy went on to relate her discovery of the blood-stained ax bearing Scully's initials as well as the presence of the trained falcon kept in the upstairs loft.

As she spoke, the look on Iris' face turned from one of disbelief to utter and complete amazement. Clearly the news was as startling to her as the initial discoveries had been to Christy.

When she fell silent at last, Iris turned away and began to pace back and forth with long, measured strides. "So it was Scully," she stated in a grim, husky voice. "I should have guessed." She paused and spun about to regard Christly openly. "Frankly, Christine, I'm afraid I've done Matthew Parrish a grave injustice. I've suspected all along that it was he who killed old Cory in order to set the people of the island against us.

"Now I can see very clearly that it was Scully. He obviously hoped to isolate us here on the island and kill us off one at a time."

"But what possible motive could he have?" Christy asked.

Iris continued to regard her levelly. "Treasure," she answered shortly. "There has always been a rumor that Scully was with Abigale when she discovered the first cask containing the map. If that were so, she would surely have sworn him to secrecy."

Once again she began her restless pacing. "You see, when Jennifer Parrish died, Abigale and Scully buried the body so no one would know the exact location. I suspect that was when they discovered the cask. Scully's known all along about the treasure map."

"But what about all those other strange occurrences?" Christy asked. "The hex signs painted on doors. The dead animals. What purpose could he have had in playing on the superstitions of the villagers."

"Very simple," Iris stated. He was simply setting the scene. It must have been he who turned them against you on the day you were attacked, although the poor fools didn't realize how they were being manipulated. And it was Scully as well who convinced me to banish them from the island. It was his idea, not mine. He knew that with the villagers gone there would be no witnesses left. Then he would be free to kill us all off and go after the treasure on his own."

"But why did he kill Mistress Cory?" Christy asked, with visions of the woman's rolling head still etched on her brain.

"She must have discovered what he was up to. That woman was uncanny. There were times when I thought she was able to actually read people's minds."

"I saw him do it," Christy blurted out, tears spilling down her cheeks.

"What do you mean, you saw him do it?" Iris demanded.

Christy went on to relate the details of her vision. While she was speaking, Iris blanched visibly, her eyes widening and darkening. It was a long time before she spoke.

"We must be very careful," she said at last. "If Scully suspects that we know what he's up to. . . ."

At this point she stopped speaking, allowing the implication of what she hadn't said to hang ominously between them.

"Why don't we go to Matthew for help? Now—to-night," Christy entreated her. "You could send him to the mainland to tell the sheriff what's happened."

"Exactly," Iris exclaimed, her voice rising in excitement. "You're absolutely right." Then suddenly her face clouded and she resumed pacing, her hands clasped tightly behind her back.

"There's only one problem with that," she offered. "We mustn't show our hand too soon. If we were to do anything out of the ordinary, Scully would surely become suspicious." She glanced down at her watch. "It'll be dawn soon. He'd see Matthew's boat leaving the island, and to be perfectly honest I don't care to be left here alone with that madman. By the time Matthew got back with help we could all be dead."

"But we could go with him," Christy put in.

"Of course you and Amanda could escape," Iris agreed," but what about the rest of us? The launch simply won't accommodate us all."

She was right, Christy reasoned. That course of action would be saving only a few at the possible sacrifice of the many. There had to be another way.

"Wait a minute!" Iris exclaimed. "I have an idea. Matthew is due to go to the mainland for mail and supplies at the end of the week. When he's ready to leave I'll give him a letter for the sheriff explaining everything. He can return with enough men, that even if Scully were to escape they would be able to track him down."

"But shouldn't we tell Matthew what Scully's about before then?"

"Do you want to see him killed?" Iris demanded bluntly. "Don't you see? If Matthew knew what Scully had done he wouldn't wait for the police. He'd go after Scully himself and most likely get his head blown off. We must not forget for a minute that we're dealing with a psychopathic killer."

She shook her head grimly. "No. Matthew's much too hot headed for his own good. We have to keep him completely in the dark until the very last minute. I want you to promise me that you will say nothing whatsoever about this to Matthew or anyone else," Iris instructed firmly.

Seeing the logic behind her reasoning, Christy nodded her agreement. Until the authorities were actually on the island they were all far too vulnerable. In addition she certainly had no desire to jeopardize Matthew's life.

Getting to her feet, she said, "All right. You have my word. I'll say nothing about this."

"Good," Iris said with a thin smile. "Now. How are you feeling?"

"Better. I'm just awfully tired."

"Then come along," Iris said taking her by the arm. "I'll accompany you back to the Pond to make sure you get home safely."

At the door she turned to Christy and said, "Remember now. You're to act as if nothing had happened. When you arrive at Falcon's Eyrie tomorrow morning, be sure to treat Scully just as you always have. I know it won't be easy, but bear in mind that by this time next week he'll be in the hands of the sheriff and we'll all be out of danger."

Christy nodded and squeezed Iris' hand in assent.

"Trust me, Christine," Iris entreated her. "And try to be strong. Our lives could very well depend upon it."

Seventeen

AMANDA stood before the easel in the spacious high-beamed studio in front of a wide expanse of windows. Beside her was a colorful selection of paints and in her hand she held a piece of drawing charcoal.

Christy was nearby, busily arranging a bowl of fruit on a table carefully positioned to catch the light. Although the room had little actual furniture, there was a dazzling array of childishly executed watercolors and oils either hung or propped up against the walls.

"There you are, dear," Christy exclaimed, standing back to observe her handiwork from a short distance. "I think you can begin sketching now."

With careful deliberation, Amanda set eagerly to work, drawing the still life Christy had so painstakingly arranged for her.

After watching her pupil's progress for some minutes, Christy moved restlessly to the windows and stood staring out at the bleak and wintery day. The afternoon fog—so common at that time of year—pressed close against the window panes and wreathed the garden shrubs. Barely visible on the far side of the lawn, the forest appeared cold and lifeless, the trees almost completely shrouded in mist.

Glancing down at her watch, she saw that it was almost four o'clock in the afternoon, their regular one-hour lesson having extended far longer than usual. The day had dragged on interminably and she was growing extremely tired from lack of sleep and her exhausting excursion of the previous night.

Once again Christy mulled over the strange meeting between herself and Iris in the mill. For the one hundredth time that day she realized how badly she had misjudged the woman. Perhaps Iris was overbearing and capable of harsh behavior but she was certainly not the monster Christy had previously envisioned.

Standing there completely immersed in these thoughts, she was brought back to the moment by Amanda's voice.

"I saw her last night," the child exclaimed without pausing in her sketching.

"Saw who, darling?" Christy asked, her voice expressing no particular interest.

"Grandmother," Amanda related with casual innocence. "She came to my room."

Christy was immediately intrigued. Turning abruptly from the windows she inspected the serene expression on the child's face. No, she thought. This time she wasn't playing fanciful games as she often did. Amanda was entirely serious.

"But you couldn't possibly have seen your grandmother," Christy informed her quietly. "She's been dead for some months now. You know that."

"But I did see her," Amanda insisted stubbornly. "She came into my room and stood for a long time beside the bed."

Puzzled by her insistent attitude, Christy stood pondering for a moment, before passing the whole thing off as the product of a bad dream.

"I think we've worked enough for one day." With a sharp whistle she summoned Jason from where he had been lying near the door. "Why don't you take Jason out for a walk. I think you could both use some fresh air and exercise."

Amanda was only too happy to comply, abandoning her sketching and eagerly slipping on her coat and mittens.

After giving Christy a hasty peck on the cheek, she ran happily toward the door with Jason frisking at her heels.

"Now don't go too far from the house," Christy called after her, "and don't stay out too long."

Then they were gone, leaving her the task of putting things away in their proper place. As she puttered about, cleaning brushes and sorting paints, Christy found herself still haunted by Amanda's words.

She recalled vividly her first night in the house and the voice she had heard calling out in the upstairs hall. Then there had been the strange unexplained episode of Abigale's portrait—the eyes almost seeming to come alive. Could Amanda have really seen someone? After all, she reasoned, she herself had dreamed on many occasions of visiting an old woman lying in a huge canopied bed.

It was not inconceivable that there was something going on in that house that could not be explained in terms of natural phenomena, Christy decided. Could it be that Abigale Falcon's ghost was stalking the mansion to expiate some secret torment?

Feeling rather silly, Christy emptied her mind of these thoughts. She was fast becoming as superstitious as everyone else on the island, imagining spirits and hobgoblins on every hand.

After leaving the studio, Christy made her way along the corridor toward the front of the house. She intended to go upstairs and lie down for awhile before dinner. During lunch that afternoon, Iris had invited her to spend the night at Falcon's Eyrie. Although she had said nothing about their encounter of the previous night, Christy suspected that she wished to speak with her further about it.

Entirely preoccupied with her thoughts, she was taken completely by surprise by Willard, who jumped out of a shadowed niche and pulled her roughly into his arms.

"I had to see you alone," he whispered hoarsely, "I couldn't stand it any longer."

Angry and shocked by his unwarranted behavior, Christy pushed him rudely away. "I'm warning you, Willard. If you ever touch me again, I'm going straight to your wife." Her eyes blazed into his. "Do I make myself quite clear?"

He stood there blinking down at her, a nervous twitch plucking insistently at his right eyelid.

"But Christy," he entreated. "I only want to talk to you for a few moments. Don't you realize how much I——"

"Get out of my way," she ordered coldly.

"But you have to hear me out," he insisted. "It's not what you think. You're in danger. I want to help you."

Before he had a chance to say anything further, she swung her arm back and dealt him a stinging blow across the face.

Willard swayed backward and his hand went to his cheek. "You're going to regret that," he said as she pushed past and hurried on down the passage.

Just as Christy reached the great hall, she heard a scream from out of doors. It was followed by Jason's sharp warning bark.

She began to run, reaching the front door only to find that Mrs. Fears had preceded her and was standing in the doorway peering out across the lawn.

"It's Amanda," she said in a low voice. "I saw a dog chasing her into the woods." Lifting her hand, she pointed toward the trees on the far side of the drive.

At that instant Amanda's hysterical screams reached them once again, accompanied this time by the harsh guttural snarls of an ongoing dog fight.

Christy fled across the terrace and down the broad steps to the lawn like a wraith. As she raced across the grass she relived in her mind the terrible and bloody events that had led to the death of the deer. Could Amanda be victim to the same fate?

Overhead, dark clouds were rearing up in the west and scudding across the sky with ominous swiftness. A few warning drops of rain began to fall, driven before the first blustery gusts of wind.

By the time Christy had gained the woods she was shivering with fear and cold. As she ran headlong in the direction of the terrible snarling sounds, the forest about her became heavy and oppressive with the smell of rotting leaves and moist earth. The trees blocked her path on every hand, standing tall and threatening in their stoic silence.

Breaking at last into a small clearing, Christy sucked in her breath at the sight of Amanda crouched back against a big boulder. She was entirely surrounded by the crouching dogs, their muzzles foam-flecked and their teeth bared in lurid snarls.

"Amanda," Christy screamed, running directly into their midst. Immediately she herself was surrounded, the largest animal in the pack flying at her and ripping at her arm with his slashing fangs. While she managed to dodge to her left, the impact of his huge body knocked her to the ground, where she struck her head against a mossy stump.

Stunned almost senseless, she fought to retain consciousness, as blood gushed from her shoulder and splattered down on her pink dress.

As the great beast spun about to attack once again, Christy's hand closed over a jagged rock buried in the wet earth. Then he was upon her, his fetid breath warm against her face, his teeth snapping and feinting as she sought to roll away from him.

Twisting to one side, she managed to wrest loose the rock in time and send it crashing against his skull. With a yelp the animal fell back stunned, retreating on lowered haunches to join the rest of the circling pack.

They seemed cowed for a moment, unsure of this new opponent. But just as Christy rose to her knees, they began to close in about her once again, their narrowed eyes glinting with a frenzied blood lust.

Lifting her rock in preparation for the second attack, she remained poised, knowing she had only seconds to live but prepared to make the dogs pay dearly for her life.

A sharp whistle rent the forest stillness and Matthew rushed into the clearing brandishing a stout stick he had snatched up at random. The dogs scattered instantly, slinking away into the undergrowth as he pursued them this way and that, raging and striking out like a man taken leave of his senses.

When the last of them had faded into the trees at a low, fast trot, he sank down on his knees and gripped the weep-ing Christy by the shoulders. "You're hurt," he gasped, staring with white-eyed shock at the bloody rent in her sweater.

Breaking from his grasp with a strangled sob, Christy looked frantically about and saw Amanda crying piteously as she rocked slowly back and forth.

A tiny flame of comprehension ignited somewhere in her throbbing head. "Jason," she screamed, scrambling to her feet and stumbling across the clearing.

Jason lay motionless, cradled in Amanda's arms. A small bundle of broken fur.

Sinking down beside the child, Christy took him gently into her arms, stroking the curly coat, which was now dark, splotched with blood. As she pulled him close against her breast, his sleek gray head swung loose, the neck broken.

Sobbing hysterically, Amanda threw her arms about Christy's waist and the two of them gave way to their mutual grief.

Christy was so numbed by sorrow and despair that she had completely forgotten Matthew's presence. At last she looked up to find him hovering above them, his face gray and stricken in the dull wintery light.

"He's dead," she whispered. "Jason's dead."

Matthew tried to draw her up but she pulled away from his touch. "This is your fault, Matthew Parrish," she said in a low, deadly voice. "I warned you that this would happen, but you refused to listen."

"Christy," he pleaded in an anguished voice, "with God as my witness I swear to you I never wanted anything like this. You must believe me. You must."

Christy had gotten to her feet by this time, with Amanda clinging to her skirts. She regarded him for a moment with eyes that were red and swollen from crying. "Don't ever come near me again, Matthew. I can never forgive you for this, and I hope what you've done continues to haunt you for the rest of your life."

Taking Amanda by the hand, she turned and left the clearing.

Jason was buried before nightfall in a small wooden box. Iris had insisted that he be put to rest beneath the sundial in a secluded corner of her rose garden.

Christy stood with head bowed as Scully filled in the open grave. She wanted to say something as one shovelful after another was thrown into the oblong pit, but no words came. Numb with loss and despair her mind refused to function, registering only an empty bitterness at the loss of her friend and faithful companion.

For a long while after the earth had been smoothed over and the sundial returned to its place, she stood there in the gently falling rain, until Iris took her by the arm and led her back inside the house.

With gentle solicitude the Mistress of Falcon's Eyrie accompanied her up the great staircase and down the long corridor to her room. Amanda had been put to bed earlier with a mild sedative. The child was inconsolable over Jason's death, and it wasn't until she had cried herself to sleep that Christy had time to examine her own grief.

Now as she opened the door to her room, she wanted only to be left alone.

"I'm so awfully sorry," Iris said, pausing on the threshold. "I know that Jason meant a great deal to you."

Christy tried to think of some appropriate response, but no words came. She was too full of her loss to do more than smile weakly and nod.

"I'll instruct Fears to bring up a dinner tray," Iris offered softly. "You probably don't feel much like joining us downstairs this evening."

Christy appreciated her kind solicitation and once again she wondered how she could have previously been so suspicious of her intentions. The picture of the avenging woman on horseback dealing vengeance and destruction had faded considerably since the discovery of Scully's guilt. Iris had simply been victimized as had all the rest of them.

"I couldn't eat a bite," Christy responded bleakly. "If you don't mind, I'd just like to be left alone."

Iris nodded sympathetically and patted her hand. "I understand completely. Why don't you just get a good night's sleep? I'm sure you'll feel better in the morning."

Closing the door behind her, Christy crossed to the bed and slumped down upon it. Now she was alone with her thoughts, totally immersed in the tragedy of Jason's death. Until the moment when she had lifted his lifeless body into her arms, she hadn't realized just how much his companionship had meant to her.

She blinked rapidly to keep back the tears. She had warned Matthew and now her worst fears had been realized. In place of the affection that had been steadily developing for him since her arrival on the island, there was now only a dulling numbness. She could never forgive him for Jason's death. Never.

Christy wasn't sure just how long she slept. It could have been minutes or perhaps hours. When she awoke the fire had burned to coals and the room was shrouded in darkness.

She had been awakened by a sound, and now as the door clicked softly shut she realized that someone had entered the room. Remaining rigid and unmoving, she listened with dread to the soft padding of footsteps crossing the carpeted floor. Whoever it was, the person was preceded by a pool of dancing candlelight emanating from a single candle.

From beneath lowered lids Christy could make out the approaching figure of a woman but dared not turn her head for a full view. Moving with great stealth, the woman drew near the bed with a whisper of starchy skirts.

Thoroughly mystified as to the identity of her visitor and her purpose in being there, Christy squeezed her eyes tightly shut and regulated her breathing to the peaceful cadence of sleep.

A hand came down to grip her arm, the fingers cold and steely. "You must come. Someone is waiting for you."

It was the voice of Mrs. Fears. Low. Emotionless. Barely above a whisper.

Surprisingly enough Christy was not in the least afraid. The concern she had seen expressed in the housekeeper's eyes that day, when they stood together listening to Amanda's screams, had convinced her that she was not as sinister as Christy had once imagined. Obviously she cared very much what happened to the child, and this single fact gave them a common bond.

Slipping out of bed, Christy accepted the dressing gown she held out to her and stepped into a pair of slippers. Beckoning her to follow along, Fears crossed the room and entered the dressing chamber.

Christy obeyed quietly, watching in total mystification as Fears opened one of the large wall cabinets, pushed back the gowns, and stepped inside.

For a moment she remained perfectly still, running her hand over the interior paneling. There was a soft, scraping noise as the side wall of the closet moved slightly inward. Fears pushed hard against the paneling with both hands and a shadowed opening appeared and widened.

Before her the narrow entrance of a secret passage yawned like a dark and mysterious cavern. "Don't be afraid," the woman murmured. "The house is riddled with passages. In the old days they saved many a Falcon's life."

With these ominous words left hanging between them, the woman stepped inside and was immediately lost to view.

After a moment's pause and a shiver of exquisite anticipation, Christy followed, finding herself inside a passage that was several feet wide and barely high enough for her to stand upright.

By this time the housekeeper had moved on down the passage and Christy had to hurry her steps in order to catch up. Making her way blindly along, she brushed at hanging cobwebs and shuddered at the sound of small scurrying feet somewhere up ahead.

After an agonizing few minutes the passage dipped sharply until they came to a small raised platform with eyeholes cut in the interior wall. On impulse Christy mounted the platform and slid the lever open only to find herself staring out into the passageway across from Amanda's bedroom.

As she did so, the ancient grandfather's clock struck one o'clock, causing her to start.

So the eyes of Abigale's portrait had been alive on that first night. Someone had indeed been peering out at her. The only question remaining was who had it been?

"Come along," Fears scolded in a dry, rasping voice as the light from the candle grew dimmer and dimmer. Her admonition caused Christy to close the aperture and hurry along the darkened passage in order to catch up. She had no desire to be left alone in that eerie, confined space that could easily become a trap.

By the time she had closed the gap Fears had disappeared abruptly down a flight of narrow stairs, her gown trailing after her step by step. At the bottom she stopped, the candlelight splashing up against a blank wall.

Once again she went through the ritual of locating and pressing the proper panel, although this time the door refused to work. Behind her Christy remained pressed up against the wall. Her nostrils were full with the stale, unpleasant odor of mice and long disuse. As she once again heard the soft rustling of small feet, she prayed silently that none of the furry creatures she was so mortally afraid of would run past her in the passage.

With these thoughts racing through her mind, the wall suddenly slid sideways and Christy found herself stepping into a room that was surprisingly familiar.

It was the room which she had visited in her recurring dream with the great canopied bed rising on a dais at the far end.

Mrs. Fears, her angular face dour, stood aside and motioned her toward the bed. Christy proceeded across the room like a sleepwalker, noticing many things she had not seen on her previous visits.

The bedroom was spacious and furnished sumptuously with a variety of antiques. It was clearly a woman's suite, upholstered and draped in eggshell ivories, muted rose silks, and pale lemon brocades. Overall there was a dim and faded elegance about it, the mirrors faintly yellowed and wavering, the Oriental rugs worn completely threadbare in several places.

Upon reaching the bed, Christy held her breath and drew back the gauzy side curtains. She stood there staring down in mute fascination, the long silent pause dragging out and lengthening from moment to moment.

The craggy face that she had seen so many times in her dream reminded her of something from a Grecian frieze depicting an ancient Medea both proud and disdainful.

A fine tapestry of wrinkles traced a face that was entirely dominated by a high-bridged aquiline nose. The hair hung in long braids about the woman's face.

"You're Abigale Falcon," she said almost foolishly. "Amanda told me that she had seen you."

The woman nodded, her eyes lucid for the first time. "Yes. I often go to my granddaughter's room . . . but I haven't dared to try and speak with her."

Christy cast a bewildered look in Mrs. Fears's direction but her expression remained unreadable.

"You see, Miss Randolph," Abigale went on in a dry, wheezing voice, "I am being held a prisoner in my own house. My daughter-in-law, for reasons of her own, has seen fit to declare me dead."

"But why?" Christy gasped.

"Because I am the only person alive who knows the location of the treasure buried by Captain Kidd."

"Then it really does exist?"

"Indeed it does, although if I had my way it should remain forever hidden."

The only illumination in the room came from the two large candleholders standing on either side of the bed. As Abigale lay there with the flickering light and shadow playing over her hollowed eyes and sagging jowls, she looked ill to the point of death.

"We haven't much time, Miss Randolph, so perhaps I had better begin at the beginning."

Abigale sighed deeply and put her hand to her heart as if to insure its continued beating. Although the years had long since robbed her of the youthful handsomeness Christy had seen in her portrait, lingering vestiges remained like the whisper of something past.

"Some years back, " she began, "I was responsible for the death of a local woman by the name of Jennifer Parrish. I shall not try and justify my action. Suffice it to say that I was wrong and would give my very life to rectify my error."

Slowly the fingers of her right hand slid across the coverlet and groped for Christy's. "In order to hide my own guilt in the affair I took my man Scully and buried the woman's body in an unmarked grave."

The wan smile that played briefly about the corners of her mouth was ironic. "What a fool I was to think that I could escape full payment for my crime. Fate is all seeing and all knowing, and I suppose mine was sealed for all eternity on that dark and terrible night."

She sighed once again, this time longer and deeper. "In any case, while disposing of the body I discovered a wooden cask with the treasure map and some other trinkets of no great value inside. I swore Scully to secrecy as I didn't want the island to go mad with treasure fever; for even at that time I knew no good would ever come of it.

"Eventually my daughter-in-law fell in league with Scully, who betrayed the secret of the treasure map to her."

Abigale's breathing was growing steadily more labored, her fingers clutching tightly to Christy's hand. "For over six months I have been held prisoner in this room. They have tried in every possible way to get me to reveal the hiding place of the map." Here she managed a low, satisfied chuckle, which was immediately followed by a coughing spell.

When that had passed, she went on. "I have managed thus far to keep them from the truth by pretending that I had gone quite mad with grief over my daughter Victoria's death."

"And that's where you came in," Mrs. Fears interrupted. "In desperation they hit upon the scheme of locating a look-alike for Victoria and presenting her to Mistress Abigale, who they thought was completely out of her senses." The woman's thin lips pursed and she made a sharp clucking sound of pure disgust.

"By the very saints, they thought that by bringing you here they could make Mistress Abigale believe that Victoria had come back to haunt her. And in so doing they hoped she would reveal the location of the map."

"But why should Victoria come back to haunt you?" Christy questioned as the pieces began to fit into place.

"I have made many mistakes," Abigale responded sadly. "It's true that the responsibility for my daughter's death rests upon my head." She was silent for a moment, her eyes blinking back the tears that threatened to course down her withered cheeks. "But we have no time for that now.

"You see, Miss Randolph, for some time now we—Fears and I—thought that you were in league with Iris and Scully. Of course it soon became evident that you were heavily drugged before they brought you to this room. Still . . . we had to be sure."

"And are you convinced now?" Christy asked.

The old woman nodded, blinking owlishly up at her. "I know how strong your feelings are for Amanda—and that is all that counts."

By a sheer effort of will she lifted her head from the pillow, her voice growing urgent. "Time is running out. I must know if I can trust you completely."

The atmosphere in the room was very still and silent, a vacuum in which nothing stirred or moved.

At last Christy nodded.

With a wave of her hand Abigale indicated to Fears that she should bring her a Bible that lay on the bedtable. When this had been done, she opened it and withdrew an old piece of parchment, brittle and yellowed with age.

With some difficulty she managed to spread it on the counterpane and beckoned Christy to lean closer.

A cursory glance indicated that it was a hand-drawn map of the island, with all the pertinent geographical considerations clearly shown.

"The treausre is hidden just above the waterfall," Abigale instructed, jabbing the map with an almost transparent index finger. "There's a clearly marked trail cut in the rock."

"But why are you giving this to me?" Christy asked, drawing back.

"Because you are Amanda's only hope. My granddaughter will be the only one left to carry on the Falcon heritage that has gone on uninterrupted for hundreds of years. It is up to you to take her safely off this island until the danger is past."

"But what about your son?" Christy asked in bewilderment. "Surely he isn't involved in this . . . this conspiracy."

"Willard is a fool and a weakling," Abigale rasped in an irritated voice. "While I'm sure he has no hand in this, he simply can't be trusted."

Folding the map with meticulous care, Abigale pressed it into Christy's hand. "You see, my dear, Iris is quite mad. She has become obsessed with the idea of the treasure and is capable of any outrage in order to get her hands on it. Unfortunately my son Willard is unable to stand up to her, and therefore he's of absolutely no use."

Christy nodded mutely.

Abigale's voice fell away and the air seemed to be full of unspoken regrets that would never be put into words.

"What is it you want me to do?" Christy asked in a firm, resolute voice.

A ghost of a smile illuminated Abigale's gray, tired features. "Tomorrow morning I want you to go about your duties as if nothing had happened. After lunch ask permission to take Amanda for a ride. Now be sure not to arouse any suspicion," she admonished her. "And when you get away from the house, go directly to Matthew Parrish."

At this point Abigale was seized by a fit of coughing and motioned weakly toward the drawer in the bedside table.

Fears immediately opened it and extracted a bottle of pills, emptying two into Abigale's hand and pouring her a glass of water from a silver container.

Abigale managed to swallow the pills and drink some of the water with Fears's assistance. Then she fell back against the pillows as if all her strength were exhausted.

"The letter," she gasped. "Give Miss Randolph the letter."

Mrs. Fears did as instructed, extracting an envelope

from the pocket of her voluminous skirts with the name "Matthew Parrish" scrawled across the face.

"See that Matthew gets this," Abigale said, her voice reduced to a whisper. "Everything is explained inside."

Her eyelids fluttered and closed, but after a moment her pale lips moved once again. "Be sure to guard the map with your life. If Iris were to get her hands on it . . . none of us would be of any further use to her."

Eighteen

HURRYING down the path toward Matthew's shack, Christy could think of only one thing. Escape from the island.

Iris suspected something. She was sure of that now. During breakfast she had been unusually silent, and several times Christy had glanced up to catch her gaze, the bright hazel eyes as cold and distant as far away stars.

If Iris was aware of her late night visit to Abigale, she said nothing and seemed to be agreeable enough when Christy proposed that she and Amanda take a ride in the buckboard after lunch.

It was a somber, gray day and as they made their way down the well-trodden path, the sand erupted from the tops of the dunes to be whipped into their eyes before a brisk northwesterly wind.

The leaden sky promised snow before nightfall. Christy could feel it in the cold, biting wind and see it in the unbroken mass of aluminum gray clouds gathering swiftly and ominously overhead.

"Look," Amanda cried, pointing out into the bay. "Matthew isn't here."

Startled by this unexpected declaration, Christy looked out to see that indeed the buoy where he usually moored his launch was empty.

Refusing to accept the obvious conclusion, she reeled away from the truth, allowing her momentum to carry her forward. If she dared to pause even for a moment, she would completely lose her nerve. That she knew for a certainty.

Of course. She should have remembered. This was Friday. The day that Matthew went to Land's End for mail and supplies.

"What are we going to do now?" Amanda demanded petulantly. She had been moody and withdrawn ever since Jason's death the previous afternoon. When they left Falcon's Eyrie after lunch, Christy had told her simply that they were going for a visit with Matthew.

Now faced with the magnitude of her mistake and the prospect of returning to the house and Iris' aroused suspicions, she didn't know which way to turn.

"Perhaps he'll be back soon," she offered without much conviction. "We'll wait for him inside."

Matthew's shack proved to be chill and bleak, the fire having burned to ashes in his absence. To occupy her mind Christy set about kindling another. It was by now midafternoon and there was still a chance he would return before nightfall.

Her task complete, Christy lit the fire and watched the hungry tongues of flame lick up over the logs. Shivering, she chafed her hands briskly, holding them out to the fire in an effort to restore warmth.

Amanda had withdrawn to a corner of the room, contenting herself with some shells, of which Matthew had a large collection.

As the fire began to take the chill off the room and banish the dark pools of shadow, Christy began to pace back and forth. The minutes dragged painfully by and from time to time she glanced anxiously down at her watch. Each passing minute was an agony thrusting her closer to hopelessness and despair.

At that moment Christy's emotions were a sea of turbulent forces and counterforces battling for ascendancy. There were still so many questions left unanswered as well as answers that had proven entirely unsatisfying.

With mounting apprehension she looked down at her watch once again. It was 3:30 and as she watched the sweep second hand creeping on to 3:31 she knew that it would be difficult for her to get up the nerve to look again.

Sinking down on one of the hard wooden chairs, Christy buried her face in her hands. She wanted to cry but there were no longer any tears left or the energy to shed them. Fear was her only pervading emotion. Fear coupled with her own sense of responsibility.

So many people were counting on her. Amanda. Abigale. Even Mrs. Fears, the woman who for so long she had thought an enemy. If she failed in her attempt to escape the island and return with help, what would be their fate?

Iris had already killed once. She would do it again.

From outside, the sound of pounding horses' hooves coming along the beach reached her ears. With a shuddery gasp Christy got to her feet and ran to the window. Looking out, she saw Iris riding astride her white Arabian stallion with Scully following a short distance behind.

A look of abject horror swept across Christy's face, sealing off all rational thought.

She recalled the map and Abigale's warning about not allowing Iris to get her hands on it. At that moment the folded sheet of ancient parchment was like a time bomb ticking away in the pocket of her sheepskin coat.

Frantically she looked about for a hiding place. Unaware of the gathering drama, Amanda continued to sort through the shells. In her childish innocence she was completely oblivious to the deadly trap into which they had fallen.

Perhaps, Christy rationalized, she could still bluff her way out of it. In any case her only hope was to stall for time until Matthew returned.

Spotting Amanda's rag doll on the table, she snatched it up and quickly made an incision with a kitchen knife. Then slipping the folded map inside, she replaced the stuffing and smoothed the calico dress back in place.

"There," she breathed. At least the map was safe. No one would ever think of looking for it inside Amanda's doll.

Just as she replaced it on the table the door banged open and Iris entered the shack with Scully following a few paces behind.

"I'm surprised at you, Christine," she said, throwing back the cowl of her long, flowing cloak. "Did you really think that I'd let you escape so easily?"

"Why . . . I don't know what you're talking about," Christy answered, attempting to compose her features into a look of innocence. A quick glance toward Amanda showed to her relief that the child was comprehending none of what was taking place. After a disinterested look in her aunt's direction, she had turned her attention once again to the shells.

"Don't you now?" Iris challenged, a thin-lipped smile playing at the corners of her mouth. "Well in that case perhaps I had better refresh your memory."

With a short nod of her head she summoned Scully from the doorway. "Take the child outside," she ordered. "We'll be along shortly."

As Scully took Amanda roughly by the arm, she broke

away and ran to Christy, throwing her arms around her waist. "I don't want to go with him," she insisted, on the verge of tears. "I want to stay here with you."

"Go along, dear," Christy urged, wanting to spare her the unpleasantness of the oncoming confrontation. "I'll be out in a few minutes." Bending down, she kissed Amanda on top of her shining head and pushed her toward the door.

After the door had closed behind them Iris strolled toward the fireplace, stripping off her long leather gloves. When she turned about a moment later, she was holding a revolver firmly in her right hand. "Now, my dear. It appears that you and I are going to have to come to an understanding."

"Understanding . . ." Christy repeated blankly. "What about?"

Iris took several slow, menacing steps forward. The shadow moving before her was grotesquely distorted by the firelight coming from behind.

Before Christy realized what her intent was, she had slapped her hard across the face. Then before she had a chance to regain her composure, Iris had twisted her arm in back of her, and after forcing her down to her knees, began forcing it painfully upward. All the while she could feel the cold snout of the gun pressed firmly against her temple.

"So you know the truth after all," Iris rasped in a low, gritty voice.

"Truth . . . what truth?" Christy managed. As the sharp pains began to shoot up her arm, she was forced to bite her lip hard to keep from crying out.

Iris' cruel laugh rang out in the room. "Don't play coy with me, young lady. I went to your room after midnight last night. You weren't there, so I took the liberty of looking around and found some very interesting gold coins."

When Christy failed to reply, the painful pressure on

her arm increased. "Now I want you to tell me exactly how much you know."

"I don't know anything," Christy gasped.

"Don't lie to me, you little snoop. You've had your nose into everything on this island since the day you arrived." The woman's voice rose in pitch and venom. "But let me assure you that whatever you've discovered isn't going to do you any good."

She gave a harsh, brittle laugh, her long fingernails biting more deeply into Christy's arm. "You see, you're not going to be around to tell any tales."

Christy fought the pain, fought the rising desire to spew out the ugly accusations and tell Iris exactly what she thought of her. Instead she steeled herself, refusing to give in.

As the silence deepened between them, Iris' breathing became a harsh rasp, her face growing mottled with rage. "Mrs. Fears took you to see Abigale last night, didn't she?"

Emitting a broken sob of pain and frustration, Christy twisted about and glared up into Iris' face. Her answer was a scream. "Yes. She took me there and I found out exactly what kind of woman you are.

"I know the real reason you brought me to this island and that it was you who ordered old Cory's death. Scully is nothing more than your tool—the tool of a madwoman."

Iris released her arm abruptly and Christy got slowly to her feet.

During the brief, heated flurry of words, her tormentor's face had undergone a distinct change. The white skin of her face had become chalky against the black velvet of her swirling cape, the eyes sparking green fire.

"That must have been a very touching scene," she said, contempt growing thicker in her voice. "I'm sure that if I had been there to see it, I should have been moved to tears."

"Doesn't it matter to you in the least that a woman is dead because of your ruthless ambition?" Christy stormed, her voice quavering with outrage. "Don't you even care that people have been driven from their homes, their lives disrupted?"

"I'll manage to recover," Iris retorted in a harsh metallic voice. "That old busybody Cory suspected the truth and I had no choice but to remove her from the scene. As for the others, getting them off the island was simply a necessary expedient."

Christy was close to despair, her quick flaring anger subsiding into hopelessness. "What kind of woman are you? Don't you realize that Abigale is very close to death? Do you want another murder on your conscience?"

"You don't seem to get the idea," Iris said, wiggling the nose of the revolver at her. "I no longer have a conscience. And as for Abigale—I want her dead. The only reason she's been permitted to live this long is because she alone knows the location of the treasure map.

"Abigale Falcon has been in my way for years," she sneered. "It's because of her that I've been forced to live a life that I despised with a man I loathe. Do you have any idea what it was like having money doled out to me all these years? To have to scrimp and save just to maintain that old mausoleum and keep this monstrous island in the family.

"Oh, I know perfectly well that you think I'm heartless and cynical . . . and I suppose it's true. But have you ever asked yourself, my dear, smug Miss Randolph, how I got that way in the first place?

"I've spent the last fifteen years of my life living with ghosts, taking care of a weak milksop and a senile old woman who treated me like a servant." A high flush had risen to Iris' cheeks and Christy read something in her expression that frightened her. "Well, it's almost over now. Soon I can begin to live my own life."

"You're completely insane."

"Perhaps you're right," Iris agreed with a mocking laugh. "If I weren't a bit mad I wouldn't have been able to do the things I've done. . . . " The long ensuing pause was freighted with innuendo. "As well as the things I have still to do."

While she spoke Christy gauged the possibility of rushing forward and attempting to wrest the gun from her hand, but quickly discarded the idea.

The distance was too great. Iris would certainly shoot her and then Amanda would be left completely helpless. No. It was too great a risk to take. It was better to stall for time and pretend to go along with whatever she asked.

"Just how involved is Willard in all this?" Christy inquired, hoping to keep her talking as long as possible.

"He isn't," Iris stated flatly. "Poor, stupid Willard is simply a cross I've had to bear. He knows nothing."

"Then he isn't aware that Abigale is alive and kept in the east wing?"

"I've managed to keep that fact from him quite easily," Iris replied smugly. "In fact my dear husband almost had a nervous breakdown when we put Abigale's empty coffin in the ground. He always was a mama's boy."

"And just what is it you expect of me?" Christy continued, holding to the offensive.

Iris hesitated a moment before answering. "I have a strong suspicion that my mother-in-law entrusted you with the treasure map during your visit last night. There is no other reason I can think of for her to have summoned you."

"But that's ridiculous," Christy countered.

"If it's so ridiculous, then why were you running away with Amanda?"

"But we weren't running away. We simply came here to

visit Matthew," Christy lied. "You know yourself that Abigale is unbalanced. . . . She told me nothing beyond the fact that she was being held prisoner against her will."

"I don't believe you."

"It doesn't matter whether you choose to believe me or not. You'll get nothing further from me."

Iris' features hardened and set. "Perhaps not. But I'm sure that Abigale will prove to be more cooperative now that she knows I'm on to her little game. For some time she had me fooled with that mad act of hers, but not anymore. I want that map, and I intend to have it."

"Even if such a map exists," Christy countered, "Abigale would die rather than tell you where it is."

"We shall see about that," Iris stated with a sardonic smile. "I had hoped not to have to do this but it appears that you give me no alternative." She took a step closer and lowered her voice to a menacing purr. "You see, Christine, one sure method of getting people to reveal secrets is to apply unpleasant and painful pressures on those closest to them."

"You don't mean that you'd actually harm Amanda?" Christy gasped, as the implied threat took seed in her mind.

"Don't be too sure," Iris replied easily. "It would be a pity but I'm quite sure that when Abigale sees Scully's brutal hands closing about that small, white throat . . . the lovely blue eyes bulging from their sockets and the tongue starting to turn black——"

"Stop it," Christy cried, shaken by an uncontrollable attack of trembling. "Even you couldn't be so cruel as to torture an innocent child."

"Don't underestimate me. As you yourself pointed out, I already have one murder on my conscience. Before this matter is concluded to my satisfaction, I should imagine that there will be several more."

Iris bestowed a deadly smile upon her, one that caused

Christy to believe her capable of carrying out her threats. "In any case Christine—it's entirely up to you. I'll give you until eight o'clock tonight to try and remember where the map is hidden. If you don't, I shall then order Scully to strangle Amanda in Abigale's presence. One of you is bound to break . . . I guarantee you that."

Christy was too horrified by the gruesome picture she painted and the determination honing her voice to formulate an answer.

"And as for you," the woman went on, "at the moment you're simply an inconvenience. I don't intend to take any chances of having Fears or my husband blunder onto your whereabouts."

There was something so openly malevolent in her tone that Christy became thoroughly frightened. "What do you intend to do with me?"

"There's an old wine cellar beneath Falcon's Eyrie," Iris related. "It lies very deep in the earth and I'm sure that you will be quite safe there from interference. Unfortunately it is awfully dank and dark and I've been told that the rats that inhabit the place are the size of fox terriers."

Her mad laugh spiraled off only to end abruptly on a high, discordant note. "And I shouldn't want you to entertain any false hopes of being discovered and liberated, because you see, my dear, no one besides Scully and myself will know where you are."

Growing suddenly impatient, Iris said, "Now come along. I have no further time to waste."

Christy reluctantly put on her coat and started for the door. Her only hope was that when Matthew returned he would realize that they had been there. Still she had to warn him somehow of the danger that faced them. Otherwise he might simply think that she had stopped in for a visit.

With a clumsy, stumbling motion she managed to trip over a low stool and fell to the ground. While Iris berated

her in no uncertain terms Christy yanked the amber keep-
sake from her neck and dropped it beneath the stool.
There, she thought as she regained her feet. When Matthew discovered it he would surely realize that something
was sorely amiss.

Outside, the day had grown colder and the air was alive
with a million fluttering snowflakes. The clouds bunching
up out of the west were purple-black, blotting the sky like
spilled India ink.

Amanda was mounted before Scully on his horse, seeming to be entirely unaware of the drama that had taken
place inside, and which held their very lives in the balance.

With Christy preceding her toward the horses, Iris took
care to hide her pistol beneath her enveloping black cloak.
Matthew's old mare had been saddled and Iris motioned
Christy to mount. Robin had been unhitched from the
wagon and was attached to Scully's horse by a short rope.
It appeared they had thought of everything.

When they were all mounted and ready to depart,
Amanda cried out, "My doll. I left my doll inside."

For an instant Iris appeared undecided, while Scully
shrugged with obvious impatience.

Christy's heart was thumping wildly, waiting to see what
would happen. Her clever ploy now seemed to be painfully obvious, with the possibility that anyone handling the
doll would discover the map hidden inside.

"Go get the doll," Iris ordered with ill-concealed annoy-
ance. "It's the only way we're going to keep her quiet."

Scully swung down from his horse, reentered the shack,
and returned with the doll long, painful moments later.

Immediately Amanda snatched it from his hand, and
without further comment they started off at a brisk trot toward Falcon's Eyrie with Robin following along behind.

Upon reaching the dune road, Iris rode up beside Christy and cantered along beside her. "I shouldn't entertain
any false hopes about Matthew appearing like a knight in

shining armor and snatching you from the jaws of misfortune," she sneered. "You see, he won't be in any condition to save anyone, including himself."

"What do you mean?" Christy demanded in a stricken voice.

"If he isn't already dead, he soon will be," Iris informed her. "I took the precaution of having Scully plant dynamite aboard the launch."

She laughed a low gurgling sound from deep in her throat, bubbling with grim satisfaction. "Matthew Parrish will trouble me no longer. I've made very sure of that."

Nineteen

CHRISTY awoke with her head throbbing and her body cramped and aching. Her mind felt slow and heavy, as if she had been drugged. Then after a moment she recalled that on arriving at Falcon's Eyrie that afternoon Iris had given her an injection. It was the last thing that she remembered.

Sitting up on the mattress upon which she had been lying, she tried to fix herself in time and space. From somewhere nearby came the steady drip-dripping of water, while a low, steady rumbling seemed to generate from below.

"The cellar," she said aloud, recalling Iris' threat to incarcerate her in the basement of Falcon's Eyrie.

Peering off into the murky gloom, she saw that rack upon rack of dusty wine bottles lined the walls. They were strung with a fine tracework of cobwebs and from beneath the racks she could hear the scurrying of small feet.

"Rats," she thought, not daring to contemplate their size or ferocity. Her flesh crawled as the soft rustling sound grew agitated and one of the furry creatures screamed.

Christy remained frozen as an invisible fight ensued. Bottles rattled in their niches and luminous eyes shone in the dimness as long reptilian tails whipped out to flail the stone flooring.

Then the furor ceased as abruptly as it had begun and she was left with the steady dripping of the water and the soft thunder of the sea in the distance.

Making a desperate effort to gather her wits, Christy rose from the moldering mattress and stood for a moment looking about her. Carefully she began a slow, cautious inspection of her prison. The stone walls appeared to be as solid and impregnable as a fortress, while the only exit was a stout single door constructed of heavy timber. There was no handle on the inside.

The only light emanated from a single window high up and shuttered over. Rubbing her arms to restore warmth, Christy crossed the cellar to a low bench, which she managed to drag over beneath the window. As she climbed up upon it, the bench swayed perilously, the ancient wood complaining beneath her weight.

Seeking a firmer footing toward the center, she pulled herself up slowly by clinging to the narrow window ledge above. Then by taking off her shoe and banging on the rusty latch, she managed to open the shutters, only to find that the ground level window was hopelessly barred.

Peering out, she was able to see nothing beyond a drifting veil of white that appeared to be falling endlessly from a leaden sky. Although it had only been snowing since midafternoon, the white crystalline blanket had by now covered everything with a ghostly unreality.

Great fluffy snowflakes, larger than any she had ever seen, clung to the grimy pane, melted slowly, and streamed down the glass like perfect tears.

Very near to despair, Christy leaned her forehead against the cold steel bars. So this was to be her prison for as long as Iris Falcon chose to leave her here. Then another thought intruded—one she scarcely dared contemplate. Was it meant to be her tomb as well?

Gradually the realization came to her that if she were to die here, her body could be secreted in the wine cellar and no one would ever be the wiser. The Lacys, her only link to the outside world, would never even bother to inquire after her.

After a long hopeless while, Christy climbed down and returned to the mattress. Slumping down upon it, she was terribly aware of its lumpy hardness beneath her body. It was filthy and spotted as well with damp blotches of mildew, but her head was throbbing painfully and she was simply too discouraged at that point to even care.

It was cold in the cellar and she chafed her hands vigorously together hoping to restore warmth and circulation. The light from the window was growing faint, and Christy looked down at her watch to find that it was now half past five in the afternoon.

Tears of frustration and hopelessness gathered at the corners of her eyes but she brushed them angrily away. This was no time for girlish hysterics. She would have to save her strength for whatever lay ahead.

Bitterly she recalled Iris' gloating announcement that Matthew was either dead or soon would be. It was clear that she had deliberately waited until the very last moment, allowing Christy to cling to the hope that he would arrive in time to save her.

Oh, why hadn't she listened to him the previous afternoon, when Jason had been killed? She had been foolish to have blamed him so completely for what had taken place. Of course he hadn't meant for it to happen and had obviously been as distressed by the incident as she herself.

Now he had gone to his death thinking that she loathed the very sight of him. The man she loved—the only one who could have saved her. And now he was dead. Yes, she had loved him, she knew that now. Now that it was too late for anything but regrets.

Sheer exhaustion and the lingering effects of the drug were weighing her down. It was by now freezing in the basement and she curled up tightly, hoping to preserve the warmth of her own body. Huddled there on the filthy mattress, Christy dreaded the coming night. Could she possibly survive the cold, the rats, and God knows what other threats to life and sanity?

The very thought of spending the long, dismal hours of night in that dank and dreadful dungeon without even a candle almost carried her to the brink of panic.

As she lay there trying to restrain her growing fears, she decided that any attempt at freedom would be worth whatever price she might have to pay. Even if it were nothing but a desperate gamble with little or no chance of success.

Christy tried not to think of Amanda or of the fate that awaited her at eight o'clock that night unless she herself confessed the location of the map. Even Abigale could not save her now, as she alone knew that it was hidden inside the rag doll which was never far from Amanda's side.

The only factor that had kept her from telling Iris the truth that afternoon was Abigale's stern warning that once Iris got her hands on the treasure map all their lives would be forfeit.

From what she had seen that day Christy had no doubts that Iris was capable of anything. Their lives would be small enough price to pay in order to gain her own ends. She had to her advantage as well the island's isolation and lack of contact with the outside world. No one need ever be aware of what had taken place here if she were careful in eliminating any who might spread the tale abroad.

The sound of approaching footfalls echoing in the passage outside and drawing steadily nearer caused Christy to start. Someone was coming. Iris? Scully? They were after all the only ones who knew where she was imprisoned.

In either case it could be her opportunity to escape, and Christy determined not to miss it if such a chance were to present itself. Feigning sleep, she remained where she was on the mattress, forcing her breathing into a deep, even rhythm.

A key ground in the lock and the sound was followed immediately by the creaking of rusty hinges. Through lowered lashes she saw the figure of a man enter the cellar and slowly approach the mattress. For a moment he remained standing above her, peering down at her prostrate form. Then bending slightly, he placed a tray on the three-legged stool beside her.

A hand came out to gently stroke her hair and she knew immediately that it was Willard.

As the increased possibilities of escape surged through her brain, she fought the urge to draw away from his stroking hand, trying to still the revulsion she felt at his touch. His presence was more than she had hoped for. More than anyone Willard provided her best chance of liberation.

Christy allowed her eyelids to flutter open and drew on a wan smile. Hugging herself against the chill, she sat up on the mattress. "Oh . . . it's you, Mr. Falcon." Then with a muffled sob, she reached out to clasp his hand in both her own. "I've been so frightened. This terrible place . . . the cold . . . the rats."

Willard's smile was sympathetic. "I tried to warn you that Iris was displeased, but you wouldn't listen, and now it's too late."

"Too late," she echoed. "What do you mean by that?"

"Only that you've in some way displeased my wife. I don't know how or why but you're obviously being punished for something." He wagged an accusing finger at her. "You've been a very naughty child, Christy. And naughty children must be punished."

Christy listened to his words with a sinking heart. She had suspected it for some time, but now she knew. Willard was completely unbalanced.

"Now then," he announced smugly. "I've brought you something to eat." He pointed to the tray. "I saw Iris and Scully carrying you down the back staircase earlier this afternoon. It didn't take much to figure out where they were taking you."

Christy found that she was unable to play along any longer. Rising to her knees, she said, "Help me, Willard. Iris is going to kill me—I know she is. I went to Matthew's to ask him to take me away but. . . ."

At the mention of Matthew's name his sympathetic expression changed abruptly, the thick, dark eyebrows knitting together and the eyes glittering dangerously.

"So that's it," he growled between clenched teeth. "You and Matthew. I was right all along.

"No," he growled between clenched teeth. "Matthew will never have you. I'd see you rot here forever rather than permit that."

The man was obviously a coiled spring of paranoia, and Christy realized too late that she had unwittingly set him off by mentioning Matthew's name.

Suddenly she remembered a psychology professor saying once in a lecture that the only way of dealing with dangerous psychopaths was to remain completely rational in approach.

"Willard," she said in a commanding voice. "I want you to listen to me, and listen carefully. There's something going on in this house that you know nothing about."

He was immediately guarded, his eyes flashing suspiciously. "Don't tell me anything. I don't want to know."

"Abigale is alive," she pursued. "Your mother is alive and being held prisoner in Falcon's Eyrie at this very moment."

Willard stared at her blankly, his mouth dropping open in surprise. "But that just isn't possible. I myself saw her buried in the family plot."

"That was only an empty coffin," Christy explained patiently. "Iris and Scully have been holding her hostage in the east wing of the house. I've seen her, talked to her. She asked me to tell you what was happening, to beg you to help her."

"Mother . . . alive," he repeated vacantly. "I can't believe it. You're lying to me."

Desperately Christy sorted about in her mind for something to reinforce her argument, some detail that might convince him that she was telling the truth. Then she remembered.

"Willard," she pleaded. "I can give you proof—proof that your mother is alive."

"What proof?" he demanded suspiciously.

"A ring. When I saw her last, she was wearing a large gold ring with a Falcon crest. The eyes were set with yellow diamonds."

"But you couldn't possibly know that," he gasped. "Not unless——"

Christy saw her momentary advantage and seized upon it. "Listen to me," she instructed. "Your wife and Scully are planning to kill Abigale unless you do something to stop them."

"But why?" he moaned, his look blank and confused.

"Because Abigale won't reveal the location of the treasure map. If you don't act immediately, they plan to kill Amanda and me as well."

It was a moment before he spoke, his voice low, his face the color of ashes. "Where is she?" he asked in a faltering voice. In that instant his eyes had gone dark and dead, like the empty windows of a long abandoned house.

"Go to Mrs. Fears," Christy instructed firmly. "Tell her where I am and she'll take you to Abigale. You can see for yourself."

Slowly Willard began to back away, his eyes wide and staring. At the door he turned and stumbled out, pulling it closed behind him. For a long suspenseful moment Christy listened intently, hoping that in his confused state he would forget to lock it. Her hopes were dashed abruptly as she heard the clank of the padlock as it was drawn into place.

Settling back on the mattress, she listened to his footsteps moving away and then dying altogether. Would he do as she had asked, or was he too far gone to be of any help? Then another thought occurred to her. What if Willard went immediately to Iris and confronted her with what he had been told?

The unhappy thought remained to tease and taunt her and Christy was forced to admit that of the two possibilities the latter seemed to be far more likely.

In his confusion Willard had departed without taking his candle. At least, she thought, that was some comfort. That along with the food. She had not eaten since lunch and although the contents of the tray were hardly appetizing, it would at least sustain her strength.

He had obviously had to sneak what he could from the kitchen without being discovered. The meager repast consisted of several shriveled winter apples, a cold turkey leg, two stale slices of bread, and some cheese.

As Christy settled down to eat, she thought longingly of the lavish meals she had enjoyed in the grand dining room of Falcon's Eyrie. She had always wondered what happened to the leftovers from these opulent meals, her practical spirit rebelling at the idea of wasting all that food.

After devouring everything on the tray, Christy leaned

back on her elbow and stared off beyond the pale circle of flickering yellow light. As the candle waxed and waned in the drafty basement, objects about her began to emerge, shadowy and far more menacing than before. It was now almost seven o'clock and the aura of danger in the cellar was so thick and persistent that she felt she was going to be suffocated.

Before long her heartbeat quickened to the sound of footsteps beyond the door. Once again the padlock was removed, but as her visitor stepped inside the room she felt her hopes collapse. It was Scully.

Swaggering across the floor toward her, he drew up a short distance away and placed his hands on his hips. A mocking laugh broke from his lips.

"Well, missy. How are you enjoying your stay so far? I admit it isn't exactly the bridal suite but ... it's ... the ..." His voice slackened and died, his gaze falling on the tray and candle nearby.

Scully's eyes turned crafty and suspicious, glinting malevolently as he leaned into the light. "I see that you've had a visitor," he sneered. "And it would be my guess that it was no less than the laird of the manor himself." The look on his face hardened into something entirely sinister and threatening. "What exactly did you tell him?"

"Nothing," she lied. "I pretended to be asleep." Christy was by now on her feet, and as the violence in his eyes intensified, she began backing away, edging toward the wall.

Slipping a long, evil-looking knife from his belt, Scully began to follow, matching her a step at a time. It was perfectly obvious that he was thoroughly enjoying the game of cat and mouse, toying with her until whatever moment he should decide to put an end to her misery.

They continued in the *danse macabre* until at last she was pressed back against the wine rack with the blade held firmly against her throat.

Scully allowed her to languish there until her eyes grew

large and bright with fear, her breathing a shallow rasp. Then with a sneer he replaced the knife in his belt and turned away.

"I have no more time to waste on you," he said. "Iris will be very interested to know of Willard's visit. I've been telling her all along that he would have to be disposed of but now he's signed his own death certificate."

Christy watched him start for the door with but one thought in mind. She simply could not permit him to leave. If she did, all hope would be lost.

With a single reflex action she pulled a bottle from the rack and rushed forward. In one explosive motion she brought it down hard on the back of his head.

The blow struck him with such force that the bottle broke, spilling wine and shattered glass to the floor. As he crumpled to the floor, Scully managed to turn and pull her down with him, the two of them falling hard and rolling over and over. As she fell, Christy's head struck the edge of the stool, leaving her slightly stunned and dazed.

Lying heavily on top of her, Scully was gasping for breath, the blood gushing from a deep wound in his scalp and spilling down his face. "Why you little vixen," he gritted between clenched teeth. "Just for that I'm going to. . . ."

Grasping her by the throat, his hands began to close like a vise, his breath fetid and warm on her face.

"No . . . no," she managed to scream before his fingers tightened and the blackness began to close in about her. He was going to kill her. She was going to die. . . .

Managing somehow to free one hand, Christy stabbed at his eyes, clawing at his face with long, raking nails. Screaming like a maddened bull, Scully rolled away, but not before her sharp nails gouged deep into his right eye.

In an instant Christy managed to grasp the leg of the small stool and brought it crashing down against his head. His body went limp immediately and a pool of blood began to form with dark certainty beneath his head.

Staggering to her feet, Christy crouched back against the wall sobbing and trembling uncontrollably. Gradually she began to regain her breath and composure, her eyes fixed on the open door.

Escape. It was now within her grasp. A quick glance down at her watch showed that it was now seven-thirty. Was there still time to save Amanda? Would she be able to overpower Iris as she had done Scully? Just the thought of the woman's formidable strength and powers was enough to chill her blood.

Standing there struggling with her own indecision, she became aware of the soft scraping sound of wood on stone. A shadow moved along one wall as the sound continued. Then an opening appeared behind the moving wine rack and the solemn dark-clad figure of Mrs. Fears swam into view holding a flashlight in one hand.

Her sharp eyes immediately took in the scene and crossing the cellar without a word, she bent over Scully's limp form.

"Is . . . is he dead?" Christy asked in a painful, rasping voice.

"Not yet," the woman answered. "But he soon will be."

"What do you mean?"

"Come," Fears instructed, choosing to ignore her question. "We must get out of here before it's too late."

"Too late," Christy echoed blankly.

Fears nodded darkly. "Yes. Abigale has decided to rid the world of Mr. Eustace Scully and her daughter-in-law."

"But what about Amanda? I can't leave until——"

Fears silenced her with an imperious wave of her hand. "Amanda is outside waiting for you," she intoned. "I'm taking you both up to an old hunting lodge. You'll be safe there until this business is settled once and for all time."

The room had stopped spinning about her, and things were beginning to fall back into logical perspective. "How did you find me?" Christy asked.

"Mr. Willard," the woman explained. "He came to me and said that you were being held down here against your will. I took him to Abigale."

"Oh . . . thank God," Christy breathed. "Then the map's still safe."

"Where did you hide it?"

Christy quickly explained about hiding it inside the doll. Then without further comment the housekeeper said, "Come. We must hurry." Taking Christy by the arm, she drew her into the opening behind the wine rack and pulled it shut behind them.

The two of them started down a narrow passage that had been carved out of the mountainside. The flashlight reflected against the moist walls and water dripped endlessly from the low ceiling. For some time they moved steadily upward until a trap door appeared in the ceiling above them. Here Fears paused, indicating that Christy should be the first to climb the metal rungs sunk into the cavern wall.

"This leads to the stable," she said in a voice that sounded hollow and disembodied. "Amanda is there waiting for us and the horses are already saddled. I've brought a warm cloak for you as well as gloves."

Grasping the first chill metal rung, Christy began to climb.

Outside, the night was a swirling white mass of great fluffy snowflakes. With Fears taking the lead and Amanda riding between them on her Shetland pony, they had stolen out of the barn and set off through the forest. For almost two hours they picked their way along the trail, moving higher and higher into the mountains.

Later Christy was to recall little of the ride. The cold was too intense, the visibility impossible. Still shaken by her brush with death, she concentrated only on clinging to the reins and keeping the sentinel figure of Mrs. Fears in view.

Beyond that her brain was too numb to even think. Too much had happened that day and she feared that if she allowed her emotions to come into play she would surely be lost.

At last they approached the top of a high rise, and Mrs. Fears pointed ahead to a long, low building nestled among the pines. They had almost arrived at their destination.

Within seconds there was the sound of a muffled explosion far in the distance. Ahead of her Amanda twisted about in her saddle and cried out in alarm.

Turning back in the direction from which they had come, Christy saw an orange glow illuminating the night sky. The snowfall had by now diminished to a few vagrant, drifting flakes and she could clearly see explosive tongues of fire licking up into the pitch-dark night.

As she watched the mounting streaks of crimson and orange growing ever brighter, Christy knew instinctively that Falcon's Eyrie was burning. So that was it. Abigale had set fire to the house. Now she knew what Fears had meant when she said that Abigale intended to rid the world of Scully and Iris once and for all time.

Seized by a sense of deep sadness, she deliberately turned her thoughts from the fire and urged her horse on up the trail. It was just too ghastly to think of Scully lying unconscious on the cellar floor as the house burned to rubble about him. No one, no matter how evil, deserved such a fate. And Iris. What of her? No matter what their sins, it was a terrible way to die.

After stabling their horses in the small barn adjoining the hunting lodge, Mrs. Fears drew Christy aside. By now the storm had cleared and star-heavy patches of night sky were beginning to appear above the treetops.

In low tones Fears explained that she planned to return to the house to make sure that all had gone as planned.

She confirmed Christy's suspicion that Abigale had fired the house and went on to tell her that it was Willard who had poured gasoline throughout the lower floors and locked Iris securely in her room.

Fears promised to return early the following morning to lead them back down from the mountains once she had determined that all was safe.

After the housekeeper had taken her leave, they made their way toward the lodge. It stood on a knoll guarded by tall pines, the air sweetened by the fragrance of incense cedar. The snow lay ankle deep and bulked up around the cabin in drifts that looked like ghostly sand dunes in the moonlight.

Upon reaching the door, they found it blocked completely and both Christy and Amanda were forced to struggle to clear away some of the snow before they were able to open it.

Once inside, Christy shut the door behind them and offered up a prayer of thanks that they had safely made their escape. It was pitch black inside the lodge and switching on the flashlight given her by Mrs. Fears, she flashed the beam about.

The lodge was entirely bare of furniture, and on closer inspection they found that there was not even any wood with which to build a fire in the fireplace. Still, in spite of the obvious discomfort and cold, Christy felt safe and sheltered after her long and difficult ordeal.

"Do you think Scully will be able to find us here?" Amanda asked.

Christy was completely taken by surprise. For the first time she was forced to contemplate the possibility that Scully and Iris had not perished in the fire. Obviously Amanda had been far more aware of what was going on than anyone had suspected.

"I don't think so," she responded vaguely. No longer, however, was she entirely at ease now that the seeds of doubt had been planted. Since it had stopped snowing, she realized that it would be very easy for anyone to follow their tracks to the hunting lodge.

"Why does he want to hurt us?" Amanda pursued with childish curiosity. Her eyes were wide and questioning.

"Scully is a very sick man, Amanda, dear. And I'm sure he won't ever hurt anyone again."

"Is Aunt Iris sick too?" Amanda asked.

Christy hesitated before answering, her mind refusing to work properly. It was late and she had been through far too much that day. "I'll explain everything to you tomorrow," she hedged. "Mrs. Fears is coming for us early in the morning and we'll return to Witch's Pond."

The satisfied expression that settled over the child's face indicated to Christy that she was not yet aware that Falcon's Eyrie was gone forever. Later, she thought. When this was all safely behind them she would try and explain.

In spite of the bareness of the lodge, they were able to locate piles of animal pelts left behind by some nameless trapper. Using Christy's cloak as a blanket, they huddled together in an attempt to get some sleep. Almost immediately Amanda's breathing deepened, and giving in to her complete exhaustion, Christy soon drifted off as well.

They were both awakened at dawn by the sound of a horse neighing some distance from the lodge. The sound echoed and re-echoed through the snowy winter fastness.

Thinking that Fears had returned, Christy got up and went to the window, which had been boarded up. Through an aperture between the planks she looked out into the breaking dawn and scanned the snowy hillside.

As she watched, Iris and Scully rode out of the trees and stopped to dismount about two hundred yards below the lodge.

The sound of her heart beating was suddenly very loud in her ears. Christy simply couldn't believe her eyes. After blinking rapidly, she looked again. No. She wasn't dreaming. It was really them. Scully had a bandage over his right eye and was forced to tilt his head as if he were having difficulty in seeing.

At that moment their own horses whinnied a greeting to the new arrivals. Iris signaled with a brief nod that they had located their quarry and they both began to tramp up the hillside, leading their horses behind them.

Crouching there before the window, Christy's fear seemed to congeal into a single burning desire that overshadowed every other consideration. She was determined that Iris and Scully would not catch them. No matter what she had to do, she and Amanda would escape. She would never stop running as long as she had a breath of life left in her.

Once Iris was in possession of the map their lives would be entirely worthless.

"What is it?" Amanda asked sleepily. "Who do you see?"

Christy took a deep breath before answering. When she finally did so, her voice was deadly calm. "Listen carefully," she instructed. "We're going to have to sneak away. Iris and Scully are coming up the hillside to get us."

Creeping down a hallway to the back of the lodge, they slipped out a back door into deep snow, striking off from the relative shelter of the outbuildings and running across a wide clearing.

Christy pulled Amanda along through the deep drifts, the two of them plunging through banks of freshly fallen snow until they managed to reach the safety of the woods. There were shouts from behind and they crouched down in the shelter of a great twisted spruce to await further developments.

With a shout Iris pointed toward the woods and ordered Scully to bring around the horses. Their escape had been discovered. Christy shivered involuntarily, but not with the cold. She dared not contemplate what her fate might be if Scully should manage to get his hands on her once again. The clutch of his fingers at her throat was still a very real agony and one she didn't intend to repeat.

From moment to moment she was growing more and more panicky. The sheltering woods surrounding them had become a trap instead of a haven. She caught a glimpse of their pursuers coming around the side of the lodge mounted upon their horses. The going was rough, the animals sinking into the deep drifts as they plunged forward with steam snorting from their nostrils.

"Come on," Christy whispered, grabbing Amanda by the hand and pulling her into a dense thicket. Silent and desperate, they forged their way through the heavy drifts that blocked their path, while high above, the wind blew through the crowns of the pines with an eerie whistling sound.

In their fright they went leaping over fallen trees, entirely heedless of low branches that lashed their faces or the thorny elderberry that tore at their clothes. Eventually the ground leveled out and they began to make better time as the trees grew further and further apart.

Amanda seemed as anxious to escape as Christy and it was the child's fortitude that gave her the courage to keep up the punishing pace. At last they ran out of the trees, only to be confronted by a gaping chasm, with a river rushing wildly between its steep banks.

A short distance upstream Christy spied a stout lodge-pole pine that had fallen across the stream. By means of this natural bridge she saw their one chance of eluding their pursuers.

Encouraging Amanda to follow her lead and cautioning her not to look down, she summoned all her courage and mounted the fallen tree. For a panicky moment she balanced high above the rushing torrent and then without faltering or pausing made her way to the far side.

To her great relief Amanda imitated her performance

perfectly and had quickly joined her on the far bank. There Christy breathed with some satisfaction. That ought to throw them off the track for awhile at least. In any case they wouldn't be able to cross the gorge on horseback, and by the time they located an alternate route she and Amanda would be well away.

As a precaution Christy broke a low bough from one of the pungent-smelling incense cedars and switched it along behind them to cover their tracks until they were well away from the stream.

"Look," Amanda called, pointing ahead.

Christy looked up to see an icy gray sheet of water just beyond the trees. It was the pond at the foot of the great waterfall. Above and beyond that lay the treasure.

Twenty

THEY paused to rest at the waterfall and share some bread and cheese that Mrs. Fears had thoughtfully provided. The pond that Christy remembered so vividly from the previous fall was now frozen about twenty feet out from shore. The surrounding woods looked glacial and inhospitable.

Removing the map from Amanda's rag doll and spreading it on a flat rock, Christy studied it carefully, noting that the treasure was hidden in a cave not too far distant from the falls.

There seemed to be no alternative but to forge on to the cave. It was the only place on the island where they would

be relatively safe. At least until Christy could decide what
their next move was to be.

One possibility was that after a day's rest they could
strike out for the far side of the island in hopes that Jeremy's father would take them to the mainland by boat. If
not—well, she would just have to think of something else.
Now the most important thing was escape.

It was by now painfully obvious that something had
gone terribly amiss with Abigale's plan. They could no
longer be sure that help would be forthcoming, and since
they had left the hunting lodge, Fears would be unable to
find them. That was of course if she were still alive.

With an effort of will Christy drove these gloomy forebodings from her mind. If she permitted her thoughts to
follow their natural course, she knew she would be quickly
overcome by doubt and despair.

After fixing the route they must take firmly in her mind,
they started out once again. With great care they began
picking their way up the mountainside bordering the falls.
Amanda appeared to have little difficulty, scrambling up
the nearly perpendicular cliffs like a young gazelle.

For her part Christy was forced to claw her way up,
clinging to every rock and tree for support. Alongside, the
shimmering cascade of water plunged downward, the icy
spray pelting her face with tiny frozen darts and almost
paralyzing her hands with the bitter cold.

From a granite outcropping high above, Amanda called
out that she had discovered a trail. By the time Christy
reached her side she found to her great relief that steps
had been cut into the rock face of the mountain. Gratefully they pressed their feet into them and continued upward
to the very lip of the waterfall.

At the very top they paused, watching as a continuous
river of water spilled over the edge to plunge two hundred
feet into the pool below. In the chill winter atmosphere the
terrible roar was strangely muted. Sounds at that altitude

did not echo or fade. Even their voices were extinguished immediately without the slightest hint of reverberation.

The first twenty minutes of steady climbing had been the most difficult. After cresting the top of the falls, the trail continued skyward at a more leisurely pace among the stunted conifers and tumbled granite boulders.

By now the winter sun had risen in the sky and burned down hard and white, reflecting sharply off the newly fallen snow. Here and there Christy spied snow flowers pushing their red tuberous heads up through the white mantle and realized with a sense of exhilaration that spring would not be long in coming.

At last they arrived at a chain of shallow pools and paused to drink. The water was sweet and pure but no more so than the air, which had warmed considerably in the late morning sun. There was no longer any wind, only a faint stirring in the crowns of the trees.

By noon they had wound their way up to just beneath the summit of the island's highest peak. Like an enormous jagged tooth, it was bathed in a sharpness of light that seemed to surround everything with a halo, bringing out the subtlest textures and colors of the rock.

The air was so fresh and clear at that altitude that every leaf, stone, and mottled expanse of bark was perfectly delineated, every shadow drawn as with an artist's brush.

After checking the map once again, they began the last leg of their climb toward the highest crest, making their way over a dizzying set of switchbacks that zigzagged upward for over one hundred feet. The path was less than a foot wide, dropping off sharply into a tumble of boulders and heaps of talus.

Then abruptly they topped the final rise, and the mouth of the cave yawned before them. They had made it.

Tired but exhilarated they paused for but a moment to catch their breath. Then with Christy clutching tightly to Amanda's hand, they descended into the darkness, both of them shivering as a damp, chill wind whistled up out of the depths.

Switching on the torch and playing it ahead of them, they began to move slowly down the narrow pathway. As they went, the flashlight darted about the cavern walls, illuminating rainbow formations of incredible beauty on each side.

They had progressed only a short distance when Amanda began to slip sideways. She was snatched back upon the path by Christy's quick action. For a moment they crouched against the cave wall, too frightened by the near accident to move.

Before starting off once again, Christy flashed the torch off to their left, exposing a gaping crevasse hundreds of feet deep. From far below, the sound of a rushing underground river drifted up to them, sounding alien and far away.

Making their way deeper and deeper into the earth, they gradually became aware of an ominous sound, which began to grow steadily louder until clouds of angry bats erupted from the depths of the cave to batter and flap about their heads in disturbed confusion.

Crouching low, Christy and Amanda clung together as the small darting creatures steamed past in a thunder of wings, moving ever upward toward the cave entrance far above.

By the time they reached the level of the running river, the cavern floor had evened out, the path becoming easier to follow. Within minutes they found themselves entering a large concave chamber with a high vaulted ceiling and giant mushroom formations on every side. Scattered all about them were fallen columns and tumbled limestone cornices that had collapsed eons before the coming of man.

They stood in awe as the torch flashed from walls to ceiling, exposing dripping stalactites and glistening stalagmites beautifully tinted with all the colors of the rainbow. The floor of the cavern tilted steadily downward, ending at last in a crystal lake as still and cold as ice, disappearing off into the far reaches of the cave.

They began walking in that direction, and as they moved along, Christy realized that the bed of the river was entirely seeded with gold coins that flashed brightly each time she played the torch upon the surface of the water.

The source, they soon discovered, was three ancient wooden chests banded by stout strips of iron. One of the trunks had broken open sometime in the past, spilling a part of its contents into the water rushing down from above.

This Christy quickly surmised was how the coins she had found below the waterfall had gotten there in the first place. At last they had arrived at the source of both the river and the treasure.

Chattering excitedly, they examined the other two trunks, only to find that they were securely padlocked with heavy metal locks of ancient origin. Turning their attention to the trunk that had broken open, they gaped in disbelief at the king's ransom in gold, silver, and jewels that had been deposited on the floor of the cave.

"How beautiful," Amanda gasped as the jewels glittered in the light. Dropping to their knees, they began to sort among the heap of coins, gold chains, and silver ingots. With a sharp intake of breath Christy retrieved a golden crown sparkling with diamonds and a brilliant shimmer of semiprecious stones.

Not to be outdone, Amanda plunged both hands into the damaged trunk and came up with handfuls of sapphires, rubies, and softly muted pearls that shone brilliantly as she held them up to the light.

When at last their excitement was quelled by their mounting hunger and ingrained fatigue, they settled down on the ground and finished the rest of the bread and cheese. With her hunger satisfied, Amanda nestled her head in Christy's lap and fell immediately asleep.

Drawing her heavy cloak about the sleeping child, Christy leaned back against a smooth rock and tried her best to stay awake. It was a losing battle and after nodding and dozing for some time she herself was soon dragged down into darkness.

Sometime later, without completely awakening, terror stole into her dreams so quietly and with such stealth that she was literally jolted back to reality.

She opened her eyes to find Iris and Scully standing silently over them. The muzzle of a gun was pointing directly at her heart. While Christy's flashlight had dimmed considerably in the lapse of time, the cave was shimmering in the light of two large burning torches planted firmly in the ground nearby.

Pressing the gun firmly against her breast, Scully leered at her with one eye, the other hidden beneath a bloody bandage. In addition there were livid scratches running from his hairline and disappearing into the ragged stubble of beard.

"Tie them up," Iris ordered in a cool voice, her eyes shining with a triumphant light.

As Amanda was shaken rudely awake, she began to whimper softly and Scully immediately stuffed a gag in her mouth. He then set about tying them both securely with a length of rope.

Finding her voice at last, Christy gasped, "But how did you find us?"

This was received with a light sprinkle of mocking laughter from Iris. "Very simple, my pet. We deliberately let you get away from the lodge so you would lead us to the treasure. The very fact that Abigale wanted you to escape from the house so badly proved that it was you who had the map all along."

"But I thought——"

"That Abigale and Willard had succeeded in burning us alive," Iris cut in. "No such luck. Scully came to in time and managed to get me out of my room."

"And Abigale?" Christy questioned, biting her lip. "Willard?"

Iris flashed a grim, sadistic smile, shaking her head from side to side. "I must admit I underestimated my poor departed husband. He had more guts than I ever gave him credit for."

Christy's whole being was slowly opening up to the dreadful realization that there was no further hope. She felt suddenly as though she were drowning, a huge wave of remorse sweeping over her. "Then they're all dead," she stated bleakly.

"Burned alive," Iris confirmed. "But I didn't murder them. At that point they were more valuable to me alive than dead. They simply refused to leave the house. The last time I saw Willard and Abigale they were standing at the railing of the minstrel's gallery with the whole place going up in flames around them."

There was the briefest flicker of an eyelid. "I think they wanted it that way," she concluded.

As Iris was speaking, Scully had been moving around sticking bundles of dynamite in whatever nooks and crannies he found in the cavern walls. They were connected to long fuses which he left carefully exposed.

Christy's apprehension mounted as she watched him move about, totally involved in these sinister preparations.

"What is it you're going to do with us?" she demanded.

Iris' eyes laughed out at her from beneath dark, slanting brows. Without answering, she moved to the open chest and scooped up handfuls of treasure. Lifting the crown that Christy had discovered earlier, she placed it upon her head, stringing a series of golden chains about her neck.

Soon her hands were encrusted with rings and her wrists encircled with bracelets stretching half way up to the elbow. Turning once again to face Christy, Iris was literal-ly ablaze with gold and jewels, the multifaceted stones sparkling and flashing in the shimmering torchlight.

"I have won," she announced in a breathless, exultant voice. "I have won at last. Now I shall have it all. Paris. London—all the places I've always wanted to see."

With a light and graceful step she began to dance about, twirling with arms outstretched, her face radiant. "There will be beautiful clothes," she chanted in a singsong voice, "expensive cars and a villa on the Mediterranean." Gradu-ally her voice rose in pitch and tenor. "It's all mine now. Do you understand? . . . mine."

"You can't possibly hope to get away with this," Chris-ty said with a great deal more calm than she felt. "There's still the curse. Whoever removes the treasure from the cave will die a horrible death."

Iris' face seemed to melt slightly at her words, the eyes becoming hooded and wary, the mouth twisting into an ugly red gash. "I have beaten the curse," she grated be-tween clenched teeth. "I am stronger than any supernatu-ral forces. There is no one . . . nothing that can interfere with my triumph."

"That's where you're wrong." It was a man's voice booming out in the cavern, the final word breaking apart into a chain of echoes—"wrong . . . wrong . . . wrong. . . ."

With her heart pounding and the blood singing in her ears, Christy looked about and saw Matthew mounted on a large boulder just inside the entrance to the cave. In one hand he held a pistol and in the other a torch shedding a blinding beam of light.

In the same instant she saw Scully reaching stealthily for his own weapon. Matthew had not yet seen him, being completely unaware of his presence.

"Watch out," she screamed.

A shot rang out and Scully grasped his hand with a

shrill scream, dropping his gun to the ground. "Wait," he cried. "Don't shoot again. I'm not going to try anything."

Motioning him toward the others with the snout of his pistol, Matthew jumped down from the boulder and strode up to them.

As he drew close he flashed the powerful beam of his torch, catching Iris full in the face. She blinked into the fierce white light, her features wearing the strangled expression of a death mask. Matthew had taken her completely by surprise and she had not yet managed to recover.

Circling warily behind, Matthew freed Christy and Amanda with a quick slash of his pocket knife. He then motioned them to set about tieing first Scully and then Iris, who still stood mute and disbelieving at this unexpected turn of events.

Suppressing the desire to throw herself gratefully into his arms, Christy followed his instructions and moved to bind Iris' wrists. "How did you manage to find us?" she asked, her voice choked with emotion.

"When I got back to my shack last night, I found the amber charm I had given you and knew immediately that something was wrong. By the time I got up to Falcon's Eyrie the house was in flames. Luckily Mrs. Fears showed up about then and told me that you and Amanda were hiding out in the old hunting lodge. It didn't take us long to discover that these two had escaped the blaze and guess that they intended to follow your tracks in the snow."

"You're supposed to be dead," Iris spat out, recovering her voice at last.

"A pity, isn't it?" Matthew replied coolly. "But you can thank your friend Scully for that. He was stupid enough to hide that dynamite charge in one of the lockers in my boat. I discovered it as soon as I started to unload in Land's End."

"And you followed us here," Iris grated out, shooting a murderous look in Scully's direction.

Matthew gave a short chuckle. "That was the easy part. The trail was getting pretty well worn by the time I came along."

There was a sudden, unexpected movement from Scully and before Matthew realized what was happening, a rock sailed through the air, striking him squarely on the side of the head.

He reeled sideways and slumped to the ground, giving Scully time enough to draw his knife and lunge forward with an angry snarl.

Matthew saw him coming and rolled to one side, but not quite soon enough. The thrust missed its intended target but the sharp blade sliced through his jacket and into his forearm.

Christy screamed as she saw the blood soak through his sleeve and Amanda buried her face against her in this new outbreak of violence.

Ignoring the wound in his arm, Matthew fixed his eyes on his assailant although his face had grown pale and beads of perspiration sprouted on his forehead.

A look of sly cunning sharpened Scully's features, his eyes igniting with a lust for blood, mastery, and death. He moved in closer, his body hunched low, arms held rigid. The knife swung down in a wide arc, only to change direction abruptly and plunge straight toward Matthew's heart.

By now thoroughly shaken, Christy turned her face away, missing Matthew's lift of his right arm and the downward chop that landed squarely on Scully's stiffened wrist.

It was only when she heard the knife clatter to the stones that she spun about just in time to see Matthew kick the blade and send it spinning off across the cavern floor.

A ragged snarl escaped Scully's clenched teeth. Like a maddened bull he charged head on, his fists swinging wildly while Iris cheered him on with the words, "Kill him ... kill ... kill. ..."

A direct blow to the jaw drove Matthew back against one of the chests and another caught him squarely in the lower stomach.

Stumbling forward, he staged a weak counterattack but was no match for the wiry Scully, who managed to weave and duck aside.

"Now," Iris screamed, and seeing his chance, Scully struck with authority, smashing his fist against the side of Matthew's head and sending him down to his knees.

He somehow managed to stagger up to his feet, but by then he had given his assailant all the time he needed to recover the knife. Scooping it up from the floor, he spun about with a victorious bellow—the blade clutched tightly in his fist.

Matthew managed to avoid the first wild swipe but not the second, the razor-sharp blade slicing across the palm of his hand. Back and forth they parried until he tripped and fell to the ground, rolling sideways to avoid Scully's booted kick.

By now Christy could see that Matthew was groggy and confused. When Scully buried the tip of his boot in his stomach with the next try, he doubled up with a low moan.

Helplessly she watched as Scully closed in for the kill. In a final desperate gesture Matthew jammed his fingers into his mouth and broke forth with a loud, piercing whistle that echoed out through the far reaches of the cavern.

There was an instant response from the shadowed entrance to the cave. Accompanied by guttural snarls and low, threatening howls, Matthew's dogs broke out of the inky darkness and streaked forward at a run.

Scully spun about just in time to find himself surrounded on all sides by the pale and ghostly animals. He dropped into a defensive half crouch and swiveled about, only to lose his balance and tumble backward over one of the treasure chests.

The enraged animals were on him in an instant, their clamping jaws ripping and tearing into his flesh with flashing teeth.

Somehow he managed to kick free and roll to one side burying his face in his arms and screaming, "No . . . stop . . . please, no. . . ."

The dogs plunged mercilessly after him, their yellowed fangs tearing at his hands again and again with maniacal persistence, while the leader of the pack went directly for his throat.

Scully roared and swore, his voice becoming a high-pitched scream that was choked off abruptly by a low, gurgling death rattle.

Christy remained stunned, unable to believe what she had been forced to witness.

"Are you all right?" Matthew said, stumbling to his feet and running over to her.

She nodded numbly, her voice frozen in her throat.

"I'm afraid," Amanda wailed, casting a terrified look at the dogs. During the entire nightmare, she had kept her face buried in the folds of Christy's cloak.

"It's all right now, darling," Christy managed, clasping the child about the shoulders.

"Come on," Matthew said, with a sideways glance at Scully's bloody corpse. "Let's get her out of here."

"No . . . you can't leave me here." It was Iris, her voice etched with panic as the dogs crept forward to form a low crouching circle about her. "Don't leave me like this. Not alone . . . in the dark."

"Don't worry," Matthew retorted gruffly. "The torches will burn until morning. And as for the dogs—they're just going to make sure you don't try and escape. His look of utter contempt eased into a bitter, ironic smile. "Surely you aren't afraid of them. So often you've said that you were afraid of nothing."

The barest flicker of an eyelid signaled a complete change in Iris' demeanor. Drawing herself up, she snarled, "You can't frighten me. Not you—or the curse of Captain Kidd, or even these mangy curs." On and on she ranted, spewing out a contagion of ugliness and accusation, gradually lashing herself into an emotional frenzy.

At that moment Christy felt almost sorry for the woman. Trussed up with her arms and legs tied and her hair a wild tangle about her ashen face, she looked old and pathetic. The glittering array of jewels she still wore only served to complete the grotesque picture. It was a far cry from the regal figure who had presided so grandly as mistress of Falcon's Eyrie.

"Iris," Christy started, but the words caught in her throat and she was afraid she was going to cry. Turning helplessly toward Matthew, she said, "We can't leave her like this. Not alone . . . it's too cruel."

"We have no choice," he countered in a steely voice.

Sweeping Amanda up into his arms, he grasped Christy by the hand and said, "Come along now. The sheriff and his deputies will be up to get her tomorrow. A night alone with the spirits of the dead is exactly what she deserves."

Turning away, they hurried from the cavern, but Christy stopped abruptly just beyond the entrance. "Listen," she whispered.

After a moment the others heard it too and turned in unison to look back. Faintly at first, then louder, the laughter grew in volume, rippling out in the cavern. Pure, rich, and mocking, it peeled forth again and again. The mellow, woodwind laughter of an old woman.

Iris heard it as well, but remained outwardly calm, her head held high. Only her eyes betrayed her fear, blinking in some speechless denial.

In complete astonishment the three of them watched as

one of the torches appeared to take flight and move through the air to set each of the dynamite charges alight.

They began to sputter and burn, the laughter growing in volume, only to be joined at last by Iris' own, peeling out in wave after hysterical wave.

It was Matthew's voice that broke the spell and set them once again in motion. "Run," he bellowed, grabbing Christy by the hand and half pulling, half dragging her up the trail.

Behind them the cavern was alive with light and echoes, the mad, spiraling laughter resounding again and again from the limestone walls.

The sound was still ringing in Christy's ears as a thunderous cannonade exploded from behind and threw them headlong to the ground.

Twenty-one

IT had been two weeks since the people of Falcon's Island had returned from their exile on the mainland.

Although the April day shone bright and sunny, the echo of winter lingered on in the brisk morning air. A timid, hesitant spring had coaxed the shy leaf buds out in full and yet it took little more than a stray cloud passing across the face of the sun to haunt the island with the ghost of February past.

The graveyard lay on a gently sloping hill a short distance from Falcon's Eyrie. The assembled mourners stood in solemn clusters as the newly arrived minister threw a handful of dirt into the freshly dug grave of Abigale Falcon.

". . . And I commend her to the earth from which she came," he intoned solemnly, raising his hand in ritual blessing.

On every side crumbling marble and limestone monuments were pressed and crowded in death, the older gravestones leaning like broken teeth. Here and there were more elaborate memorials. Some bore sculptured angels peering up into the sunlight with sightless eyes while reaching out to the heavens with supplicating arms. Others were marked by only a simple inscription and the dates of birth and death.

In the stones themselves was written the history of the island. The same names being repeated over and over. Bishop. Jenkins. Cabot. Calvert. Dorn. Godwin, Parrish, and Falcon.

While the Falcons who had lived and ruled, rested beneath monuments both grander and more elaborate than those of the villagers, they were covered alike by the same pale green moss and creeping lichen.

Christy stood at the head of the grave with Matthew and Amanda on either side of her. A dark mantilla was drawn about her head and shoulders in mourning. A few steps behind stood Mrs. Fears.

A light breeze sifted through the stately sycamores surrounding the graveyard and gently fingered the folds of Christy's veil. It passed like a sigh, whispering of the past that was now dead and gone forever.

In her hands Christy held a leather-bound Bible. It was the same Bible that had rested at Witch's Pond for so many centuries, listing within its yellowed pages those women who had served as midwife to the island's people. Now the line of succession had been broken. There would be no one to take Mistress Cory's place, although Christy had made arrangements for a doctor from Land's End to take up residence in the near future.

Abigale's grave lay beneath a great spreading oak. Christy had chosen the plot herself, finding it peaceful and yet significant with its view of Pirate's Cove, the ruins of Falcon's Eyrie, and the island stretching beyond.

There had been three funerals that day, and the newly covered graves of Willard Falcon and Mistress Cory were but a short distance away. Since their return from the mainland the islanders appeared to accept Christy completely. While still reserved and distant, they treated her with respect and the distrust was gone from their eyes.

"And may our sister Abigale Falcon rest in peace forever," the minister concluded solemnly.

A murmured "amen" emanated from the people gathered about, all of them dressed in their somber Sunday best. Slowly they filed past the grave with lowered heads and prayerful hands, each of them offering a brief nod of farewell.

Then it was over. Slipping her arm through Matthew's and taking Amanda by the hand, the three of them started for the wagon, with Mrs. Fears following a short distance behind.

Matthew had just lifted Amanda up onto the front seat of his buckboard when a strange occurrence began to take place.

Slowly the newly returned islanders led by Elder Dawkins began to file past in procession before her. The women curtsied with downcast eyes and placed a sprig of greenery or a small bouquet of spring flowers at her feet, while the men doffed their caps and bobbed their heads in obeisance.

Christy stood watching in speechless wonder. It had not occurred to her until that very moment that Amanda was the last surviving Falcon and therefore heiress to the island under the original feudal charter.

Even more surprising was the child's strange acceptance of the archaic ritual. She sat perfectly still and erect with her head held high and her tiny gloved hands folded neatly in her lap. Amanda Falcon. A proud flaxen-haired princess accepting her just due from her new subjects.

Christy glanced from Amanda to Matthew with questioning eyes. His own countenance was sternly disapproving as he regarded the feudal display. "It has always been so," he murmured bitterly as the procession continued to file slowly past. "They just don't know any better. In their eyes Abigale the queen is dead, and even though they hated her—long live the queen."

As the last of the villagers filed by, Christy and Mrs. Fears mounted the wagon and settled themselves in the back seat. Matthew whipped up the horses and they drove back down the hillside in the mellow, moving sunlight, all of them strangely withdrawn and silent.

Approaching the turnoff to Falcon's Eyrie, Christy put her hand on Matthew's shoulder. "Please," she whispered. "I'd like to go and see."

Without a word he clucked to the horses and guided the wagon between the stone gateposts with their sentinel falcons still standing guard.

Proceeding along the wide, curving drive, Christy allowed herself to be submerged in the idyllic beauty of the place once again. The tall, mature trees of elm, maple, beech, and hemlock shook the sunlight from their branches as they passed, and it fell in deep pools of dappled shade along the roadway.

Soon, very soon she knew, the drive would become choked with tall grass and the trees would throw out their branches to impede the progress of anyone foolish enough to trespass.

At last they drew out of the cool, sheltering forest and Matthew brought the wagon to a halt at the top of a low rise. Beyond they were greeted by the sight of what had once been Falcon's Eyrie.

The mansion was now little more than an empty shell, a tumble of blackened stone and brick, shattered chimneys and smoke-blackened beams. In the very center of the great hall the magnificent marble staircase mounted off into nothingness.

All about was ruin, desolation, and emptiness. The fire had spread quickly to the stables and greenhouses, destroying them as well. Even the birds seemed hushed in the trees; the song of the crickets chirruping in the grass had an empty, wistful note to it. Only the distant wash and whisper of the sea remained constant, unchanged.

It had been just three short weeks since the fire and already the grounds had begun to return to the wilderness from which they came. Secretive and silent, the weeds had begun to spring up across the lawns and Iris' lovely flower beds were already choked with nettles and whispering barley grass.

Christy sat lost in thought, contemplating the many dreams that lay buried in the ruins of the once great house. Dreams of power, treasure, and mastery over men. There were other dreams and hopes buried as well—moments of great beauty she would always remember with a vague, fluttering sadness.

The fierce regal pride of Abigale Falcon, the final nobility of her son Willard, and always somewhere in the back of her mind there would be Jason, her friend and companion. No. She would not soon forget them.

Staring out at the desolation before her, she cast her thoughts back in time and tried to remember the house as she had seen it from the sea on that very first day. The diamond-paned windows had reflected the morning sun and friendly trails of smoke curled lazily up from the mellowed brick chimneys. How long ago it all seemed and what a different person she had been as she wondered what lay behind those mysterious beckoning windows.

Now she knew.

Without a word Matthew turned the wagon around and they started back toward the road. Feeling the hot burn of tears, Christy knew that she would not return to Falcon's Eyrie again. At least for a long, long time. Perhaps one day when the steadily creeping ivy had lent a gentle grace to the broken portals and the pain of those last dreadful days had subsided.

Then she would go back. But that day was far in the future. Now there was only sadness.

They drove across the island in the country stillness of early afternoon. The day was windless and mild. Overhead the sky was a harmony of soft cerulean blue, bordered at the horizon by tattered wisps of snowy clouds that appeared to be smoking from their outer edges.

Cresting a rise in the distance, the old windmill revolved slowly in the light breeze, its tattered sails catching the light and flashing brilliantly in the sun. In spite of all that had taken place, Christy still liked to think of them as welcoming arms, just as she had on that very first day.

Falcon's Island had become her home. It was not really an island of horror and death, nor was it any longer a place of exile. It had simply been sleeping, guarding the traditions of another time, another century. Waiting with the patience of the ages for someone to lift the curse.

Now that the treasure was lost forever they would be free of the past. The island would live again, Christy vowed silently. Together she and Matthew would bring it to life once more.

Christy was thinner now than she had been the previous fall and looked somewhat older than her years. The finely sculpted cheekbones were more prominent and the lovely eyes expressed a depth of sadness that had not been there before.

Observing the tautly erect figure of Amanda seated primly on the seat in front of her, Christy realized that she had changed as well. No longer was she the emotionally disturbed child she had taken under her wing those many months ago. Now she appeared to be far more mature and was given to long periods of silent introspection. There were times when Amanda was almost a stranger.

Once again Christy recalled how the people had come up to her that morning after the funeral service. There had seemed to be some unspoken bond existing between them, something beyond Christy's comprehension.

Upon reaching the cottage, Mrs. Fears had taken Amanda upstairs for her nap, leaving Matthew to stoke up the fire and Christy to prepare tea.

When it was ready, the two of them sat before the hearth staring into the roaring blaze and sipping from delicate china cups. Finally without a word Matthew got up and went to stand by the windows with his back turned.

"Matthew," Christy called after him. Ever since leaving the graveyard that morning it had been clearly evident that something was troubling him.

When he failed to answer or to turn around, she got to her feet and went over to stand beside him, leaning her head against his shoulder.

"I'm so sorry," she whispered, giving voice to the regret that had haunted her ceaselessly these past weeks. "So terribly sorry for those things I said to you on the day Jason was killed. I should have believed in you, trusted you."

"I guess we both have a lot to forgive and forget," he said, slipping his arm about her waist and drawing her close.

"What is it, Matthew?" she asked, staring up at his granitelike profile. "What's wrong?"

Turning, he took her face between his hands and peered into her eyes. "Do you love me very much?" he asked.

It was a moment before she could find the words with which to answer. "More than anything," she said at last.

Bending down, he kissed her softly on the forehead, before drawing away and turning once again to stare out at the marsh. "Then you must take Amanda from the island."

Christy stared at him blankly, her hands twisting, the palms moist.

"But I don't understand. This island is her home . . . her heritage. She's the last of the Falcons."

"That's exactly the reason you must take her away. Once she leaves, Falcon's Island will revert to the people. For the first time in over four hundred years they will be free men and women."

Christy turned her face away in confusion. "I can't think . . . I'm confused."

Gripping her by the shoulders, Matthew forced her to look up at him. "Listen to me," he demanded. "You saw what happened up at the cemetery today. What you witnessed was the ancient feudal oath of fealty between mistress and serf. Must it be propagated again and again? Don't you see? For the first time in our history there's a chance for these people to move into the twentieth century."

"If I'm willing to sacrifice Amanda," Christy said in a bleak, empty voice.

"Yes," he stated bluntly. "It's too bad, but that's the price that has to be paid."

"Matthew," she said after a long pause, "there's something you don't know. Christy's face was pale and drawn, her dark eyes tortured. "I've been putting this off . . . not quite knowing how to tell you."

Crossing the room to where her knitting bag rested on the table, she opened it and extracted a letter. It was the letter Abigale had given to her on the night of their meeting. "I think you should read this."

Crossing to where she stood, he slipped the single sheet of paper from the envelope and began reading aloud.

Dear Matthew,

There comes a time in each of our lives when we are forced to own up to our mistakes. Unfortunately that time usually arrives when all hope is lost on this side of the grave. We can only pray that a compassionate Maker may forgive us our misdeeds and take note of our suffering in expiation of our sins.

I have done you a great wrong, Matthew. Perhaps in more ways than you can now imagine. You are well aware that it was I who was responsible for the death of your poor mother so many years ago.

I have wronged you as well in my failure to acknowledge you as the son of my half brother Sebastian. In this I have been guilty of the sin of pride, and I beg your forgiveness.

Still for all the wrongs I have done, there is yet something you don't know. Something I must now confess or suffer the consequences for all eternity.

I was fully aware of the love my daughter Victoria bore for you and did everything in my power to discourage it. When I found out that she was carrying your child, it was I who persuaded her to reject you and marry another man. In so doing, I was responsible for her untimely death.

You see, Matthew, when Luther Holland found out that Victoria loved another, he threatened her life. I am convinced that it was he who scuttled the boat that night after leaving Falcon's Island, although it is I who bear the burden of guilt.

Having but a short time left upon this earth, I beg your forgiveness for all that I have done, while at the same time I leave you with a legacy. Amanda is your daughter. A child who combines the two worlds of

Falcon's Island through her joint heritage. It is through her that there can be a new beginning.

While I have never deigned to beg in my life, I must now beg you not to let the sins of a foolish old woman prevent you from giving her the love and guidance she so desperately needs.

Try and forgive the past, Matthew. And bear it well in mind that the fate of this innocent child and the island we both love so well rests entirely in your hands.

It was signed simply, "Abigale."

Matthew's face had gone ashen, and for the first time Christy noticed how gaunt and drawn he had become of late.

"It's a lie," he said at last. "A trick. The desperate ploy of a despotic senile old woman."

"Oh, Matthew," Christy entreated. "Look into Amanda's eyes. They're your own. Even Mistress Cory knew that Amanda was your child. She made up a poem about it and taught it to her. One day she knew the truth would have to come out."

It was a long moment before he spoke. During the ensuing seconds, she saw the disbelief slowly subside, only to be replaced by a cold, unreasoning anger.

Shaking his head stubbornly from side to side, he said, "So Abigale's won at last."

"Won? What do you mean?"

"By giving me the gift of my daughter, she has condemned this island to another hundred years of serfdom."

"But Matthew . . . it doesn't need to be that way. Abigale said herself that the child will need your guidance. It's within your power to change things here. Don't let your hatred of the Falcons blind you to the truth."

"The blood of the Falcons is poisonous," he shot back. "Tainted."

"How can you say that?" she countered. "Surely you loved Victoria."

"Love can sometimes turn to hatred. How do you think I felt when she rejected me because I was of too lowly a station? Oh, yes, I was good enough to be her lover but not her husband or the father of her child.

"It's true that I loved her once but now I feel nothing but bitterness and resentment. For all her beauty and charm Victoria was a shallow, selfish creature, who thought of no one but herself."

"Is that why you destroyed her statue?"

"Partly . . . and partly to frighten Iris," he admitted. "You see, she believed that Falcon's Eyrie was a fortress, that she was completely safe as long as she remained there. I wanted her to know that forces beyond her control could reach out and touch her when she least expected it."

He turned away. "It's no use, Christy. The Falcons have beaten me. There's nothing for me to do now but leave the island. I refuse to remain here and be subject to my own daughter. My pride is too strong for that."

Without another word he strode to the door and slammed out of the cottage.

Christy stood listening to his footsteps receding along the gravel path and then the wheels of the buckboard rolling away in the distance. Surely he would return, she reasoned. He just needed a little time to think, time to adjust to his new state of affairs.

Sitting with Mrs. Fears before the fire, she waited throughout the long afternoon. By the time the older woman got up to light the candles, Christy knew that Matthew would not be coming back. He was lost to her forever.

Putting on her long cloak, Christy left the cottage and crossed the dunes to the outer beach. It was the moment at which the twilight held the day and the night apart. The sky was brimming with early evening light and the sea had darkened in ever receding bands from pale green to deepest indigo.

Slowly she began walking along the water's edge as the twilight deepened to dusk about her. The ocean had lost its wild wintery anger; the waves seethed up the glistening sand and then slid back into the sea with barely a whisper.

One by one the stars began to appear, until the clear, high sky was thick-sown, the sea below a shimmer of pale light. Christy raised her face to the coming night. From somewhere on high she heard the fluttering of mysterious wings. Then moving like white phantom shades she saw them, and all else was forgotten.

A flight of wild swans was passing along the coast, remaining well out to sea. They were flying low and traveling very fast, their course as sure and direct as if they had been arrows shot from a marksman's bow.

As she stood watching, the glorious white birds swept past in the April night. A river of life flowing swiftly across an infinite blue sky.

A sound escaped her lips as she called out to them, experiencing a feeling of exhilaration as sharp as pain. It was more than the wild music of their wings or the sad, plaintive piping that filled the night. The birds were a portent of life forever renewing itself, an omen of renewed faith and hope for the future.

Now she knew that she had done the right thing. No matter what Matthew might think of her, or what cost she would have to pay in loneliness and pain, she had not failed her trust. Falcon's Island was Amanda's heritage and in some strange way Christy realized that the people needed their small mistress just as much as she needed them. The specter of the great glowering mansion was gone forever, and all of them working together could make a new beginning.

The sky was now empty except for an immense slice of pale moon that banished the deepening shadows and lighted the golden crests of the dunes. Far in the distance Christy could still hear the lonely cry of the swans growing ever fainter and farther away, until at last she was left alone once again with the wash of the sea and the night.

Still she remained where she was with tears streaming down her cheeks, her eyes searching the sky. It was a moment she would always remember. A moment of grace from on high. Although the swans had vanished into the night, they had left something of their wild, hopeful spirit behind.

"Christy," a voice cried out from somewhere behind her. "Christy. . . ."

She spun about to see Matthew running along the dunes. Wild, erratic, his long dark mane of hair whipping loosely in the light breeze. There was something in his voice that told her he had returned—this time for good.

With a sob Christy began to run as well, her heart pounding madly in her breast. He had come back to her— the man she loved had come back.

They met at the water's edge, and sweeping her up into his arms, he spun her around and around. Then he kissed her. Tenderly. His lips warm and sweet on hers.

"I was wrong, darling," he managed in a gruff, uneven voice. "So terribly wrong. What a fool I was to think that I could ever leave you. That I could abandon Amanda."

"It's all right," she whispered, pressing her fingers to his lips and thrilling to the strong, male warmth of him. "Everything's going to be all right now."

As they stood there forming a single silhouette, a great wave—larger than any that had preceded it—shouldered up out of the sea to break on the beach and foam high about their legs.

With their laughter mingling in surprise and delight, Matthew lifted her into his arms and began walking back up the beach with Christy clinging tightly about his neck.

In the distance the firelit windows of the witch's cottage

beckoned in the night. "Home," Christy sighed, savoring the word on the tip of her tongue. "Oh, Matthew . . . we're going home."

Invest $6.95 in a better marriage!

Every year, one half million American marriages break up. Very often because of sexual ignorance, frustration, boredom, and apathy.

It doesn't have to happen. Not to you.

You can enjoy more sexual satisfaction. You can know the secret of woman's "cycle of desire."

You can enjoy more sexual freedom.

A Marriage Manual is a tactful, illustrated guide that delves into every aspect of the art of marriage from the first sex act to Vatsyayana's Kama Sutra. It has already sold three-quarters of a million copies.

▼ **AT YOUR BOOKSTORE OR MAIL THIS COUPON NOW FOR FREE 30-DAY TRIAL** ▼

Today they're playing word games.
Before he's five, he can be reading 150 words a minute.

HOW TO GIVE YOUR CHILD A SUPERIOR MIND

A remarkable new book tells how you, yourself—at home—with no special training can actually add as much as thirty points to your child's effective I.Q....how you can help him move ahead quickly in school and enable him to be more successful in an education-conscious world.

Best of all, your child can achieve this early success without being pushed and without interference with a happy, normal, well-adjusted childhood.

GIVE YOUR CHILD A SUPERIOR MIND provides a planned program of home instruction that any parent can start using immediately. *You will learn:*

1. How to awaken your child's inborn desire to learn.
2. How to teach your child to read.
3. How to help your child streak ahead in math.
4. How to give your child the power of abstract reasoning.
5. How to increase your child's effective I.Q.

At all bookstores, or mail coupon today.➡

P 63/2